One Last Secret

Ella Perri Mysteries Book 2

A Novel by Krissy Baccaro

First paperback edition October 2021

Book design by Ebook Launch

ISBN 978-1-7346217-4-7 (paperback)
ISBN 978-1-7346217-3-0 (ebook)
ISBN 978-1-7346217-5-4 (hardcover)

www.krissybaccaro.com

For my mom who instilled a deep love of reading
For my dad who sparked my love of mysteries
Both inspired me to write.

Chapter 1
Ella

It happened on a sweltering morning under a hot sun. I was kneeling in the garden, covered with dirt and bug spray, when my mother burst into the backyard waving a sheet of paper.

"You'll never believe what I found in the ancestry report I ordered!" she yelled.

My mother had said she'd stop by for a quick visit to see my gardens. Five hours later we were still side by side, shovels and weed pullers in hand, talking and laughing at nothing. Our voices floated above us with occasional whispers of Italian ancestors and quests for truth. We didn't have to say it; we felt Poppy's presence all around us and a sense of peace at knowing I'd uncovered my uncle Luca's secrets in Italy. She seemed so happy in the garden beside me, talking about distant relatives, that I decided not to tell her—yet—about the package I'd received in the mail.

"Remember those?" she said, pointing to the sundrop garden.

Poppy had loved sundrops, magic yellow flowers he claimed expelled sadness from one's heart. A neighbor had given him a few dozen one day, and I remember when he brought them home, their skinny, wilted stems slouching over the rim of a plastic bucket. He'd strategically placed them in the prepared soil one by one, allowing for room to spread. At the time I had thought how pitiful they looked trying to stand in their new home. My eight-year-old self stood beside Poppy as he pointed to them like my mother was now. "Wait 'til next year, Abriella," he'd said. "There'll be so many you'll get lost in them!" None of us could imagine it then, but the following year they had doubled in size and number.

"Yes—look at them!" I said, gesturing to the sea of yellow spread before us, covering most of our side yard that ran adjacent to Skaneateles Lake. How could they not expel sadness?

It had begun as a perfect day. But it wouldn't end like one.

When we had finished planting and weeding, I arranged the sprinklers near the gardens while my mother chirped about finding a connection to a relative in Northern Italy.

"What if it's Gianna?" she said, wiping her brow. Gianna could be living in northern Italy. In Poppy's diary, he'd said Gianna's family had moved to Tuscany after they left the neighborhood, but he never mentioned where. "Maybe she returned to her home after—" She stopped, and we both knew why. "Do you think she became part of the Resistance?" my mother continued. "Wasn't that in Poppy's diary?"

"Yes," I said. "Gianna wanted to help, but Poppy discouraged that. He said it was too risky. But I suppose she could have become involved somehow. It's so hard to even contemplate. We just don't know where she might have gone."

"Could she have known someone in Tuscany who might have helped her?" my mother suggested. "Maybe she confided in a family member or a friend?"

"If it were me," I said, "I think my first instinct would be to go somewhere familiar, somewhere safe—maybe where I grew up. But if the person who tried to kill me ever learned I wasn't dead, that would be one of the first places he'd look."

Our conversations about Gianna trailed into several possibilities, but no matter where they took us, we always circled back to two unanswered questions: Was it possible Gianna had returned to her hometown in Tuscany? And could the central Italian relative on my mother's ancestry report and Gianna be the same person or someone close to her? The excitement that her real mother could be just within reach was palpable.

With my laptop propped open on the picnic table, amid the soft sounds of the sprinkler, we sipped lemonade and studied the online report of the mysterious Peragrapo family tree that was set to "private." To seek more information we would have to send a message. This person was listed as having a "close family" relationship.

"'Close family,'" I read aloud, "'could range from two to four degrees of separation and could be an aunt or uncle, niece or nephew, grandparent or grandchild, great-grandparent or great-grandchild, a half sibling, or a double first cousin. Someone who appears in this category is rarely a first cousin. You will share about 1,450 to 2,050 centimorgans with a half sibling, niece, nephew, grandparent, grandchild, or an aunt or uncle.'" I glanced at my mother, whose report revealed 1,992 centimorgans. "That means it's probably not a parent or full sibling, but it still could be a relation to Gianna."

"It must be, right?" she said, looking confused.

"It has to be," I said. "The Perris—Poppy's whole side—is strong in Southern Italy, especially Calabria."

I showed her the relatives we knew and, with a simple click, we confirmed our relationships with them, connecting to their family trees. Those great-aunts, uncles, and cousins had already sent in their DNA and were all set to public visibility, making an easy connection with them. The only relative set to private was the one in the northern Tuscan region.

Together we crafted a note to the Peragrapo relative:

Hello,

I recently received my ancestry report, and it appears we may be related in some way. I am interested in connecting with you if you are comfortable with that. However, I respect your privacy and understand if you do not wish to connect. Thank you for considering.

Best regards,
Gabriella Perri

My mother finished typing and sat with her hand on the mouse, the cursor anxiously hovering above the "send" button. After a few seconds, she clicked it and the message disappeared into cyberspace.

We looked at each other earnestly.

I powered off my laptop, placed it in the shade, and we sat beneath our beloved Storybook Tree, a sacred place where we'd spend hours reading or sharing intimate secrets below its branches. I prayed for a cool breeze to break through the haze, but the trees, the flowers, and even the blades of grass remained still, as if the world was holding its breath.

We sat in silence for a few moments as the mist from the sprinklers lightly tapped our skin. My mind was captured with imagining possibilities of our connection to the Peragrapo family member.

"I can't stop thinking about who it could be," my mother said. She had been thinking the same thing. "This could be it—our connection to Gianna. We could really find her, Ella."

"Once we figure it out," I said, "there will be other connections too."

"I hope they write back."

Our voices filled the air with eager chatter until I noticed my mother staring curiously at something near the edge of the lake that bordered my yard. I followed her gaze to the trees that were moving in just one spot, yet there had been no breeze.

My stomach tensed. "Not again," I said.

"What did you say?" she asked, looking at me.

I kept my eyes peeled on the trees, regretting that I'd said that out loud. I pointed, and her eyes returned to the trees.

"What's going on?" she said. "Is someone . . . there?"

"I don't know," I said.

"Maybe it's a breeze finally?"

We glanced at each other, and our eyes held the same expression. It was not a breeze.

"I thought I'd been imagining it before, but—"

"Me too," she replied.

"What—"

I was interrupted by a flash of movement in the poplar trees at the edge of the lake—peculiar movement in that one area, while the nearby hemlocks remained still and lethargic, as were the surrounding wilted sundrops, their heads hung low. Not a fluid, rhythmic waving of branches created by a passing wind but jagged, agitated, unnatural. A twinge of fear rushed through me and kept me seated. We were frozen, holding our breath, staring at the trees.

Chapter 2
Ella

My heart drummed fiercely in my chest as I peered through my dark sunglasses. This was not the first time I'd been watched, but it was the closest I'd felt to my stalker. Only a couple hundred yards of grass and gardens stood between us and the trees bordering my side of the lake.

I removed my hat and ran my fingers through my hair, pretending to be relaxed and unaware, but in my mind fear and panic seized me. My mother hadn't moved at all. She continued to stare into the moving branches ahead.

A sudden upheaval in the branches formed an opening, and I sensed a presence drawing near. I planted my feet on the ground, eyeing the back door. My mother did the same. I dabbed at the sweat pouring into my eyes, my heart wedged in my throat, our shallow, rasping breaths echoing above us. As much as I wanted to run, I wanted to wait this time. Just another second . . . to see who it was.

Is it him?

I straightened myself while placing one hand on my phone. I slid my sunglasses down with the other and stared directly at the menace hiding within the trees. I pointed, feigning bravery, while fear gripped my insides.

Twigs snapped. A tumultuous chaos within the leaves ensued as if a wild animal were breaking from its captors. Whoever was in the woods was coming out.

I grabbed my mother's hand and we bolted toward the back door of the cottage. The grass between us and safety seemed to multiply and lengthen with each step. I glanced frequently over my shoulder, fearing I'd see him and fearing I'd miss him. My legs felt heavy as we stumbled to the door. My mother was right beside me, a crazed look in her eyes, heavy breaths in my ear.

My unsteady hands fumbled with the doorknob. Finally it released, spilling us onto the floor. I slammed it shut so that the windows rattled. The bolt refused to align with the door frame, swollen and warped from the heat. I clicked the smaller lock on the knob. It would have to do for now.

We closed the blinds and raced to the kitchen window near the sink. It was high enough to view out and angled just so that if I stood off to the side it afforded me a perfect view without being seen. I spied the trees along the lake from the kitchen window, fearing he'd slip away and I'd never know.

But just as abruptly as it had started, the commotion in the leaves ceased, and then the parting of branches slowly began to recede, feathering backward until it no longer existed. As if it had never occurred.

A chill ran down my spine. I held my shaking arms and looked at my mother who was standing a few feet behind me. Her face had blanched, contorted in a horrified expression. She approached me cautiously and placed her hand on my arm. Together we stood by the window looking out at the wooded area of our beloved lake.

Soon another terrifying thought consumed me. We'd spent hours outside, gardening and weeding all around the yard. Although the front door was locked, we'd left the back door open so we could come and go into the cottage as needed. We weren't always near the back door. In fact, most of the gardening we did wasn't even within sight of the door. Someone could have easily slipped inside without either of us seeing.

I desperately needed to search the cottage to reassure myself we were safe.

My mother looked at me as if thinking the same thing. "The cottage," she uttered, and I nodded.

While she stood watch beside the window, I did a thorough search inside the house and thankfully found no one else there. But something still tugged at my stomach. Something wasn't right.

When I returned to the kitchen, I finally told my mother what I hadn't yet told anyone else—that over the last few weeks, I had without a doubt been watched and followed. I was surprised at how relieved I felt to finally say it out loud, to release the fear just a little bit and let someone else know.

I described moments when I jogged, as the path lengthened into less populated areas, how the feeling would suddenly change. A shift in the air. Leaves rustling a little more than they should, footsteps on gravel but no one around. Other times, headlights in my rearview mirror seemed to go wherever I went. And then that time I came home after working a double shift at the hospital and realized I hadn't locked the front door, which was odd because I always double-checked everything.

Separately, each time seemed like a coincidence, but collectively they became increasingly alarming.

My mother listened intently as the fan hummed in the background. She insisted we call the police, but I said no; I was pretty sure I knew who it was. I just needed proof. And I would get it. I was on the verge of telling her about the mysterious package and the video I'd found in the study when she cupped her hand under my cheek.

"You don't need to protect me," she said. "You know that, right?

I'm not afraid of anything anymore. I can handle disappointment."

I recalled her reaction on that sad day two years ago when I'd had to unleash the news which caused that disappointment, seeing the soft wrinkles at the corners of her eyes as I revealed Uncle Luca's secret and betrayal. He had framed her father—his own brother—for kidnapping and murder. The victim, Gianna, was the love of her father's and my Poppy's life, and Gianna had been carrying his baby or, as we later came to know, babies—twins—and my mother was one of them.

I hadn't even finished what I had to say that day, yet she knew. Her knees had nearly buckled as my words confirmed what her mind had already acknowledged: her real mother was Gianna, the one Luca had buried in a shallow grave in Italy. Nonna had raised my mother as her own, but she hadn't given birth to her as she claimed she had.

The vision of my mother crumpling to the floor, crying, remained fixed in my mind. Everything she'd ever known had been a lie.

After some time had passed, my mother began to accept the truth, refusing to allow it to swallow her. Sadness had turned to curiosity, and she wanted to know more. A fire grew within her, forging a new path for her life.

I knew I didn't give her enough credit, but I worried she'd get hurt again. What if we couldn't find Gianna? Or Grace, the lost twin she never knew? What if they didn't want to be found?

Now my mother stood before me, confident and strong, but I noticed something shift in her eyes. She looked away and tucked a curl behind her ear.

"I have something to tell you too," she said. "Strange things have also been happening to me. A couple days ago, while I was at the mailbox . . . it's hard to describe . . . it was a feeling, like you said. An eerie feeling came over me. Gave me chills. It felt like someone was right there, close to me. I thought maybe I was being paranoid at the time because of everything that's happened, but it felt so real." She seemed to hesitate before pulling her phone from her pocket. She tapped in her lock screen code and turned her phone toward me. "Yesterday I got this," she said.

I read the text out loud:

"I know something about you."

"What the hell?" I said. "Did you reply?"

"No," she said firmly.

"Is that a familiar number?"

She shook her head.

I jotted the number into my phone to check out later. "Maybe it was meant for someone else and you got it by mistake," I said, but I didn't believe that.

"Should I block it?"

"Not yet," I said. "Let's see if it happens again."

"You think it's Luca?" she asked. "Do you think he's the one watching us?"

"I don't know." I glanced out the window, regretting the few seconds I hadn't paid attention. "Do you really believe Aunt Lena hasn't seen him over the last two years? Or heard from him?" I asked.

"For the longest time I was sure she hadn't, but . . . I don't know anymore."

"I don't like not knowing where he is," I said.

"For all we know, her crazy nephew, Marco, shot him," she said. "He ran after him with his gun, right? Luca could be dead somewhere in those woods in Italy. I never even knew she had a nephew named Marco."

"He's not dead," I said. "I know it deep in my bones. That man is *not* dead."

"I hope you're wrong," my mother said, her eyes wide.

And like every other time Luca's name was mentioned, a brief discussion of my last encounter with him followed: The confrontation in the woods behind the vineyard in Italy two years ago. Marco, standing, his gun aimed. Luca running like a coward away from a grave that wasn't there—a grave he intended to be there. Jamie, Nico, and I sprinting in the opposite direction as Marco pursued Luca instead of us. We floated as we ran, our minds faster than our legs. Stumbling at the car while Nico searched frantically for the keys. Finally speeding away. The smell of rubber burning against the road as Jamie and I peered through the rear window all the way back to Angelina's.

It was a brief discussion that quickly became a heated conversation, resulting in more worries and less answers. I stared through the window at the calm trees peacefully standing near the water's edge and began to second-guess my reaction. But a voice inside my head resisted. *He's out there,* it whispered.

Chapter 3

Luca

Italy - 2 years earlier

A crack echoed through the forest, closer than the last. Thick, monstrous trees obscured his vision, but Luca knew these woods well and continued to run along a familiar path until he found a place to hide.

He had always feared this day would come, but when months became years, he thought he'd gotten away with it. This should have happened decades ago. Not now. Sure, he was still fit, but much older.

Luca knew Marco was determined to find him and would hunt through the woods until he did. He regretted pulling Marco into his affairs. He should have known better. Marco was his nephew only through marriage; he wasn't blood. He didn't deserve to know what he knew. Luca should be the one pursuing *him*, because now he knew too much.

Luca knew Marco didn't care anymore. He had nothing to lose. He knew Marco had a burning fire deep inside his soul etched with Luca's name. He began to sense Marco's disdain for him not long before they ended up in the woods behind the vineyard. Luca had orchestrated so much chaos in Marco's life, which eventually resulted in his wife, Sophia, leaving him. He had seen it in his eyes days before—Marco's regret mixed with anger for the dreadful things he had done for Luca for practically nothing; crimes he'd helped Luca keep secret.

Marco undoubtedly regretted trusting Luca, but he'd been raised without a father, and when Luca married Lena, Marco's aunt, Luca had immediately taken Marco in and filled the empty space in his heart. Luca knew this. He had fooled Marco into believing he actually loved and cared about him. For a time, it felt like love to Luca too. Marco felt like family, someone he could depend on and be his real self around. But like everyone else in Luca's life, Marco was just a tool to get what he wanted.

Slowly and methodically, Luca had lured Marco into his secret life, gradually sharing more and more, and Marco became his confidant. Luca remembered how elated he'd felt when Marco had finally accepted the assignment to follow Ella when she came to Italy. Luca had needed someone there to make sure she didn't dig too deep and find out what she ultimately discovered. But Luca never would have thought Marco would actually fall for Ella in the process. And he never could have anticipated that Marco's wife, Sophia, would discover Marco's deceptions and turn on him, divulging everything to Ella. Luca had sent Marco on a quest, and he lost everything, including his wife. That's why, when Luca bolted into the woods, he knew Marco would pursue him and not the others.

Luca ran as memories flashed through his mind. Memories of his beautiful mother grounded him in goodness and kindness, creating a fight within his conscience to be better. Memories of his father compelled the blackness from within his heart, creating a stark contrast to his mother's bright hopes for him. As the years had passed, the lines between good and bad and reality from fantasy in Luca's mind became so blurred that they no longer existed.

Another shot whipped through the trees, close to Luca as he bolted, weaving and ducking through the forest. How far could he run before his heart exploded? Pain arced across his chest. He feared his legs might buckle beneath him, causing him to fall and become vulnerable and exposed. He slowed his steps to calm his ragged breaths.

Crouching low within the wild brush, Luca looked at his dirt-caked fingers, crusted around his knuckles, much like that day when he'd buried her. Sickness welled within him, and he clenched his teeth to keep from vomiting. He swallowed hard and examined his time-worn hands from the life of a mason and a life of crime. As he moved his fingers to loosen the drying earth, that one small movement brought him back to that day.

She was so beautiful standing in the doorway at Maria's house that day, waiting for him at the foot of the steps, her hands resting on the handle of the baby carriage. Her supple skin radiated a beauty she possessed both inside and out. Her soft rose-petal lips made his heart race. Her unruly locks gave him a thrill. But it was the brown-and-green swirl in her eyes that captured him the most. How they held both the softness of a lamb and the fierceness of a tiger was intriguing to him. As he approached the steps, her eyes taunted him. She must have known it.

Gianna took Luca's outstretched hand and held it while guiding the carriage with the other. When she eventually wriggled her fingers out of his grasp, it deeply bothered him. He tried to decipher the look in her eyes. Was it confusion or repulsion? He reasoned that the heat had something to do with it. Or maybe two hands could guide the carriage more precisely.

"Luca, I've been thinking," she said when they'd reached the park.

Luca didn't answer. He was mesmerized by her wavy brown hair bouncing against her shoulders.

Gianna continued, "I know I said I wouldn't go to the vineyard anymore because of Franco, but today . . . I'd like to."

Franco. Why had she mentioned his name? It was a dagger through his heart every time. Perhaps going to the vineyard would finally rid Franco from her mind and she could move on. With him.

"You're sure you want to go?" he asked.

"I'm sure."

"Then let's go," he said. "We'll go anywhere you want."

But when they reached the vineyard, the carriage wheels caught easily on the brush and became difficult to push, so Luca suggested a safe spot nearby where they could leave Gabriella safely sleeping in the carriage and still have a perfect view of it while furthering down the path. Gianna reluctantly agreed but for not more than a few minutes. Luca locked the carriage wheels and folded the top closed to keep out bugs and protect Gabriella while she slept.

Vultures circled high above the treetops as they would prior to descending upon the dead. It reminded Luca of his last day with Gianna, there in those same woods, only it was the chickadees weaving from branch to branch slightly above their heads as they walked. Luca remembered paying more attention to Gianna's lips and her voice than the words floating from them.

Her smile flashed in his mind again.

"Do you think there's a way to get through that?" she asked about the thicket before them. "I heard the most beautiful meadow is just beyond all this." She waved her arms at the overgrown brush and old, fallen trees intertwined in an intricate puzzle. "I'd love to see it."

Luca resisted the urge to hold her hand. "Perhaps we'll come again tomorrow and I'll bring shears. Then we'll see what lies beyond."

"It might be more difficult than we think," she said, frowning, "but it's worth a try."

She looked at him in that special way again. He hoped—he believed—that after all that time apart from Franco she'd lost her love for him, accepted his death, and grown closer to Luca.

A loud snap pierced the air, and Luca dropped to the ground. He tried to get his bearings. Marco was gaining in proximity. Had he seen him?

"I'm on to you, old man!" Marco's voice echoed in the distance.

He was closer than Luca thought. Luca held his breath and listened as a chill swept through him. Like the chill he'd felt when his hand brushed against Gianna's on their way back to the carriage. A rush of fear mixed with thrill.

Twigs snapped close behind him. Luca kept his head to the ground and lay very still, inhaling an exhilarating mix of pine, earth, and decaying leaves. It was the same scent he'd smelled just before he pulled Gianna to his chest, pressed his mouth against her lips, and kissed her hard. She'd gotten angry and pulled away, calling him ridiculous and mad, telling him she could never love anyone besides Franco.

Luca remembered that precise moment he'd snapped and could no longer contain the rage inside. All the actions that followed could not be undone. He had felt a shift within himself as the darkness inside him took over. He'd gripped Gianna tightly and snatched her close again. He remembered the sting he'd felt when she pulled one arm free and hit him in the eye.

He slid his hands from her arms to her shoulders. And then to her throat. She struggled and fought against him, kicking and hitting, but he overpowered her. His fingers pressed into the soft skin around her neck as rage pumped through his blood. Her eyes that had once pulled him to her now repulsed him, and he watched as they shifted from confusion to fear to desperation. Luca squeezed until her body slackened, her eyes gently closed, and then . . . slowly he let go and watched her fall to the moist ground below. Luca crouched beside her beneath the shadows of the forest.

A bird swooped by Luca's ear, then another, and the movements startled him, whipping him back to the present moment. How long had he been hiding in the trees, his mind drifting back to that life he'd left behind?

He listened as an eerie silence filled the forest. When he felt it was safe, he got to his knees, cautiously scanned his surroundings, and stood crouched among the trees. Marco must have gone past him or changed directions. Was he safe? He fought against the need to stand tall and stretch. His aging body had been compacted, crouching low for much too long. What had he missed? And where was Marco?

Chapter 4

Ella

Shadows lengthened as the late afternoon sun hid behind the hills. The lights inside the cottage glowed behind the curtains as the outside lights facing the lake and the road burned brightly. We jumped at even the normal sounds of a settling house, and when we spoke, our voices expressed the fear in our minds.

My mother tried to keep busy by re-reading her ancestry report. I watched as she examined it, her chin resting in the palm of her hand, her wavy hair falling over her shoulders. She was beautiful inside and out. I admired how she had raised three kids alone with an element of grace and confidence I could only dream of having. I was proud and sad at the same time.

For as close as we were, there was a lot I didn't know about her. I knew by heart the beloved stories of her childhood that she told over and over again. On rare occasions, she'd share a high school or college memory, but they were fleeting: brief descriptions of friends gathering at a bonfire or sledding at the high school hill; whispers of summer nights with her best friend sneaking out of the house just to roam the neighborhood. My ears perked at these hidden treasures of her life. I'd listen desperately for more, filling in the missing pieces with my imagination.

I had so many questions. Who was her first love? Did she love my father like she had her first love? What were they like together as a couple? How did the hunting accident that claimed my father's life really happen? Had she accomplished what she wanted in life? I knew these were complex questions. It had to be difficult for her to talk about, or maybe it was too hard for me to ask. I anxiously scratched my arms. I wanted to know more.

She lowered her glasses and squinted at me. "What?"

"Nothing. I was just zoning."

She smiled and went back to her papers.

"Mom?"

"Yes?"

"Why don't you talk about Dad?"

She removed her glasses and sat up. "What made you ask that just now?"

"Can't I ask?"

"Of course you can," she said, setting the paper aside. "You can ask me anytime. Did something make you think of him?"

"I always wonder about him. I don't know a lot about him."

She arched her eyebrow. "What would you like to know?"

"Anything. What did you love about him?"

She threw her head back in thought and then looked at me with a wide smile. "He was a very generous man. Always wanted to help people. He was very handsome. He had a scruffy beard that I begged him not to shave." She laughed and then stared at the wall. I could tell she was lost in thought, back in time.

"And the accident . . . What caused it?" I regretted asking as soon as the words came out.

She clicked her pen vigorously and looked at me, her brow furrowed. "It was a hunting accident. You know that."

"But they never figured out how it happened."

"It was just him and a friend of his," she said. "The other hunters didn't know they were there. . . ." She trailed off. She shifted in her seat and looked at me through angry eyes. Angry at me or angry at life, I didn't know which. "Let's talk about this later. Now is not a good time."

I nodded. It never was.

But the lack of answers made me eager to know more about the missing branches of my family tree. The fullness of my mother's side held multiple vines connecting to others, now including Gianna and Grace, while my father's side had a twig with no leaves. How could I not know about an entire side of my family?

I was about to ask when my mother put her papers down again, removed her glasses, and stared at me. She leaned in close and proceeded to tell me about a peculiar visit she'd recently had with Aunt Lena.

My mother shared with me how Aunt Lena and Nonna had come over to her house for lunch. After lunch, Aunt Lena had gone into the living room and sat on the sofa. She was very quiet, unlike her normally talkative self. She had half-smiled with a distant look in her eyes as my mother approached and sat next to her. My mother asked Aunt Lena if she was feeling okay, and she had said she was fine. When Nonna joined them in the living room, she too commented that Aunt Lena looked unsettled, and Lena didn't like that.

"Nonna suggested to Aunt Lena that they should spend more time together," my mother explained, "and Aunt Lena said, 'You've seen me plenty, Olivia,' which I thought was odd. But Nonna insisted and tried to convince her that, since they were both alone, they could have sleepovers and it could be fun."

"Nonna is so sweet," I said.

My mother arched an eyebrow. "Lena looked at Nonna and yelled, 'NO!'"

"'No'?" I said, surprised.

"Can you believe that?"

"Of all people, Lena would never talk to Nonna like that," I said.

"Nonna wouldn't let up," my mother continued. "She insisted Lena not be alone and offered to stay with her for as long as she needed. And—you're not gonna believe this—Aunt Lena got all fidgety and anxious, kept shifting in her seat, and then she yelled, 'I'm not alone!' Then she looked horrified at what she'd said and covered her mouth with her hand."

"'I'm not alone'? She said that?"

"Yup."

"What did Nonna say? What did *you* say?"

"Nonna and I stared at each other, and Aunt Lena started to backpedal. Said she meant to say she's not *afraid* to be alone. She made excuses—her house was a mess, she's not ready for visitors, maybe another time. When was the last time she cared that her house was a mess?"

"You're right. I can't believe it," I said.

"I know. Nonna was so fired up," my mother continued. "You know how she gets—can't let it go, swears in Italian under her breath loud enough to hear but not so you know what she's saying. She was visibly upset with Lena. It was very uncomfortable after that. Lena didn't speak to either of us the rest of the night until I brought her home."

"Well, it's obvious she slipped," I said, "and she knows it. I've always feared it; known it. Uncle Luca is back, and she's hiding him in her house. That's the presence we feel." Even when he wasn't in front of us, he still haunted us. Stole our security. I glanced at my mom and placed my hand on her arm. "Our family hasn't been the same since I came back, and it's partly my fault. I know Aunt Lena blames me for what happened."

"None of this is your fault," she said. "You did what most of us could never do, and you risked everything for it. That's why Poppy confided in you. He knew you would expose the truth when he couldn't. I'm proud of you for that, and so is he."

My eyes swelled thinking about Poppy. He couldn't have known this would be the outcome.

I thought about the family dinner I'd had a few weeks after I got back from Italy. When Aunt Lena had excused herself from the table, the conversations had quickly shifted between predictions about Gianna's whereabouts to fearing Luca's next move. I remembered the worried look on Nonna's face when I said Gianna's name. I had reassured her that, no matter what, we all thought of *her* as our mother and grandmother, not Gianna. But we were curious and needed to know where she was and what had happened to her.

Nonna's eyes had widened as Aunt Lena returned to the table.

"Stop this right now," Aunt Lena had said. "I'm tired of all of you constantly thinking Luca is coming for you or hiding out there somewhere"—she waved her hand toward the backyard—"like he's spying on you. It's ridiculous." She'd grabbed her purse and marched to the front door. But before she left, she turned toward us and yelled, "Luca is not here anymore! Stop thinking he is! He's never coming back thanks to Ella!" She had left the door wide open as she stomped to her car. Mom ran after her just as Aunt Lena's car sped away. When Mom had come back inside she looked at me. "Ella. You know she didn't mean that." But I knew she had.

Everyone had blamed Aunt Lena's outburst and accusations on pent-up frustration because it had been so hard for her to deal with Uncle Luca's lies and now his disappearance. That may have been partly true, but I knew it was also because of me and the secrets I had exposed. They had changed us all.

Not once since my return from Italy had Aunt Lena ever expressed relief or happiness that I was okay, unharmed after the confrontation in the woods. She never acknowledged how scared I must have been to have a gun pointed at me. She never showed any empathy at how shocking it must have been when Uncle Luca had led me to the storage unit he'd rented which housed Gianna's belongings. She never seemed upset about *that*.

"I don't even blame Aunt Lena for hating me," I said to my mother. "Everything is different now. Look at us—we're fearful, less trusting even of each other. Just like Poppy's and Uncle Luca's father was. Just like Uncle Luca. He doesn't want us to find Gianna. As soon as he saw that she wasn't buried in those woods, he set out to find her, like we are now. What if he gets to her first? We can't let that happen. We need to go back to Italy. Now."

"Ella, how can we? Didn't you just get approved to go next month before your fellowship?"

I resisted the urge to tell her what I'd been thinking and planning for my fellowship—that I'd all but accepted an offer in the Doctors in Italy fellowship program in Rome to complete the last required step before becoming a heart specialist. Although it was something I'd wanted more than anything, it was hard to imagine being so far away from my mother, which is why I had put the conversation off for so long.

Instead, I changed the subject once again and chose to tell her about the thumb drive in my pocket, another secret I had kept from her. I'd transferred videos from the DVD I found in Poppy's study. It was Poppy himself describing a specific house in Tuscany. The urgency in his voice, the details and features of the house and his thoughts about it made me extremely curious. But the box at the end of the hallway, an odd and somewhat disturbing package I'd received two days ago with peculiar items inside, caught my attention, reminding me of the main reason I needed to talk to my mother.

I stared at it, ignoring her question about the fellowship. "There's something I want to show you," I said as I went to retrieve the package.

On my way back to the kitchen, the slam of a car door froze me mid-stride. *Who's out there?* I looked out the hall window toward the driveway, but the dusk obscured my vision. I suddenly felt anxious about the approaching nightfall surrounding my home. A loud, sudden rapping on the front door made my heart stop. I placed the package behind a chair next to a pile of private investigating books and slid to a window adjacent to the door, peering through a crack at the edge of the curtain. The light above the door illuminated a shadowy silhouette standing beneath it.

Chapter 5

Ella

I watched as the shadowy figure on my porch stepped back and the light unveiled a familiar face. It was Jamie standing at the door, her right hand resting on her hip.

An uneasy feeling crawled through my skin. We'd spoken very little since we returned from Italy. I held my breath, contemplating whether to let her in or pretend I wasn't home. Why would she stop by this late?

Jamie's eyes scanned the front windows and then looked at her watch. As she reached for the doorbell, I opened the door.

"El!" She seemed surprised.

"Hi, Jame."

"May I come in?"

"Of course," I said, stepping aside. We hugged briefly as she entered, and she followed me down the hallway to the living room.

"You would love London, Ella. I'm telling you, it should be our next adventure." She tossed her hair over her shoulder and smiled.

I returned a forced smile, recalling the day she'd phoned from London, well over a month ago, to say she'd gotten married. It was love at first sight, she'd said. They just clicked. Next thing she knew she was off to London to tie the knot, like a dream. *Not my dream.* No invitation, no party. Nothing. Her husband's clean-cut blonde hair and always-well-dressed appearance was something I only knew through photographs.

"I'm sure it was amazing," I said. "Can I get you anything? Something to drink?"

She hesitated but then said, "Yes, I'd love a glass of water." She threw her jacket over the back of the sofa and sat down.

Water over wine?

My mother, who had followed me into the living room and waited there as I answered the door, stood by the sofa as Jamie entered.

"Gabby!" Jamie approached my mother as soon as she saw her and hugged her.

"Welcome back," my mother said with a slight sting to her voice. She'd become very cautious of Jamie since her questionable behavior in Italy.

Although Jamie said she hadn't known of Uncle Luca's ill intentions when he'd asked her to keep an eye on me while we were in Italy together, I still had a hard time believing her. She'd even cried when I told her that *she* was the one he was playing with, not me; that he wasn't genuinely concerned for my safety and well being, but he was worried that I'd discover things he didn't want me to know.

I remembered how concerned he was when I first told the family I was going to Italy to do what Poppy couldn't do: resolve the disappearance of his lost love and clear his name in the process. Luca had used Jamie for his own gain and she'd happily obliged. Almost as soon as we'd gotten to Italy, I sensed something was off about her but couldn't place it, just like I felt now.

Jamie smiled at my mother and then her eyes slid to my walls. "I thought you'd put Gianna's painting there," she said, pointing above the fireplace where Poppy's Italian neighborhood painting was displayed. It was an exact replica of the streets of Scilla that he and his brother and Gianna and her sisters would run through and play along all day—one of my favorites. I never would have imagined that, just a few decades later, I would wander those streets as well, although for very different reasons. I felt immense pleasure and pride in Poppy's paintings because they were pieces of his life that told a story.

"I wanted to," I said, "but I can't find it. It's missing. Do you remember what I did with it?"

As a child, I'd always been curious about the mysterious woman in the painting, the wide brim of her hat gently resting on golden shoulders. At the time, Poppy had said he didn't know who she was, but, of course, after my trip to Italy, I discovered that was far from the truth. The mysterious woman was Gianna.

"They were in the back seat of your car," she said. "After you had them matted and reframed. I saw them there." She twirled her hair, and the rock on her finger momentarily snagged. "You wouldn't let them out of your sight—wouldn't even let *me* touch them."

I refrained from commenting.

My mother stared at Jamie. "I'm sure it'll turn up," she said. "We'll keep searching until we find it." She smiled.

Jamie smiled back and then opened her purse and retrieved a thin envelope. She opened it and pulled out several professional photographs from her wedding and honeymoon. She seemed truly happy. Still selfish, but happy.

But like before, something was off about her. Since her betrayal in Italy, my view of Jamie had changed. When I'd learned she had acted as Uncle Luca's spy, she'd claimed she had my best interests at heart and was only doing it because Uncle Luca feared for our safety. She swore she hadn't known his true intent, that he'd used her to find out what I knew about his secrets. It eventually made sense why Marco would appear everywhere we were.

Jamie was my best friend. Someone I could trust and confide in.

She had been an integral part of my healing after Jack died. I trusted her with my life. But after Italy, things were different. I realized things about Jamie I never had before. I saw her for who she really was, and that was not my best friend.

It plagued me after I returned from Italy and moved into the cottage that, of all the paintings, the one of Gianna was missing. I remembered putting it aside near the sofa because I planned to fix the broken wire on the back. I'd left for the hardware store to pick up some new wire the next day, and when I got back it wasn't there. We were so busy that week moving my things in and Nonna's out. In all the chaos, someone must have moved it so it wouldn't get damaged. But no one remembered doing that or even having seen it in the first place.

Poppy's paintings were far deeper than a particular moment in time. They were a life and a story. When I was little I used to imagine I could put myself into those paintings and be part of their story.

It took a while before I was ready to display the beautiful painting of the vineyard. To me it signified deep love shadowed by deep sorrow. What once was a beautiful escape for Gianna and Poppy became a terrifying nightmare. But I convinced myself to remember the reason that had moved Poppy to paint it. He never knew the terrible things that went on in the woods behind it. To Poppy, it represented happiness, and when I looked at it now, that's what I chose to see.

"How's Nico?" Jamie asked, interrupting my thoughts. "It must be hard to be apart."

"It is, but we're good." I smiled, pushing away that uneasy feeling again. "I'll see him soon."

"Are you going back to Italy?"

"No. He's coming here next," I lied.

"We should get together!"

I was about to say probably not when Hercules charged in, tossing Jamie's water to the floor. He stood crouching, his hackles raised on the back of his neck. A loud, incessant barking rolled to a low growl. His muscles twitched as he stared down the door. My mother, Jamie, and I stood close.

"Hercules, what is it, boy?" I said, stepping cautiously toward him.

His eyes were locked on the door.

I raced upstairs to the front guest bedroom window to get a better view. Jamie and my mother followed and waited in the hallway. I kept the lights off and stared out the window into darkness. Something was near the old white spruce near the mailbox at the edge of my front yard—an obscure figure, hard to make out, but the more I watched the more I was convinced it wasn't some*thing* but some*one.* Suddenly it bolted from the tree out into the road and out of sight.

"El, what is it?" my mother whispered from the doorway.

Jamie peeked over her shoulder.

"I saw someone run from the tree out front by the road," I said, turning from the window. My hands were shaking.

"Did you see where they went?" my mother asked.

"No, just toward the road. It was too hard to see. We should call the police."

"We should have done that hours ago!" she replied, dialing.

"Do you see anything else?" Jamie asked, approaching the window.

"It's too dark," I said. My chest tightened.

"What can the police do if he's gone?" Jamie said.

"'He'?" I echoed.

"Whoever. . . . Probably a man. Isn't that usually the case?"

"Ella lives here alone," my mother said. "We need the police."

I brushed past them, and they followed me down the stairs. As we neared the last step, Hercules turned his attention to Jamie and barked repeatedly at her.

"Hercules! No!" I yelled.

He stopped barking but remained crouched. He sniffed Jamie and came to my side. His tail wagged despite the spiked hair along his neck.

"Something's got him spooked," Jamie said.

Officer Spalina arrived soon after I called. He asked several questions and then investigated the front and back yards and the adjacent houses but found nothing. He reassured me that if someone was out there, at least now they knew we were aware. And Hercules's vicious bark might have been enough to scare whoever it was away. He assured us it probably wasn't personal.

I convinced myself this couldn't have been Luca. He was too smart to allow himself to get this close and cause a scene. But it could have been someone working on his behalf.

After another look around, Officer Spalina left.

"What's that?" Jamie asked, pointing to the package I'd hidden behind the chair. "Are those private investigating books?"

"It's a package for Nonna," I lied. "I still get her mail sometimes." I ignored the question about the books and the doubtful look in her eyes.

My mother and I looked at each other. I'd tell her about the box later.

"Ella . . . this is scary," Jamie said. "Has this ever happened before?"

"No, never," I said.

"I guess I have great timing," she joked, but no one laughed, not even Jamie. Instead, she had a distant look on her face as if something else was on her mind. "Any updates on Gianna?"

It was just like Jamie to be blunt. I couldn't tell if she was trying to change the subject or if she genuinely wanted to know. And if she did want to know, was it out of caring or for her own agenda? I still didn't trust her completely.

"No, not yet."

"You'll no doubt be going back to Italy, then, to find out," she said. "And if I know you, it'll be soon. I can't believe it's been almost two years since we were there." She cracked her knuckles and bit her lip. "So, Ella, I need to talk to you—"

We froze as the piercing sound of breaking glass exploded at the back of the house. We listened and scanned the doorways. I ran toward the back door where the sound had come from as my mother yelled for me to wait. Shattered glass at the foot of the door littered the floor. My heart dropped seeing the door partially ajar. Had someone gotten in? Jamie and my mother came quickly, my mother frantically tapping her phone to call again for help.

"Oh my God! Hercules!" I yelled, stomping over crushed glass as it cut into the soles of my feet. "Hercules!" I heard the shrill hysteria in my voice as it echoed in the night.

But Hercules didn't come. He'd bolted after someone, and he'd stop at nothing until he got him, or at least he'd fight like hell trying.

"Help!" I shouted, running across the backyard searching desperately for Hercules while also being watchful of the intruder who could be anywhere out there. My calls for help seemed to be swallowed in the air. I felt exposed and fearful running along the lake in the direction I thought Hercules might have gone, near the trees that earlier had harbored a mysterious disturbance. I continued to call for help and shout for Hercules, the muted sounds of my mother's frantic screams in the distance.

Chapter 6

Luca

Italy - 2 years earlier

Crouched and hiding uncomfortably beneath a dark sky and thick canopy of trees, Luca seethed with anger, brought back against his will and better judgment to the same spot he'd lied about years ago. The exact place where he'd carved a shallow pit in the dirt and laid to rest the love of his life.

Plagued with emotion, he struggled to accept the implications of an empty grave. How could this have happened? She had been dead before his very eyes.

And now it was he who was running from a madman.

He heard the snap of a twig.

Then another.

Marco was getting closer.

Luca prayed that Marco would walk by and never see him hiding there. As he prayed, a tiny piece of guilt pierced his soul because he knew he didn't deserve for his prayers to be heard.

Luca almost lost his footing as a prickling sensation crawled through his sleepy legs. As he tried to catch himself, he caused the leaves at his feet to rustle. He stopped moving and, from where he stood, he had a perfect view of Marco.

Marco must have heard him because he whipped around and pointed the gun directly where Luca was hiding. Marco waited, scanned the trees, and moved on.

"I'm gonna find you, old man! "he yelled. "And when I do . . ." He whistled an eerie tune and disappeared into the shadows.

Suddenly, from a different direction, Luca heard something brush against leaves—a *snip-snap-whoosh* sound blasting through the trees and approaching fast. Luca was tucked beneath a low-hanging branch, hardly standing. He peeked between the leaves and at the same time saw Marco stop. He watched Marco's silhouette turn toward the noises.

Luca winced at the sharp pain in his knees. *Just a few minutes more and then I can move. Just wait. Don't move.* But the pain was too much. Luca considered shifting his weight, just enough to give him relief and buy him some time, but the pain was too strong and he let out a small gasp.

Marco spun around to face Luca's hiding place.

Luca knew this was it. This was where he met his end. He tried to push his body farther into the brush, but it was too thick and his legs were too weak.

Marco took a step in Luca's direction. He held up his gun and aimed. He took another step.

A loud *CRACK!* exploded around Luca, and he no longer heard the sounds of the forest. Luca slumped down, unsure if he was alive or dead. He opened his eyes, looked at his hands and feet, then he looked out at where Marco stood . . . but he was gone. Luca waited to see what might happen next, and, as he was about to stand, a large shadow of a man stepped into view.

The man approaching the spot where Marco stood a moment before had a hulking, muscular build. Probably at least six feet tall.

Luca saw the man looming over Marco's body, giving him a slight nudge with the butt of his gun, but Marco didn't move. The man bent closer to Marco and then spoke into his phone.

"It's not him," he said gruffly. "It's the other one. Yeah. I'll take care of it."

Then he hoisted Marco's body over his shoulder and gave one final scan of the forest. Moonlight glimmered through the trees illuminating the high, structured cheekbones and square jawline of the hitman before he disappeared through the trees.

Luca felt a chill spread through his body. He'd seen this man before—an apprentice of his father. "He does the dirty work," his father would tell him when he'd come along with him. "You don't ever want to cross him," he'd say, laughing. His father had only shared his secret life with Luca, and Luca felt privileged to be part of his inner circle.

Something Franco would never have.

But the features of this man's face were so much like the man his father had worked with. He was much younger then. Was it him? Or could it be Gianna's husband, Carlos? Could Carlos still be looking for Gianna after all these years? Or was Carlos now looking for Luca?

Luca contemplated bolting out of the forest, but fear paralyzed him, rooting him to the ground. He waited a little while longer and then made his move. Once out of the forest, he took back roads and got on a train headed north to a house he hadn't been to in well over thirty years.

Chapter 7
Ella

I sprinted through the backyards of the next two neighbors and had to stop running to catch my breath. Hercules was long gone, and I felt vulnerable out in the open, exposed to my intruder. Whoever had done this could be watching me. I knew I had to turn around and go back. I shouldn't have left my mother alone with Jamie, and I felt with some confidence that Hercules would find his way home . . . if he wasn't harmed.

As soon as I arrived in my own backyard, I ran toward the back door and immediately saw a message in Italian painted in black across it, causing the hairs on the back of my neck to raise:

BASTA
Moriranno…
I tuoi amici

"Stop. They will die . . . your friends."

I raced inside and locked the door.

My mother was a hysterical mess. She hugged me tightly and then stepped back. "You shouldn't have run out there like that!" she scolded. "Anything could have happened!"

When I told both Jamie and my mother about the writing on the door, Jamie thought the message was referring to her, but I had a strange feeling it was meant for Angelina, or maybe Nico. Why else would it be written in Italian?

Now I was convinced Luca had to be the one behind this. And he *wanted* me to know. He was playing a game, and he thought I would play along.

I called Nico right away, but it went to voicemail. Officer Spalina returned as I was about to call Angelina. He and another deputy followed us around the back of the house to see the message.

Officer Spalina listened to our story while stroking the stubble on his chin. Something about his dark hair and his chocolate brown eyes reminded me of Nico. His partner, Officer Carey, asked if I thought I was being stalked. I sighed and explained to her everything that happened over the last few days as well as my growing concerns about Luca. She scribbled notes on a notepad and looked up when I mentioned the package I'd received a couple days ago. Jamie's eyes burned through me. The officers asked to see it, but I hesitated. I didn't want to open it in front of Jamie, especially since I hadn't even shown my mother yet.

Officer Spalina suggested we first drive around the neighborhood and then open the package after we returned. Officer Carey agreed and resumed searching the house and the yard. I was relieved to go with Officer Spalina, not only to put off opening the package in front of Jamie but more importantly to help him find the intruder and possibly spot Hercules. I hoped while we were gone my mother would keep an eye on Jamie. Jamie would definitely try to peek inside that box if she thought she wouldn't get caught. And who knew what else she might snoop around for.

After almost an hour and no sign of Hercules or anyone else, Officer Spalina and I returned to the cottage. I tried to convince myself that Hercules was smart and he'd find his way back.

As soon as we stepped inside the house, Officer Spalina asked to see the package. Reluctantly, I placed the box on the table.

"You said that was for Nonna," said Jamie with her arms crossed.

"I know I did," I replied, "but it was actually addressed to me."

Everyone watched as I lifted the cover, reached inside, and carefully pulled a long chain from the neatly wrapped tissue. The chain fell gently through my fingers as I presented it. My mother reached for the intricately designed pendant and ran her fingers across the antique roped edge to the smooth, turquoise oval stone in the center, a deep-blue stone that reminded me of Italy's beautiful Tyrrhenian Sea. Within the blue were three concentric ovals of black, gold, and white, shaped like an eye that I only recently came to know as the "evil eye."

Instinctively I reached for the Italian horn hanging on my neck and thought of Angelina. I'd worn the Italian horn every day since she gave it to me. She had proclaimed that wearing it would provide peace and safety against evil—an evil she was convinced surrounded my family and me.

"I knew what it was immediately when I pulled it out of the box," I said as they passed it around.

"Maybe it's from Angelina," said my mother. "Maybe she's still trying to protect you."

"I thought so too and tried to call her to find out, but she didn't answer. And there's no return address. Angelina would have included one." I removed the other items from the box. "These were also inside," I said, placing two black-and-white photographs on the table. One was a picture of a mansion, and the other was a picture of a beautiful older woman. I handed the picture of the woman to my mother. "If I had to imagine what Gianna might look like as an older woman—based on the painting and the pictures Poppy had of when she was young—this would be it."

My mother reached for the photograph and held it close to examine its details.

"I don't understand," Jamie said. "Who would send you these? Why?"

The officers were intrigued by my story and examined the necklace, the pictures, and the empty box. They asked about Luca and wanted to know more about our family. I knew they were doing their job, but I didn't want to say anymore in front of Jamie. I briefly explained the meaning of the evil eye and the curse that many Italians believed could be put upon another and the connection between Gianna and Uncle Luca. The officers gasped when I said that Uncle Luca thought he had killed and buried Gianna.

"Your uncle *thought* he killed someone and buried them—alive? But you didn't find the body?" Officer Carey asked.

"Correct," I said.

"But we found a gold necklace," Jamie added.

I shot her a look.

Then the officers asked if I had ever seen either of the pictures before or if they meant anything to me, and I told them no . . . although that wasn't entirely true. I didn't want to say in front of Jamie that I believed the house in the picture might be the one Poppy had mentioned in the DVD, the one he thought Luca was connected to.

"Your uncle's an old man now. You think he's up to this?" Officer Spalina asked.

"He's not a typical old man," I said. "He's strong and resourceful . . . and corrupt. He might have even hired someone to work on his behalf. He's got connections. I'm surprised you haven't heard of his father, Gabriel Perri."

They glanced at each other but said nothing.

"But now that Luca's secrets are out," Jamie said, "why would he care now? What does he have to prove?"

I eyed her up and down coldly. "Gianna being alive is a threat to Luca. He knows I'm not going to stop until I've found her and uncovered every last secret of his, and trust me, he doesn't want that to happen."

Jamie shrugged her shoulders and looked away, annoyed.

Both officers appeared sincerely concerned for my safety and promised to have a car patrol the neighborhood for the next few days. They recommended I look into home security options and also suggested that, as soon as I had any proof that my Uncle Luca was behind this, we would get an order of protection against him.

Officer Spalina handed me his card on the way to his car. "Call if you need anything," he said. "We'll be right outside."

Jamie offered to stay the night, but my mother said there was no need since she'd already planned to sleep over.

As the officers approached their cars, something in the trees at the end of the driveway moved wildly. The officers stepped away from their vehicles and assumed a ready stance, their hands on their holsters. We were still as we watched, preparing ourselves for the unknown.

Hercules emerged from the brush. When he spotted me, his ears flew back, his tail wagged excitedly, and he bolted into my arms. I hugged him as he trembled with energy. He smelled of outdoors and wet dog, and I loved every bit of it. I plucked pine needles and small twigs from his fur as he licked my face.

The officers, still unsure if anything else would burst through the bushes, remained fixed to their positions. After searching the area and finding nothing, they came to inspect Hercules.

For a moment, we all relaxed. I wished Hercules could tell me what he saw out there. I cradled his face in my hands and noticed blood near the corner of his mouth. I examined the inside of his mouth and saw blood surrounding his lower canines.

Once inside the house, I cleaned him up and examined him more closely. There were no cuts or bruises that I could see in his mouth or on his face, and there appeared to be no blood coming from anywhere on his body. The blood dripping from his mouth moments ago couldn't have been his. It must have belonged to whoever was still out there in the woods. I removed his bloodstained collar and gave it to Officer Spalina for inspection by the forensics lab.

I noticed something just beneath his collar. When I removed it, a small, shredded piece of denim fell to the floor, surely from the intruder as well. Someone out there had had a good fight with Hercules, and now they were hiding. And wounded.

Chapter 8

Ella

A warm amber light glimmered through the cottage windows revealing an awakened and busy household. I was determined to make sure the intruder knew the people in this house would not drop their guard. I felt slightly at ease knowing one officer was parked in front of my house and the other was patrolling the nearby streets.

Hercules remained beside me, following me from room to room, yet he was restless and wouldn't lie down or even sit. He stood and panted and whined, and his eyes never left sight of me.

I had a hard time settling myself and decided to do some research online: light reading about psychopaths, serial killers, and private investigating. My mother dove once again into her ancestry report, her laptop propped upon her knees. She tried to keep her mind off the last few hours, but I could tell she wasn't paying attention to anything on the screen. Her eyes wandered from me to her phone to the door and back to her screen, never staying in any one place for long. Sometimes, when she'd get up to go to the bathroom, on her way back she'd pace back and forth down the hallway from the kitchen to just beyond the view of the back door before returning to her laptop again.

Before the officers had moved outside, they boarded up the broken window on the back door and confirmed that the lock was still intact. I went into the study where I often found solace and inspiration. I sat in Poppy's desk chair and flipped the thumb drive between my fingers over and over, recalling how I'd stumbled across the DVD shortly after moving into the cottage. I had found it almost by accident on a shelf in the closet among other home videos. A note attached to the inside was simply labeled *"Box."* But it never made it into the box he'd hidden, the one he wanted me to find, the one I *did* find tucked into the dark crevice of a particular bookshelf obscured by tightly packed leather spines. Had he forgotten to put it there? Had he changed his mind? Or could the note be entirely unrelated?

I knew all the family movies on those DVDs by heart and had watched them dozens of times over the years, never tiring of them. I remembered coming to the cottage as a teenager and spending time looking through old photo albums and watching old DVDs with Nonna and Poppy. Before we sat down to watch, Poppy would make his famous banana splits and, aside from various ice cream flavors and bananas, he had all the fixings: whipped cream, nuts, chocolate toppings, sprinkles, hot fudge, and even pineapple. "Pineapple?" I'd said, making a face the first time. "Just try it," he'd said. "It'll make it schmeckle!" And I was glad I had. It was just the right ingredient to balance all the rest and definitely made it "schmeckle."

Poppy had always encouraged us to try something first before assuming we wouldn't like it. More often than not, we loved whatever new and unusual food we tried at his table. My stomach rumbled at the memory.

A few days ago, I had come to the study to gather all the DVDs in hopes of having the family over to watch them and reminisce about Poppy. I stood in front of the shelves and looked at the collection: twenty-five meticulously labeled jackets in Poppy's flowy handwriting, with the dates and events written along the spines, lined up in neat rows on two shelves. All had been labeled except one.

Curious about the unlabeled DVD, I pulled it from the others and popped it into Poppy's old DVD player to have a look at it, excited for the memories it contained. Sadly the DVD player no longer worked, so I transferred all the DVDs to thumb drives for each member of my family. Something told me to watch the unlabeled one before sharing it. I was glad I did.

It wasn't what I expected, and I wondered if Poppy had meant for it to be on the shelf among the others or if it was meant to be kept somewhere else. I wondered if anyone else had seen it or known about it.

When I inserted the thumb drive into my laptop, a younger Poppy with salt-and-pepper hair, smiling eyes, and a plump belly was speaking into a microphone. It was the same microphone used by my sister, brother, and I when we belted out countless made-up songs while we were growing up. It was the Poppy I knew best from my childhood. He must have propped his video camera on a tripod, unless someone else was filming him. He had to be in his mid-fifties. My heart melted at the sound of his soulful, warm voice as if he were in the room speaking directly to me.

In this particular video, he spoke passionately about a house in northern Tuscany he'd never been to but was adamant existed. He said he planned to go there someday. I was intrigued by his insatiable curiosity about this house. I recognized the sparkle in his eyes as he talked about it.

But his excitement was fleeting, and sadness resumed as he acknowledged that he'd probably never be able to get there. Something was always in his way; usually it was Nonna. Nonna meant well, but she could be very controlling, especially of Poppy. He said he'd never be able to go without Nonna but knew he could not bring her there either. So he remained stuck in a place he didn't want to be.

I was lost in the soulful drone of his voice and his unique mannerisms, but my ears perked when he mentioned Luca. He was resolute in his belief that Luca had been to this house and on more than one occasion. Poppy said one time he had overheard Luca talking to someone on the phone and heard him say something about arriving in Tuscany. Luca had kept his voice low, but he couldn't prevent Poppy and Aunt Lena from overhearing. Poppy said he had noticed Aunt Lena's eyes widen as they listened to Luca's conversation. Something about a visit to his home in Tuscany. He was sure Luca had said *his* home. Poppy confronted Luca, but he had brushed it off saying he was visiting the home of a colleague while he went there on business.

Poppy looked directly into the camera with an expression I'd never seen before. His eyes grew serious, fierce, and he spoke as if Luca were right in front of him. "Luca," he said, "you're a liar. You don't have clients in Tuscany. Tuscany was beneath you—remember when you said that? All this time you say you've been going to Milan or Venice, but it's not there that you go. I know where you really go for weeks at a time, sometimes more. I know what's there . . . or should I say *whom?* It doesn't matter *how* I know. And if I'm right—so help me God, if you've done what I think—someday you will pay." Poppy made a tutting noise and shook his head. He looked once more straight into the camera. "You may have fooled everyone else, Luca, but not me."

And that was it. There were no further recordings after that. I watched it three more times and was desperate to know what had happened. I needed to know if Poppy had ever proved what he believed.

My mother's reaction was the same after she saw it. She wanted answers as much as I did. We hoped we were the only ones who knew about the DVD. What if it had fallen into someone else's hands?

Would they have brushed it off as a jealous brother or an old man captivated and obsessed with a mysterious house? Or would they be as concerned as we were? Could Poppy have known it—planned it—that I'd be the one to find the DVD just like I'd found the box?

My thoughts ventured to a darker side. Could criminal genes be passed within a family? I knew mental illness could. How closely were the two linked? Maybe they lurked within our cells, dark and deceptive, almost invisible until a trigger released the darkness that could no longer be contained. Maybe that was what had happened with Uncle Luca and his cruel, angry father—how our seemingly adoring uncle became a criminal right before our eyes. Pretending to be one of us, acting like us, sounding like us, seeming to be the same as we were, but disguised all the while as a weed.

My phone chimed loudly and I jumped. A text from Angelina:

Ella…thank u for the gift. It's lovely, but…I don't understand.

Gift? I hadn't sent her a gift.

Chapter 9
Gianna

Italy 1939

Her eyes opened but the darkness remained.

Was she dreaming?

Something gritty on her lashes fell into her eyes, and they stung and watered. She blinked, but it only intensified the pain. Something soft tickled her nose, caving into her nostrils and into her partially open mouth. It caught at the back of her throat making her cough and choke. Her teeth crunched into the grainy, tasteless matter. She spat and coughed again as a powdery substance loosened and cascaded around her.

Panic coursed through Gianna at the frightening realization that she could only draw in brief gasps of air, short, rapid, dust-filled air, into her lungs. And all at once she felt an alarming sensation of confinement.

Wake up!

Fear gripped her insides as a musky, sulfuric scent and moist earth engulfed her. Was it her surroundings or her own fear she smelled? Soon something familiar dominated—sweet pines and cedar—telling her more than she could accept. This was not a dream.

Her body ached, imprisoned, heavy. But a slight movement of her fingers and toes instilled hope that she might still be alive. Gianna grasped at fragments of her memory, pulling at the moments that had led her there. Confined to the musty dampness of the earth, Gianna's skin crawled, as did her mind, as she became keenly aware of her dire situation beneath the soil.

How long had she been there? She listened to muffled footsteps padding over the earth nearby. She convinced herself not to attempt to scream but to remain calm, fearing the footsteps above may belong to the one who had put her here. She prayed she could endure her tiny grave until they were gone.

All at once a desperate ache swirled in the pit of her stomach as two names echoed in her heart: *Gabriella and Grace.* Suddenly, the horrifying moments that had led her here returned, and she felt she might slip away, consumed by fear. Gianna forced herself to focus and concentrate on breathing and praying.

Soon the footsteps faded away, and Gianna's heart pounded loudly in her ears. *Get out, Gianna. You must get out. For the babies.* She wriggled her shoulders and tried to bend her knees against the tightly packed earth. Sweat beaded along her forehead and dripped into her eyes. Her chest squeezed against her ribs. She concentrated on a pattern: move her shoulders, then her knees, then her arms and legs, pause briefly for small breaths of dirt-filled air, and pray for strength. She repeated this sequence until slowly the space around her began to widen.

With effort she was able to bend her arms and kick her legs. She drew her arms toward her chest and punched at the rigid earth, her knuckles scraping against dirt and roots. At times she paused to spit clumps of soil that had fallen into her mouth. She felt depleted of air and energy but feared that, if she stopped now to rest, she might not start again. So, with her babies' faces fixed in her mind, Gianna stubbornly forced the earth aside. At once, Gianna moved every part of her body as mounds of dirt fell around her. Her bloodied hands pushed through and gripped the dead branches purposely laid upon the earth. She used them to pull herself up to a seated position. Crisp sounds of the forest echoed in the night, and the cool air rushed to her weary lungs.

She wiped dirt from her face and brushed it off her body. She threw aside branches and tangled vines that had disguised her burial and hoisted herself against a branch until she could stand and climb out of that hole. Gianna's limbs shook as she stood, finally free, peering at her grave below. She drew her hands to her sore neck and throat, and her pulse quickened as she visualized the face of the man who had done this to her.

Luca.

Although Gianna felt vulnerable, alone in the woods, the only thing she cared about was finding Gabriella. After getting her bearings, she scanned the trees for movement in the shadowy forest and, when she felt it was safe, she bolted to the spot where she was sure she'd parked the carriage, fearing she may never find it or, worse, find it empty. It was nowhere in sight. Her heart sank as she listened for her baby's cries, filtering out the sounds of tree frogs, insects buzzing around her head, an occasional, distant hoot from an owl. *Nothing.* A sickness welled within her, and she fell to the ground and vomited.

Lights from the vineyard glimmered in the distance as did the yellow glow of eyes not far from where she stood. She prayed Luca hadn't left Gabriella alone in the woods, that he had taken her back to Maria's or to his own home where she would be safe. She wiped her cheeks, feeling helpless and defeated. She thought she had done the best she could to love and protect Gabriella in the three months she'd raised her. She'd never had the chance to meet Grace, stolen in the minutes that followed Gabriella's birth, and now they both were missing. She had failed the one thing she'd promised herself: to keep her daughters safe.

But she had to think clearly, to be vigilant. What good was she to her children if something happened to her now? Luca might return or even be there watching her now. Maybe he'd seen her crawl out of the grave he had dug and was waiting for the right moment to put her back in it for good.

Her eyes filled again as she thought about her daughters, twins separated at birth by her own mother. Gianna had gotten so close to learning what had happened to Grace. She had trusted her mother, and how could she have known not to? She had trusted Luca and believed he was nothing like his father. But he was just like him. She questioned her lack of judgment about the people closest to her and her lack of confidence in her own decisions.

If Luca was out there, she and her children weren't safe. Gianna desperately wanted to run but feared he might see her. For now, she was safest in the small hiding spot she'd found among the bushes. Safe from wild animals and safe from Luca. Under the dimming moon, she imagined how she would find her children. Her tired legs gave in and her body slid gently into the dense brush. She fought against the lulling sounds of the forest and the heaviness in her eyes.

Chapter 10
Ella

I called Angelina as soon as I read her cryptic message, and she picked up on the first ring.

"Hello, dear!" Her voice was bouncy and full of life even though it was five o'clock in the morning in Tropea, Italy. "I see you got my text! How are you?"

"Hi, Angelina," I said, putting the phone on speaker when my mom came into the room. "I'm okay. How are you?"

"Wonderful!" she said.

"Angelina, I got your text, but . . . I didn't send you a gift."

"Nonsense! It came late last night. I just opened it now. You remembered the story of the *malocchio*," she said. "Who else would have sent it?"

"*Malocchio?* The evil eye?" I said.

"Yes, of course, the evil eye."

My stomach twisted as I held a similar gift in my hand. The evil eye, known to Italians as the *malocchio,* was a curse that someone cast upon another, wishing them harm. The last time I'd been to Italy, Angelina was convinced I had been cursed. She had performed a test using oil and water, which confirmed I had the *malocchio.* Immediately following the test, Angelina had created a remedy and said a prayer that dispelled the curse. She'd given me an Italian horn necklace the next day to ward off any other evil. I'd worn it every day since.

"I don't know who sent that to you, but it wasn't me," I said. I heard her rummaging through something and mumbling to herself.

"Hold on," she said. "I thought there might have been a card, but there isn't one. No return address either. Very strange. If this isn't from you, who's it from?"

"I have no idea. Describe it to me," I said, looking at mine. "What's it like?"

"Well, it's an oval . . . like an eye. Almond-shaped, actually, with a beautiful blue stone in the center and—"

"Two circles around that? Black and gold?" I interrupted.

"Yes."

"A roped edge . . . antique gold on a long, gold chain, right?"

"Well—yes. That's correct," she said. "How would you know if you didn't send it?"

"I'm holding the same thing in my hand right now. I got a package yesterday. No return address. No note. I thought it might have come from you."

Angelina seemed to stumble over her words. "No, I—I'm confused. I don't . . . know what to say. . . ."

"Was there anything else in the package?" I asked, holding the photographs as if showing them to her.

"No, just the necklace. Why?"

"I found two photographs in an envelope with mine," I said. "I almost didn't see them in all the tissue paper. You're sure you looked through everything carefully?"

"Yes," she said. "I emptied the whole box. What were the pictures?"

"One of them is an older woman, maybe in her fifties. The other one is an old mansion."

"Mansion? I know a lot about mansions," she said, her tone

pregnant with curiosity. "Tell me more about it."

"It looks old and rustic but stately. Like it might have been beautiful at one time. Kind of hard to see because it's black and white. There's a lot of land around it and hills. Looks like there's maybe a fence or a gate around it. And I think that's a swing hanging from a big tree in front."

"Can you send that picture to me?" she said, her voice tight.

"Sure. Do you think you'd recognize it?"

"Old mansions tell a story," she explained. "I've always been secretly obsessed with them. And I might have even been there. There are several abandoned mansions in Italy, especially the further north you go."

"Yes, I'll send it to you."

"Thanks, *cara*, dear," she said. "But so you understand, Ella, this isn't a coincidence. Someone is sending us a message." Angelina's voice was low and conspiratorial. "They know something. Or they think they do. It could be a warning."

"A warning about what? No one else knows what we said about the evil eye that day except for us."

Angelina paused. "And Jamie and Nico. And anyone else you may have told when you got home."

That was true. I had told my family everything that happened in Italy, including what I learned about the evil eye, something Italians believed could ward off the curse of the *malocchio*. Of course, they all knew what it was.

Then I thought about Aunt Lena, but she wouldn't know how to reach Angelina, would she?

"Vinny was with us too," I added.

"Yes, of course, and Vinny." Angelina gave a nervous laugh and then whispered loudly into the phone, "I don't like this. Something bad is going to happen. I feel it. The evil eye pendants have a purpose.

It doesn't matter if someone does or doesn't know what we discovered about the evil eye the last time you were here. The photographs are also connected. *Everything is connected.*" She emphasized each word. "And it's personal. If I've been to this mansion before, I'll know it when I see it, and . . . maybe I'll check it out."

"No, Angelina. Wait until I get there and we can go together. Promise me you won't go without me . . . or at least bring Nico. It could be dangerous."

"Okay, fine. Send me that picture as soon as possible. . . ." Her voice trailed off into a prayer for protection.

I glanced at the clock. Two hours until my shift at the hospital. My mother and my sister, Liv, insisted on staying at the house while I was gone. I didn't like leaving them at the cottage and could never forgive myself if something happened to them while I was away, but I knew I wouldn't win that argument. And I was anxious to speak to one of my patients, Mr. Jones, a convicted murderer who needed a heart transplant. My colleagues joked about it—a murderer without a heart—but I couldn't laugh. It wasn't until I'd spent time with him that I realized what I needed to do. To get ahead of a psychopath I had to start thinking like one.

***

The door to Mr. Jones's room was slightly ajar. I moved closer, trying to mask the fear from my eyes. Anyone else would have been fooled, but somehow he always knew what I was thinking. I could tell by the way he studied me, particularly my eyes. He was observant and calculating, familiar with the strange and unexpected. While explaining the endovascular aneurysm repair I would be performing on him this week alongside Dr. McCarthy, I noticed how he watched me. His head was tilted to the right, his top lip slightly curled. He appeared proud of the thoughts roaming his mind. Confident and cocky.

I pulled a chair closer to his bed to address any questions he might have about his procedure and glanced at the door not far behind me. He stared into my eyes, and I felt like he was reading my soul. It gave me goosebumps.

"Has anything changed since your last visit?" I asked.

"Plenty," he replied, folding his arms across his chest.

I opened his electronic chart on my laptop, prepared to add additional symptoms or concerns to his file.

"On my first visit," he began, "you asked me something I didn't want to answer at the time. But now I do. Do you remember what that was?" He smirked.

I froze on the inside while forcing a calm exterior and nodded. I remembered exactly what it was, and he knew it. It had been bold of me to ask why he killed that girl. Then I asked him what had happened in his brain to make him do that.

I got the feeling that he knew my interest in the well-being of his vital organs paled in comparison to my intrigue for his mind. When I learned I'd be treating a criminal, someone who had willfully taken the life of another, I made sure I'd stand out among the other newly practicing doctors so I would be chosen as the primary assistant to Dr. McCarthy. Dr. McCarthy noticed my efforts right away and recommended me. I knew that climbing into the mind of a sociopath would be disturbing and possibly even dangerous, but it might provide an understanding as to why Uncle Luca did the things he did. And what he might do next.

With Luca's estranged nephew, Marco, it was easy to figure out what motivated him. He'd been wronged by Luca, who had used him as his pawn to do terrible things to others based on lies. Marco simply wanted revenge.

But Luca was more of a deviant. He fooled the people who walked beside him each day, those who loved him and trusted him. He presented himself as a quiet lamb while a dark wolf prowled inside. I needed to know how someone became this way.

Mr. Jones never liked to answer my questions right away. He seemed to take pleasure in watching it all unfold in front of him, leading me to the conclusions he drew. He was edgy and sarcastic, but throughout the last couple of weeks, we'd built somewhat of a rapport with one another. Maybe on some level he trusted me. At least today he seemed willing to talk.

"You've got balls," he said, shifting on the table. "I'll give you that much. You asked me that question about someone in your family . . . a criminal . . . after I'd just told you I'd done time for murder. I could have hurt you, but you were too curious to care." He bit his dirty fingernails, and I gagged inside. He leaned back, chewing whatever was between his teeth. "Before I tell you anything, I want to know—why do *you* want to know? And are you sure you want to know?"

I swallowed hard and began to share bits and pieces of my story. "We've been deceived by someone in my family," I began. "Someone we loved and trusted with our lives. This person did something terrible a long time ago, and I discovered it. I exposed him and his secrets, and he's been missing ever since. I think he may be watching me . . . may want to hurt my family or at least me. So I'm trying to understand why or how he became this person I don't recognize anymore. I want to stop him from hurting anyone else."

Mr. Jones eyed me up and down. "People are deceitful," he said, grinning. "Some of us are better at it than others. Some do it without intending to. Others have intent. Everyone is flawed. Even you," he said, pointing at me.

I could tell he liked to have the upper hand. He liked being in control. Luca was someone who was always in control, had always led the family alongside Poppy. Sometimes I felt like he wanted to be the patriarch, but he was always in Poppy's shadow.

"To deceive with purpose," Mr. Jones continued, "takes practice. It takes time to build those skills. Hone them in. Perfect them. Someone who is an expert at deceiving can easily lead a double life. And he can live those lives simultaneously and flawlessly."

"How? How can anyone do that?" I asked.

"Compartmentalization," he said with one finger on his lips, as if to deeply ponder that word. "This person you're asking about—what did he do?"

"He took—kidnapped—a woman. He thought he killed her and then he buried her in the woods. He let someone else take the blame for it."

"That's not surprising," Mr. Jones scoffed.

"I'm the one who figured it out and called him on it. Made him go back and dig up her body—"

"*You* did that?"

"Yes, with a little help," I said. "We kept a gun aimed at him and watched him dig for hours. When one area turned up empty we made him go to another until there was nowhere left to dig. She wasn't there."

"How do you know you were in the right area? Maybe he led you to the wrong place on purpose."

"He marked the spot so he would be able to find it. She wasn't there. I saw the shock in his eyes. He wasn't expecting it."

"Or he wanted you to think that."

I ignored that comment and continued. "That same night he ran for it, even with the gun aimed at him. Someone chased him into the woods, and I ran for the car. He's out there somewhere, and I know he wants revenge. On me."

"Makes sense," he said, nodding.

"There's more he's hiding," I said. "I know it."

Mr. Jones appeared captivated by my story. He leaned his elbow on the bed. "Yes, there is always more than what's visible on the surface. More than what you *think* you know. Sometimes it's best not to know."

"Well . . . I was wondering if . . . you might give me some insight? About what you did or, more importantly, why?"

I knew I was pushing the limits with this man. He could shut down and refuse to say another word. He could explode in anger and call attention to others. He could hurt me. I also knew Dr. McCarthy or any other doctor could walk in at any moment and see us in an intense discussion—a discussion that should have been quick and explanatory. Not emotional. A discussion that should have been over by now.

I glanced through the window in the door and then at the clock. "We've only got a few minutes and then I'll need you to change into your gown so we can begin the procedure. But, please, anything you can share . . ." I felt his eyes on me as I examined his chart. "Dr. McCarthy will be joining us any time now to discuss your post-surgery requirements," I added to entice him.

"Why don't *you* just tell me," he said, the corner of his mouth upturned. "Come sit." He patted the edge of his bed. When I didn't move, he swatted the air with his hand. "Eh, you're not my type anyway."

Repulsed and intrigued at the same time, I moved toward the edge of the bed but didn't sit. I wanted to continue our conversation about Luca. I wanted to know what was going on in his mind.

Mr. Jones scanned me from my feet and up to my eyes, where he held his gaze uncomfortably long. "Make no mistake—you don't know everything," he said, crossing his arms against his chest, "and you might not ever."

"I need to finish this," I said. "My family needs closure."

"You should mind your own business," he said.

"My family *is* my business." I noticed Dr. McCarthy approaching the long hall before our room. I grabbed a gown from the drawer below the bed and tossed it to Mr. Jones. "Everything comes off," I murmured. "I'll be back in a few minutes." I exited the room, my heart pounding as I passed Dr. McCarthy.

"See you in a few minutes," he said.

I smiled and nodded as I ducked into the restroom to catch my breath.

Chapter 11
Ella

"You're quiet, Ella," Dr. McCarthy said as he stood beside me at the sink.

He was right; I hadn't spoken much as we put on our gowns and scrubbed our hands. Normally we'd engage in light conversation as we prepared, nothing too deep that might distract us from the impending procedure.

"Everything okay?"

"Yes, everything is fine," I said, forcing a smile.

But everything was far from fine. My family was not fine. I was about to perform surgery beside one of the best surgeons in New York and I was nervous. It wasn't the first time I'd assisted Dr. McCarthy with a minor heart procedure, but it was the first one I'd ever performed on a criminal, at least as far as I knew. And this criminal had gotten into my mind.

I thought about the irony in the situation. Mr. Jones had decided the fates of the women he tortured and killed, as if their lives had less value than his own. Today I would be manipulating the instruments to make the necessary incisions into his groin. I would be guiding and assisting as the stent graft was inserted into his arteries. If I wasn't the kind of person I was—if I'd instead inherited the mind of a psychopath—I could stop him from ever hurting anyone again. I held a power of sorts.

Those were the thoughts that plagued my mind as I'd rushed into the bathroom after my chat with him. I'd gone there to meditate and quiet them; the result was my silence as I prepared for surgery.

Compartmentalization. Mr. Jones had mentioned it before as something he'd done to live a double life. That's what I needed to do now.

"I reviewed the articles," I piped up. "I'm ready."

"Good," he said. Dr. McCarthy often rehearsed his procedures and encouraged those he trained to do the same, even sending us articles about the procedure days beforehand so we felt confident and prepared.

He summoned the nurses and anesthesiologist and together we reviewed the steps. Mr. Jones would be sedated using general anesthesia. A breathing tube would be inserted, and he would be connected to a ventilator. A small incision would be made in each groin, and X-rays would be used to guide a stent graft as it was inserted through the femoral artery and advanced up through the aorta to the aneurysm. The stent graft would be inserted in a collapsed position of the aneurysm site and then expanded, attaching to the wall of the aorta and supporting it. After checking for leaks, Mr. Jones's incisions would be sutured and dressed. Then he'd be sent to ICU and, if recovery went well, he would be released in a couple of days back to the prison.

***

"You think he's in Italy," Mr. Jones whispered only hours after the breathing tube had been removed. He'd been wheeled from ICU to a regular hospital room, where Dr. McCarthy had assigned me to check on him.

"What did you just say?" I asked, studying his oxygen levels and respiratory rate.

"You did a good job, Doc," he said, his voice still raspy. "Look . . . I'm still here!"

"Of course you are," I said. "How are you feeling?" I adjusted his pillow and handed him a cup of water. "What's your pain like?"

"Not good," he said.

"I'll get someone in right away to adjust your medication," I said, pressing the call button to alert his nurse. "I'll be back in a bit to check your incision. Is there anything else I can get you?"

"That's a loaded question," he smirked.

I shook my head and walked toward the door, but before leaving, I turned once more toward him. "What was it that you said when I first walked in? Something about Italy?"

"I don't remember," he said. "I don't think I said anything. Oh, wait, you're right. I did say something." I knew he was playing with me. "Hmm . . ." he tapped his finger against his lips. "Now what was it?"

"Nevermind," I said, knowing I'd be back later and didn't need to play his game right now.

"Ah, that's right. I remember," he said. "I said, 'You think your uncle's in Italy right now.' Right? That's what you told me. Your boyfriend or someone saw him."

"Yes, he thought it was him but he wasn't sure," I said, recalling the day Nico thought he had passed Luca on his way to his volunteer job at the library.

"But you also think he's here, in Skaneateles, trying to kill you. Or scare you or something. I mean, who else would be following you?"

I remained quiet. I wanted to hear him process it.

"So, how does he do it?" Mr. Jones continued. "How is it that he can be all the way over in Italy *and* here in the US at the same time? He's resourceful. Fascinating. I'd like to meet this guy."

"He *is* resourceful," I said. "He's an old man who—"

"Age doesn't matter," he said. "It's the craving."

"Craving?"

"For the kill. Or the thought of it. He'll risk anything for it," he confided. "You'll never find him if he doesn't want to be found. And if he wants to kill you he will. Maybe that's not what he wants, or maybe he's waiting for the right moment. It's hard to say."

The little hairs along my neck raised, prickling my skin. I wasn't sure I wanted to hear anymore, but my feet were rooted to the floor.

"Sounds like he's gone to great lengths to craft and cultivate these lies to a perfect reality. If he believes in this reality, then they are no longer lies. They are the *truth*." Mr. Jones tapped his temple. "He'll do what's necessary to keep his truth alive. Anything. Even if it means killing someone who gets in his way. Even you."

"Unless I find him first," I said.

"Highly doubtful." He clasped his hands together in finality.

"I will find him," I said, "and Gianna."

"Gianna . . . Such a pretty name," he mused. "Doubt you'll find either of them."

"We'll see about that," I replied.

"Sometimes we don't know who we are or what we're capable of until we break." He snapped his fingers. "Then it's too late to go back. The person you were before that moment can no longer exist with who you are now. Forever changed."

"You could have stopped yourself after the first girl," I said. Anger was like a vice around my heart. I saw a version of Uncle Luca in Mr. Jones, and it was all I could do to stop myself from lunging at him. I wanted to cry and scream and hurt him for all the pain Uncle Luca had caused our family, but a strange feeling of pity pulled me back. I couldn't let him get to me.

"It was too late for that," he said. "I was hungry. I knew I shouldn't have it but I craved it. Ever smoke?"

I shook my head no.

"You're missing out." He licked his lips. "It's sensory—the whole experience. The taste of tobacco on your lips. The deep pull of the drag as smoldering embers crackle. The burn against the back of your throat. Releasing it through your mouth and nose. You need it and it needs you. It's a partnership." His cheeks flushed a crimson red, his eyes were wide with passion. "When I see someone holding a cigarette between their fingers, before they even light it, my mouth waters and my heart pumps fast. I can smell it a mile away," he said, wetting his lips again. "Like the hunt of a kill."

"Is that . . . how it was with each victim? Your last victim? The one you're being investigated for now?"

He squinted and furrowed his brow. Through gritted teeth, he uttered, "I told you I'm not guilty of that one."

"I guess it's for a jury to determine," I said.

He shot me a long look of disgust but quickly wiped it clean. "I think our talks might be coming to an end," he said. "Once I'm released, it's back to prison for me . . . that is unless you need me to stay here longer. I could help you." He smiled, studying my face. "What I'd give to take you out sometime . . . If I weren't your patient—"

"Not happening."

"Too good?"

"I don't date patients—even former," I snapped.

"I don't see a ring," he continued. "The only reason I'm telling you anything and being nice is because *you* have fixed *my* heart. I mean, you could have easily done something—you know, *accidentally*—that could have been fatal."

"I would never do that," I said. "Even if I wanted to. I'm not that kind of person. Even with someone like you." I quickly regretted what I said. His eyes narrowed and his jaw clenched. "What I meant was—"

"Time's up, Doc," he spat. "I'll take those meds now."

I blew it. I could have gotten more. I turned around and exited his room, but I'd be back later to try again.

What Mr. Jones had said made me wonder what Luca was thinking when he tried to take Gianna's life. What urges did he have? Had they stopped with Gianna, or had he too developed a hunger that couldn't be satisfied?

Chapter 12

Ella

It was quiet and still dark when I left the hospital. The roads held a ghost-like emptiness, making it feel as if I were the only one alive. Not a soul in sight.

It had been a long night. My body sat in the car and drove me home, but my thoughts were somewhere else—lost in conversations with Mr. Jones, his surgery, and everything that had occurred in the last two days. I had no recollection of the drive home.

I emerged cautiously into my neighborhood, keenly observant of my surroundings, absorbing every detail as I passed each house. I scanned the trees between the houses and studied their corners to see if someone might be trying to hide there. But everything remained still, like a picture, everything in place.

A well-lit house glimmered before me as I pulled into my driveway. All the outside lights were lit and a golden glow spilled from every window, except for the rooms where Liv and my mother were sleeping. I nodded on my way to the front door, acknowledging Officer Spalina who was sitting in his car looking at something on his phone. Although I was exhausted, I couldn't quell the rising anxiety in my stomach.

The glint of the moon shone through an open space in my bedroom curtains, casting eerie shadows from the objects on my dresser. I moved them into one of my dresser drawers and finally lay down in the middle of the crisp, downy cushions on my bed. I thought of what Mr. Jones had said about the hunger and urges of a psychopath. If Luca had that hunger—if his urges were as uncontrollable as Mr. Jones's were—then there was no way he'd stop looking for Gianna if he thought she might still be alive.

Maybe it had been Marco and not Luca who'd been watching me all along. Marco could be the one who broke into the house. Maybe he knew there was something Luca wanted from the cottage and he was trying to get it before Luca. But I couldn't imagine what it could be.

***

A muffled sound echoed in the distance. A roll of thunder. Obscure like in a dream. The second time I heard it I knew it was real. I must have drifted off to sleep. Something exploded, and a deafening silence followed. My eyes popped open. A jolt of fear stilled my heart. Yes, it was real.

Hercules sat tall at the foot of my bed, his ears perked high, his head tilted. He watched the bottom of my bedroom door and went over to sniff it. The wind whipped against the side of the house making us jump.

A loud thud came from just outside my door. I shot out of bed, searching for a makeshift weapon. Hercules barked as I grabbed the lamp from my nightstand and yanked out the cord. I tore off the shade and held the base in my hands, unsure of how I'd use it, but at least it was something. My hands shook as I texted Liv in the guest room next to mine. Had she heard it too?

Suddenly the door flew open. I raised the lamp base, and Hercules charged through the doorway. He quickly backed down seeing Liv there, clearly shaken.

"You heard it too?" I whispered.

Liv nodded. "I thought it was Hercules," she said.

I raised a finger to my lips as the floorboards in the hallway creaked, my heart nearly stopping. It was my mother emerging from her own room. She joined Liv and I in the doorway, and we listened breathlessly for the sound to return.

A creak rose from the floorboards in the kitchen directly below us. Footsteps drew close to the stairway. I closed my bedroom door and held my breath as I clicked the lock into place, its sound echoing in the hallway. Hercules continued barking from behind the locked door as I steadied my phone to call Officer Spalina.

Liv mouthed, "Closet?"

I shook my head and pointed to the window.

"Ella, we'll be trapped," my mother said.

"Our chances are better out there," I said, pointing to the roof, "than in here."

Liv climbed out first, then my mother. I looked at Hercules as I pulled myself up and out onto the roof. "It's okay, Hercules. Good boy," I whispered.

My entire body shook as I searched my contacts list for Officer Spalina's number. He picked up immediately. "He's in the house!" I whispered. "Hurry—he's coming!"

From the roof, I heard my bedroom doorknob rattling as someone tried to get in. I remembered the car app on my phone and frantically pulled it up. I pressed the emergency horn, praying it would scare the intruder or alert someone in the neighborhood. An outside light flashed from the house next door as the horn blared repeatedly against the police siren, blue and red lights churning in the night sky.

The rattling knob ceased, and footsteps retreated down the stairs, pounding through the house. A second set of heavier footsteps followed, moving fast.

Please catch him. Let this be over.

My mother was the first to climb down the fire escape, but she stopped abruptly as someone darted from the house toward the trees at the back of the property. Officer Spalina followed, shouting warnings to stop, but the intruder never did. We watched as the sleek, dark figure disappeared into the night.

Upon further investigation, it was confirmed that someone had been looking for something. Books and items from shelves were tossed haphazardly in both the study and in the living room. Mail was spread across the counter, cushions upturned. But in all the mess and upheaval, primarily in the living room, study, and kitchen, it didn't seem as if anything had been taken. The TV and my laptop were still there. My wallet was lying on the kitchen counter, untouched. Even Poppy's gold watch I kept on the mantle next to his picture remained. Someone was looking for something very specific. Had they found it? Why had they come upstairs?

Officer Spalina led me to the study. "Didn't you say you normally kept this door closed?" he asked.

"And locked," I said.

I stepped past him, horrified at the sight before me: Drawers opened and fully extended. Files and papers strewn across the desk. I noticed the side drawer of the desk was slid open partway. A key was needed to open this drawer. I slid it open the rest of the way and was relieved that Poppy's secret box was still there, the box he had wanted me to find two years ago. Thankfully, its contents were still there, all except for the diary. *Which is in my bag,* I thought with a sense of urgency. *I need to find my bag.*

"If you notice that something is missing—" Officer Spalina continued, but I couldn't wait for him to finish. I ran to the closet where I kept my bag. My heart sank as I approached the partially opened closet door and saw the contents of my now empty bag spread across the floor. I searched the mess, looking for the one thing I cared about most. But it wasn't there.

I held my nauseous stomach and described the soft, well-worn leather, slightly frayed at the corners. Its seams gently bulged as it hugged hundreds of crinkly pages, some of which had been added and stuffed long after the last page had been used. A lock that no longer worked after I'd busted it open with the pointy end of a rattail comb.

It wasn't just the beautiful leather that held Poppy's flowy handwriting that I loved; it was the words contained on those pages—a story of a life filled with love and passion and regret. I had tried to explain its significance to my family, but my words didn't do it justice. It felt as if some of the life I'd lost after Poppy's death, which the diary had somewhat restored, had been taken away again.

I knew now that the only person who could be interested in the contents of the diary was Luca. I explained my suspicions to the officers, telling them that if it wasn't Luca himself, it had to be orchestrated by him. I wondered if Luca thought Poppy might have mentioned something in the diary about his suspicions of the house in Tuscany.

Officer Spalina, now joined by Officer Carey, had asked again if I was sure it was Luca. I emphatically told them yes. I knew without a doubt that this was Luca, and now that he had the diary, I feared what he might do next.

Chapter 13

Ella

Officer Carey's face was stern as she whispered something to Officer Spalina. Then they both looked at me. "I need to show you something in your backyard," she said.

My mother, Liv, and I followed the officers around the side of the house to the backyard, their flashlights carving a path through the darkness. I held my breath as we walked, feeling a chill in the balmy night.

"Step over here," Officer Spalina said, directing us around a trail of footsteps in the dirt that led through the mulched gardens and away from the house.

We stopped in the middle of the yard, and Officer Carey flashed her light where the footprints began at the back of the house, illuminating their trail until they disappeared at the edge of the property near an opening within the trees. "There's a set of tire tracks," she said, pointing, "that start on the other side of those trees and go straight through the next property and then out to the road. A neighbor walking her dog says she thinks she saw a black SUV driving west around that time. We're following up on that."

"Do you think more than one person could be involved?" I asked.

"Too early to say," she answered. "There are footprints coming to the house and leaving, but it appears they're from the same shoe. It's possible someone else could have been waiting in the car."

"To and from the house?" I repeated.

Officer Carey nodded. "There's something else you need to see," she continued.

My stomach churned as she led us to the back window of the study. A third officer I hadn't seen before snapped pictures of the footprints, the windows, and various places in the yard. Officer Carey nodded to him as he passed and then pointed to the fallen screen on the study window. It looked as if it had been sliced open with a sharp object.

"They cut through the screen and broke the window lock," she said. "That's one point of entry."

"One?" I gasped.

"How often do you use your attic?" she asked.

"My attic? Not often . . . just for storage. Why?"

The officers exchanged glances and moved out into the yard a few feet away from the house, motioning for me to follow. All of the back house lights were lit, brightening the exterior of the cottage.

"See that?" Officer Carey pointed to two windows side by side, framed by black shutters beneath the attic's peak. The highest point on the back of the cottage. Quaint and charming, they created a poised and charismatic look from the vantage point of the Storybook Tree.

I squinted to bring into focus the details of each window. At first, I didn't see it. But when Officer Carey aimed her light on the windows, I noticed something awry with the window on the right. Had I not been looking for it, I would never have noticed that the curved edge of the window frame was crooked.

"The top frame on the right?" I asked.

"Yes," she said. "I'm almost certain the second point of entry is through there." She swept her flashlight to the fire escape that led from the attic to the second-floor roof. Another set of stairs began there and ended near the ground.

"How do you normally access your attic?" Officer Carey asked.

"There's an old sewing room upstairs," I said. "A door in that room leads to the attic. Do you think someone was in there?" I found it hard to breathe, as if all the air had been sucked away.

"It's possible," she said. "Could just be wear and tear over time too. But it's worth a look, especially since you've had an intruder."

I showed her the way inside, leaving the other officers to continue their investigation in the yard.

Officer Carey, my mother, and Liv followed as I led them upstairs and down the hallway to a small corridor on the right. The only two rooms on that side of the cottage were Nonna's sewing room and a guest bedroom. I opened the door to the sewing room and my heart dropped. Just beyond the sewing table, resting against a wall of fabrics and sewing tools, I saw the door to the attic. It was wide open. My heart raced as I pointed to the door.

Officer Carey motioned for me to stay back. Liv was beside me and grabbed my hand. My mother was pinned to my other side. With one hand on her sidearm and a flashlight in the other, Officer Carey stepped through the attic door and out of sight.

We waited, fixed in an eerie stillness. I released Liv's hand and walked cautiously toward the attic entrance. Liv followed but remained in the doorway as I slipped through, following Officer Carey.

I slouched under low beams, pushing through cobwebs until I could stand with ease. Boxes were stacked on the left and right, their contents labeled in Nonna's handwriting: "seasonal," "sentimental," "Christmas." Boxes she chose to leave here when she left.

One box caught my eye: "Ella and Jack's Wedding." Poppy and Nonna had gathered supplies for an event that would never be. I'd had no idea it was here. I brushed my hand against the top as I passed, releasing a mini-explosion of dust particles into the air that caused me to cough and sneeze.

Officer Carey glanced at me and then at one particular spot on the far end of the attic. I followed her gaze and saw a bunched-up blanket at the end of what appeared to be an air mattress. One edge was flipped back as if someone had risen from a slumber, hastily threw back the blanket, and scrambled away.

Someone had been in here. It sent a chill down my spine. I covered my mouth to block the noise that wanted to come out. The officer put her finger to her lips and continued searching. As she did, I spotted something leaning against the wall next to the air mattress.

A white sheet disguised the item, but I could tell it had corners, like a box. I approached the object cautiously, but before I pulled the sheet away, I knew what I would find. It had to be what I'd been looking for since I moved into the cottage: Poppy's painting of Gianna.

But why was it in the attic? Nonna would never have been able to maneuver her frail, arthritic body through the attic door, let alone to the far end. Everyone knew I'd been looking for it, so why would someone put it here, knowing how much it meant to me?

"Everything all right?" Officer Carey was at my side. "What's that?" she asked, pointing to the painting.

"Something I thought was lost," I replied, "but I guess it's been here the whole time."

"All clear," she said into her radio. She looked at me. "Who else has access to the attic?"

"I'm the only one who lives here, but anyone in my family has access if they want to." I glanced at the blanket on the floor and then at the officers. "Other than my mother, my sister, and my grandmother, it's been weeks since anyone else has been here."

I thought about Jamie, but she'd only been here for a few hours and always within sight of me or my mother . . . except when I ran upstairs to get a better view of the front yard when the intruder first made himself known. But she came upstairs minutes later.

"Anyone who had access to the attic would not have put the painting here, knowing I was looking for it. And everyone knew it was missing."

"What about that?" Officer Carey pointed to the mattress and the blanket.

"They're mine, but I didn't leave them like that. The mattress was stacked against the boxes over there," I said, pointing to the other side where I'd entered the attic. "The blanket must have come from there." I pointed to a box labeled "bedding."

"Well," she sighed, "someone's been making themselves at home in your attic. For how long I don't know."

I was sick at the thought that someone had been in the attic this whole time as we went about our lives beneath it. We could have easily been harmed. I worried about what they might have seen or heard. What if there were two people? What if the person in the attic and the one who just broke in were not the same?

"Look closely at everything," Officer Cary said. "Your diary might not be the only thing missing. Is there anything else with sentimental value that someone might want to take?"

Other than the painting, I couldn't think of anything else. And then I remembered the letters, the ones that revealed the forbidden love between Poppy and Gianna. A love that Luca hated. Those couldn't have been stolen because they were locked in a safe.

"El, what's going on?" Liv poked her head through the attic doorway.

"Where's Mom?" I asked.

"She's talking to Officer Spalina." Liv walked over to where we were standing. "What's all this?" she asked. When I showed her the painting and told her what Officer Carey thought may have happened, she became enraged and demanded to know what the police were doing about it. "The person you've been chasing out there has been inside this house the whole time? How? How is this happening right under our noses? It has to stop!" she insisted. "It's not acceptable."

"I know you're upset," Officer Carey said. "I would be too. We don't know if we're dealing with one person or two yet, but we've collected a lot of evidence, including a utility knife that was found in the grass which might have been used to cut the screen. We'll find whoever is responsible."

Liv threw her hands to her head and paced. I agreed with Liv, and we discussed possibly staying somewhere else while the officers completed their investigation.

If this was Luca's doing or someone connected to him, then the diary and the letters were not the only things he wanted. If he wanted to harm us, he had had plenty of chances. What was he waiting for?

After the officers had filed a report, it was decided that Officer Carey would keep watch from her car while Officer Spalina stayed inside the house with us. The third deputy would obtain an imprint of the footprints and tire tracks. But before he did that, he asked to see all the shoes in the house, so I gathered every one I could find, threw them in a plastic bin, and handed it to the deputy.

Over the next couple hours, we sealed the attic window using an old board I had in the garage and my nail gun. My mother opened her laptop and searched for a locksmith to change the locks on all the exterior doors. Liv took pictures of the wreckage in the house before putting everything back to the way it was. But it would never really be back to the way it was.

Chapter 14

Ella

A lonely and fearful silence filled the cottage as we attempted to assume our normal activities in the midst of an abnormal day. My mother resolved to stay with me until the police figured out who was behind the break-ins and stalking. Liv chose to take some time from work to be at the cottage to ensure that, when I worked my next shift, my mother wouldn't be alone.

Officers Spalina and Carey remained resolute in their promise that at least one of them would be just outside our house. It was somewhat reassuring that the cottage would never be empty, that someone would always be there waiting. Prepared.

I jumped when my laptop chimed, announcing a video call from Nico. Just what I needed. He'd become enraged when I told him about the attic and was emphatic that I should leave the cottage until everything was resolved. He'd argued that I should stay at my mom's or come to Italy sooner, but I'd said no, it was better to be home. He'd called me stubborn and irrational. Our conversation became ugly and I had cut it short, fearing that we'd say things we couldn't take back. I didn't like the way it had ended. I needed to reassure him. And myself.

Wavy black locks fell against chocolate eyes, past chiseled cheekbones, and just below his chin. An electrifying smile spread across his face. "*Ciao, bella,*" he said, and warmth spread through me. "Are the police still there?"

"Yes," I said. "The replacement officer just arrived for the next shift, and Mom and Liv said they'd stay for a while until . . . you know." Something was off in his eyes. Probably worry over me and what had been happening lately. "You okay?"

He cleared his throat. "Yes. . . . I wish I was with you. I don't like this. You shouldn't be there."

"We've been through this, Nico. I promise we're okay."

"No, Ella. You shouldn't be trying to catch him. Risking your life. Let the police do their job. Come to Italy sooner. Come now."

"I want to, but it's not that easy," I said softly. "The hospital is—"

"Inflexible." He rolled his eyes.

Yes," I said. "I accepted that long ago. It's a commitment to be a doctor." I knew what I was getting into when I chose this path. I hoped someday he'd understand. Still, something didn't seem right. He appeared agitated. Distracted.

"Ella, I have to tell you something," he blurted.

I waited, staring into his eyes, as if I might be able to see what it was before he said it.

"Luca is not the one harassing you. He's not the one who broke into the cottage."

"What?"

"I saw him," he said, and my stomach tensed. "I've been looking for him every day with no luck, but this morning I was up early, so I went to the market for a few things. There was a man . . . not more than a hundred feet away. He was talking to a vendor facing away from me. The way he stood, the way he carried himself—it was just like Luca. He turned quickly as if he felt me staring at him. He looked right at me. I think he remembered who I was." The veins at Nico's temples bulged on the screen.

"Are you sure—"

"I'll never forget those eyes."

"Oh my God. What did he do? Did he say anything?"

"No, he turned back around fast. Kept his head low, paid the vendor, and took off. I followed him all the way to Via Fosse Ardeatine. He was so fast, cutting in front of people, knocking things over. I was afraid I'd lose him. *Diavolo Veloce.* Fast devil. I don't know how, but he got away!" Nico slammed his fist on the counter. "Next time he won't be so lucky."

I couldn't believe what I was hearing. If Nico had seen Luca in Italy this morning, then it wasn't Luca who had been here.

"Marco," I said. "It must be Marco. He must be the one responsible for what's happening here." My voice shook as I said his name.

"It could be anyone tied to Luca," he said. "He's smart and he's got connections. There's no telling what he'd do or the kind of person he'd send to do it. That's why you need to get out of there."

Nico was right about that. If I had learned anything from Mr. Jones, it was that someone with a mind like Luca's was unpredictable. And dangerous.

The look on Nico's face was indecipherable. "What are you thinking right now?" I asked.

"*Niente.* Nothing. I'm worried about you," he said.

"There's something else. Tell me."

He raked his fingers through his hair and his face grew stern. Frustration and worry that had inhabited his eyes moments ago faded, replaced by sadness. "It's Angelina," he said, his voice cracking.

My heart sank. I tried to prepare myself.

"She's okay now, but—oh God, El—she was attacked. She's in the hospital. Vinny called me—"

"No—!"

"She was found in an abandoned house—a mansion."

"Mansion?" My throat swelled, recalling our last conversation. She had asked me to send her the picture I had received from the mysterious package. After seeing it, she was convinced she knew where it was. I had begged her not to go alone. I told her to wait until I came to Italy. This was my fault. "What happened? When did this happen?" I wanted to know but dreaded hearing the words.

"Yesterday. She doesn't remember much," he said. "Some kids in the area heard screams and they called for help. She was . . . it was bad."

Rage coursed through me until I felt sick. "I just talked to her a couple days ago." My head throbbed. I swallowed hard against the knot lodged in my throat. "Vinny—" I choked.

"He hasn't left her side." Nico clenched his fists.

"Do they think she'll be okay?"

"They said she's coming along," he explained vaguely.

I blotted my cheeks with the arm of my shirt. "My God. How could this have happened? I have to see her. I should be with her." Then I thought of something dreadful. "What if . . ."

"What if what?"

"What if Luca had something to do with this? I couldn't handle that, Nico." Angelina was one of the sweetest people I've ever met. The most generous, loving, incredible human I've ever known. She was so much like Poppy, which was probably what had endeared her to me so quickly.

"We don't know that," he said. "We might not ever know that."

"This has to stop," I said, reconciling what I knew had to be done. Once again I would be pulled in two polarizing, opposite directions—adhere to my responsibilities and what was expected of me or expose the truth to protect my family no matter the cost. I had to find a way to do both.

Nico was right. I should let the police do what they could here. I should trust them. Maybe I could get my brother, Sal, to stay at the cottage while I was gone.

"Yes, this does have to stop," he said, "but I'm afraid it won't stop until Luca is caught. I won't stop looking."

"I'll see what I can do to get there, but I don't know," I said.

A slight smile appeared on his lips.

Nico had seen Luca, so he was definitely in Italy. He might be close to finding Gianna, and I couldn't let that happen, not after everything. And Angelina—what had happened to her was my fault. If I hadn't sent her the picture of the mansion, she would never have gone. I needed to get to Italy. I'd speak with Dr. McCarthy about beginning the Doctors in Italy Fellowship early. I was prepared for it; I just needed to officially accept. Dr. McCarthy would only have to make a recommendation that I begin sooner.

"I'm going to the hospital this afternoon," he said.

"Please tell Angelina I love her so much and . . . I'm sorry."

After our call ended, I splashed cold water over my face and prepared to relay the news of Luca and Angelina to my mother and Liv and to tell them that, if they were coming with me to Italy, they should start packing.

Chapter 15

Luca

Italy - 2 years earlier

Luca kept his head low and tried to look unassuming as he sat waiting for the train to depart. His limbs hung motionless, his breathing shallow. The woman across from him would never have known just to see him that his mind was wild with fury. He felt defeated, tricked, that he'd been fooled somehow. He prided himself in being smarter than others. More prepared. He was the one who orchestrated events, pulled the strings. Other people were his puppets, not the other way around. He felt cheated, not only because Gianna had fooled him into believing she was dead but also because he'd lived a whole life without her. He needed to know where she'd been all this time. He demanded to know.

The overhead light reflected on Luca's hands resting in his lap. Luca looked at them and realized how dirty they were. Dirt caked into his knuckles and deep inside his fingernails. Dark soil matted into the hairs on his arms to just past his elbows. No wonder that woman gave him such a look of disdain. He was filthy from digging and then hiding from Marco in the woods.

His hands looked just like they had on the day he'd buried Gianna in the woods behind the vineyard. He remembered the fear, regret, and curiosity he'd felt as he shook her lifeless body. He'd called her name several times, but she never opened her eyes. She didn't move. *There was no pulse.* He'd had no choice but to bury her. How could he explain what had happened without being blamed for it? Luca remembered scooping her into his arms and carrying her deep into the woods; then, using only his hands and the sturdy ends of two fallen branches, he dug through the first layer of pine needles, scooping up the loose soil, removing as much as possible to the side. He had worked methodically, like a machine, until he had it the way he wanted it.

He'd covered her body with dirt, her beautiful face last. He'd pulled vines and branches over top to assume a natural blend with the woods. How could she have survived with no air under all of that?

Luca leaned his head back against the seat and closed his eyes. A pain pierced his side, reminding him of the pain he'd felt knowing he had to leave Gianna in the woods. And then, just as he was leaving, he'd found part of her necklace in the soil. He knew it was the right thing to do, tucking the necklace in Gabriella's carriage on the day he left her at the doorstep of his parents' house. *Gabriella should have a piece of her mother too,* he had reasoned. No one would have known Luca had put it there. They'd assume it had fallen off while Gianna was taking Gabriella out of her carriage. Luca had plenty of other special items that belonged to Gianna; he could give up this one.

If he hadn't heard Gabriella's tiny whimpering, he might have left without her. He remembered thinking that the strange noise in the distance was a bird, but then, as he listened, he realized it was the baby. He knew he shouldn't leave her there, so leaving her with his parents was the most logical decision. His mother would open the door first thing in the morning to let out the dog, and she'd see the carriage. Everyone would think one of two things: Gianna had left her child and run away with someone, or something had happened to Gianna and the person responsible had left the baby. A smile spread across Luca's face as he recalled the moment he'd done exactly that.

But his smile quickly disappeared, and a tear crept down Luca's cheek, leaving a trail across his dirty skin. He closed his eyes again and, as if observing from above, he saw himself sitting on the train, just as he had that day when he'd felt a deep connection to his mind but not his body. He was slipping away again. A chill raced through him remembering Gianna's lifeless body. In that moment, he reconciled that he was more like his father than he'd ever realized. Maybe worse.

Luca sat taller and looked at the train's destination display. He'd been lost inside his head and almost missed his stop. He texted to alert his driver that he would arrive shortly. His next destination was a place he had once called home.

***

Luca stood breathless in front of the old house he had once known intimately. In its prime it had been an impressive place, the most beautiful house in the neighborhood, noble and stately on the outside yet dark and devious within. Crooked, rundown peaks on the lofty rooftop pointed at Luca, mocking him as he stood there. Scant color clung desperately to the once-brilliant dwelling, now a shadow among unruly shrubs. It didn't look at all as he remembered. The house appeared to be bulging. Oozing. Swollen with secrets. The house with a secret, whose menacing memories remained locked in Luca's head. A house of lies, silhouetted by the rising sun, conjured up a baffling combination of despair and yearning in Luca.

Luca wiped his brow and tried to calm his ragged breaths as he contemplated going inside or turning away. But he'd come all this way to see it . . . to know if someone else had been here too. Had they discovered this place or was it still one of his secrets?

A strange feeling crept through him as he neared the house, ignoring every instinct to turn around and go back to the car, just as it had the very first day he was brought here as a child. When he was a young boy, he and his father had stopped at this house, which was being painted at the time. Luca was told to wait in the car while his father ran inside for a minute. Something on the side of the house had caught Luca's eye. He remembered watching his father and another man carrying a trunk to the side of the house. He wanted to know what was inside the trunk and what they had done with it.

If it weren't for the intense fascination he'd felt as a young boy that had lured him into that cellar, maybe things would have been different. Maybe if Luca had turned around and gone back to the car as his father had ordered, he might not have ever learned what was happening in that house. He might not have become what he became.

Luca brushed the memories aside and eyed the doorway, once a prominent feature of the house. How small and dark it looked now. He pushed against the stubborn door and stepped inside the dust-filled entrance.

Chapter 16
Ella

Silvery stratus clouds overshadowed the beautiful countryside I'd come to love so deeply. They spread above us, low and dense, like a downy blanket scarcely touching the tops of our heads. A gloomy, ominous haze obscured the natural elegance of the landscape. I wished for the sun to slice through the close-knit clouds and reveal its true beauty to my mother and Liv, whose first encounter with Italy was beginning now.

I sat between them on a bench outside the airport doors as we waited for Vinny's car to pull into the pick-up area. The feeling of being in Italy again was just as strong as it had been when I'd first stepped onto its soil almost two years ago. I felt it in every fiber of my being. I belonged in Italy.

I hadn't told my mother the real reason I was able to come sooner than we had planned. That would come up later. It was all thanks to Dr. McCarthy, who had helped to put the plan in motion. He had spoken highly of me with the cooperating doctors in the fellowship program in Italy, fostering an expedited opportunity for an interview while I was here. Dr. McCarthy had been proud of my determination and motivation and pulled me into surgeries and procedures more often than other doctors he'd trained. Not long after I'd begun working with him at the hospital, he'd said he knew I would be a brilliant heart surgeon.

My mother squeezed my hand, and my stomach tightened. I was happy we were together in Italy, but fear remained a shadow that clung to my side. There were so many secrets yet to be unraveled.

Nico and I had been playing phone tag ever since our last conversation about Angelina. He'd texted me shortly after that call to say he had seen Luca again and followed him to a plaza. He'd stayed and waited in the parking lot, but, even after the plaza closed, Luca never came out of the doors he'd entered and never went back to his car. It was very peculiar. Nico couldn't stay any longer, but he said he would try to go back the next day.

I was hoping we'd video chat once more before my trip to Italy, to find out what had happened when he went back and to discuss my arrival plans, but we weren't able to make it work. I wanted him to know I was coming a little sooner than expected, but my calls were going straight to voicemail.

The thought of seeing Nico excited me and, at the same time, it overwhelmed me. It had been so long since we'd seen each other in person. Would we easily fall into a normal comfort zone with one another, or would it take time to adjust and reacquaint ourselves again? Would he be happily surprised at seeing me sooner than he had expected? I imagined the warmth of his skin and how the mere touch of his hand soothed me. I stared across the busy road, picturing a warm smile on his beautiful face.

Across the way, I saw Vinny pull into a temporary parking area and wave his hand through the car window. The roads were too congested for Vinny to drive to us, so we made our way to him. We waded through the crowded street like herded cattle, our arms brushing against other people slowly headed in the same direction. I noticed someone standing near Vinny and waving their arms vigorously. I squinted my eyes to see who it was. Had Vinny told Nico I was arriving today and now *he* was surprising *me*? But as we drew nearer, my heart sank as the man I thought was Nico swept two children and a woman into his arms.

When Vinny and I embraced, he said, "Angelina is very excited to see everyone, especially you, Ella. I told her not to come to the airport. She's still a bit stiff." We squeezed our luggage into his trunk and, just before I slipped into the back seat, he whispered, "She wants to tell you something."

***

I took in the beautiful scenery, feeling nostalgic as we passed the cypress trees and olive groves—a charming small-town feeling just as Poppy had painted it. As we drew near the house I could see the faint outline of Angelina through the open spaces between the trees. I remembered this road so well. Angelina must have seen us coming, too, because she rose from her chair on the porch as soon as we entered the private drive to the villa. As we neared the corner and passed the lemon trees, she continued to stand, waving beside her chair until we pulled onto the curved road before the porch. Angelina's smile was wide, tighter than normal, subtle signs from the attack still visible.

We gently embraced and then Angelina cupped my face in her hands and kissed me on both cheeks. "It's so good to have you back again, Ella," she said.

"I'm so glad you're okay," I said tearfully.

On our way inside the villa, I introduced Angelina to my mother and sister. She greeted them as if she'd known them her whole life. The most welcoming smells of homemade pasta, meatballs, and sauce floated through the air and greeted us at the door. We sat at the kitchen table, and I ran my hands across the soft wooden planks, happy to gather around it once again. I smiled as I recalled hushed conversations and revealed discoveries of Gianna's disappearance. I remembered Angelina's encouraging words to call Nico and explain that there was nothing between Marco and me. It seemed like a lifetime ago. The pinot noir that filled our glasses magically put our minds and bodies at ease.

I wanted to ask Angelina how she was feeling. I wanted to know exactly what had happened to her, but I got the sense that she might be trying to avoid that conversation. She was busy asking my mother and Liv the kinds of things you ask people you're getting to know for the first time. "What do you do for a living?" "Have you ever been to Italy before?" Liv began telling her about her work with interior design, which made Angelina ask her opinions about her kitchen.

It didn't take long before my mother reached for her bag.

Angelina watched her curiously. "What are you looking for, Gabby?" she asked.

"Well," my mother smiled sheepishly, "I don't know if this is the right time, but—"

"Of course it is," Angelina replied. "It's always the right time."

Gabby placed the papers from her DNA report on the table and said, "This is my ancestry report. I thought maybe I could get your opinion?"

"Sure," Angelina said. "About what, exactly?"

"Well, first, do you know anyone from the Peragrapo family?" she asked.

"Peragrapo . . . ," Angelina repeated. "Hmm. It's a familiar name, but I don't think I do. Why do you ask?"

"The family tree that may be connected to mine is from the Peragrapo family," she said. "Their online tree is private, so I had to send them a message to see if they'd be willing to talk to me to see how we're connected. Ella helped me write it."

"Have you heard back from them?"

"Not yet," my mother said as she smoothed out the wrinkles from the report she'd printed and placed it in front of Angelina. "You see how there's a strong presence of potential relatives in Tuscany?" She pointed to the pie graph and map included with her report. Angelina nodded. "I knew we had relatives around here in Tropea, and even down in Calabria," she continued, "but I was surprised to see such a strong presence in Tuscany. And according to the numbers here, there's a high probability that it could be a parent or a sibling. What do you think? Could it be Gianna?"

Angelina turned to me. "If I remember correctly, in your grandfather's diary, he said Gianna's family moved to Tuscany after some irreconcilable issues with his father. Is that correct?" I nodded. "So, if she spent a good portion of her life in Tuscany, which eventually became her hometown, then I would think it's very possible that when she escaped those woods, she would have gone there first. It makes perfect sense to me . . . unless she had reason to be afraid to go there."

My mother's eyes widened. "Do you think so?"

"Well, yes, especially since Nico thinks he saw Luca close to that area. That's not a coincidence. I think Luca knows where Gianna is already."

Those words made me sick with worry.

"Nico saw him in Tuscany?" my mother asked me.

"I haven't had a chance to tell you that yet," I replied. "We've only recently known about it—just a couple days ago. I had hoped to talk with Nico again to make sure before I said anything."

"It wasn't in Tuscany exactly," Angelina said. "This area," she tapped the paper where my mother had referenced, "is Pistoia. It's further north. And, yes, your family does have a strong presence in Pistoia, but Nico saw Luca in Montepulciano, down here." Angelina drew her finger lower to an area in southern Tuscany. "Right here—in this little province of Siena—is where Nico saw Luca."

As Angelina spoke, my mother scribbled notes along the paper's edge.

"What is he doing?" Liv asked.

"Protecting his lies," I guessed. "Protecting himself any way he can. He genuinely looked surprised when Gianna's body wasn't where he buried her . . . or anywhere."

"Could be an act," my mother said.

"An act? That would mean he already knows where Gianna is," I said. "Maybe he's always known. He could have orchestrated it all from the beginning. We could be playing right into his hands, just the way he wants us to."

Chapter 17
Ella

The weight of those words rested heavily upon us and we sat in silence for a few moments. The rain began to fall and tapped wildly on the roof, and the walls of Angelina's little villa screeched and cracked against the gusty wind.

Her eyes met mine. "Did you bring it?" she asked. I knew immediately what she meant.

"Yes," I replied, retrieving the pendant from my purse. I placed it on the table, smoothing the kinks in the chain. Angelina retrieved hers and laid it beside mine. The shiny, gold chains glimmered beneath the pendant light. Two turquoise-blue stones hung at the bottom of each—blue centered amidst swirling white, like the eye of a hurricane, captured by a flared golden rope at its edges. They were an exact match. We stared at each other. "What does this mean?" I asked.

"I believe it's a warning," she said. "It could mean someone is aware that we're in danger and they're warning us to be vigilant. Or it could be a warning from someone, and they want to use our fear of the *malocchio* against us. They want to scare us—or worse." She made the sign of the cross and kissed her fingertips.

"I think Uncle Luca wants to scare us," Liv said, "to stop us from finding Gianna before he can."

"He might even have someone working on his behalf," I added.

"You said your brother is staying at your house while you're here, yes?" Angelina asked. "I'd hate to have your house empty after everything that's happened there."

"Yes, he's there," I said. "I'm worried about him being there. I'd never forgive myself if something happened to him, but Sal insisted. And the police will be watching too. I just want them to find out for sure who is responsible for the break-ins."

"You must have been so scared," Angelina said.

"I was. . . . I still am."

"You're safe now, here with us," she smiled, then picked up her pendant. "We should either wear these like a necklace," she said, gesturing, "or hang it on the wall in our rooms."

I slipped mine over my head, and Angelina did the same. I placed my hand on hers. "Why did you go to that house alone?" I said. "I thought you were going to wait until I got here."

"I thought the same," Vinny said, entering from the living room. He stopped at the table with his hands folded across his chest.

Angelina rolled her eyes. "I needed to, Ella," she said. "After we discovered that we both got the same necklace in the mail, with no return address, and then you sent me the picture of that abandoned house, I just couldn't stop thinking about it. I knew it was possible that I had been to that house. I wanted to wait for you, but I became obsessed with it and started researching abandoned houses in Italy. I weeded through hundreds of them and came across one that looked a lot like the one in the picture. It was eerily familiar. Then I found a documentary that I'm positive was on the exact house.

"It's haunted, you know. I'm pretty sure I was there as a child. I remembered there was a red-and-white swing set in the backyard. I'd swing so high I thought I might fly away. The girl who used to live there was sort of a loner, but I had befriended her. She'd invite me to come and swing on her brand-new swing set. Hardly anyone had one at the time, so I felt special being able to do that. As we grew into teenagers we drifted apart and then, a few years later, rumors spread that there were dead bodies in the basement—one of them might have been hers. No one ever proved it, though," she finished. "I'm sorry, Ella, but I knew we'd be pressed for time when you got here, so I took the train one day while Vinny was with his brother . . . and I went to see it. I had to know if it was the house I'd been to. And I'm glad I did."

"You could have been killed!" I said, shaking my head. "I would never forgive myself."

"Nonsense," she replied with a slight smile.

Liv leaned in and asked, "Do you think this is the same house Poppy mentions in the DVD?"

"It could be," Angelina said. "But this house is dark, evil. I don't get the sense that the house your Poppy referred to was dark like this one. There are hundreds of abandoned houses in Italy. There might be some connection, but I don't get a strong feeling about it. I don't think it's the one."

In the short time I had gotten to know Angelina, there was one thing I'd learned: she was usually right about her predictions.

Then Angelina stood abruptly and motioned for us to follow her into the living room. She called up a recording of the documentary on the TV, and what I saw gave me chills. I held up the picture of the old mansion I'd received and was shocked to see so many similarities. We paused the video several times to examine it closely and compare it to the photograph. It was uncanny. The walkway, the prominent windows in the front, the grand entrance—everything; even the striped swing set that peeked from behind the house was the same.

"You must have been so scared when it happened," my mother

murmured, grasping Angelina's hand.

"Never been so terrified in all my life," Angelina said. "Not just from the attack but the house itself." Her eyes widened. "Something's not right in that house. You'll agree when you see it. Do you want to go there now?"

Vinny slammed his fist on the table, and an argument ensued as Angelina insisted she would be safe if we all went together. Vinny threw his hands in the air and stormed out of the room.

"Perhaps now isn't the best time," Angelina conceded. "We can talk more about it tomorrow. But there's something in that house we can't ignore. This town has grown over the years, but at its core it's still very small. We are all connected in some way, just as I used to play in that house with my friend many years ago and then I never saw her again. So many years of wondering where she went. I still don't know. And then you were sent a picture of the same house; the pendants we both received in the mail; the break-ins at your cottage; the stolen diary. There's so much more to all of this," she said. "*So* much more."

She stood and gathered the plates and glasses, placing them into the sink.

"I got it!" my mother cried suddenly, looking up from her phone. "I got a reply from the Peragrapo relative!"

We raced to my mother and stood behind her, anxiously waiting as she pulled up the email notification.

Chapter 18

Gianna

Italy 1939

Dawn emerged, and an emphatic trill from the sparrows commenced as they gathered on the branches above Gianna. Some dove through the treetops in cheerful song, rousing her from a restless slumber.

She opened her eyes and panic seized her, recalling the treacherous predicament she was in. She scanned the trees for movement, fearing a wild animal or, worse, Luca. When she felt it was safe, she hurried to her feet and continued to search for Gabriella. But even as the sun brightened the forest, Gianna could not find her baby anywhere, not even a slight indication that she had once been there. Despair filled her, but she forced herself to think about what she needed to do so she could find Gabriella without alerting Luca to her whereabouts.

Gianna was sure that, as the hours had passed from nightfall into day with no sign of her returning home, her sister, Maria, would definitely have called the police. Maria would be crazed with worry. She would have told her mother and her sister, Sienna, and she might have even told Luca that Gianna was missing. She was sure they would search for her, but Gianna had never told anyone where she and Luca were going that day. They would have assumed she'd gone to the park as she they most days. No one would ever think to look in the woods behind the vineyard. If Luca was with them, he'd make sure of it.

She began to see Luca in a different light. His obsession with her began long before she and Franco came together. She'd ignored his attentions, casting them off as harmless jealousy, but as she recalled several moments with Luca, after Franco left for the war, she started to see him clearly, as if the veil that had obscured his true identity had been lifted, and now it was crisp and clear.

The way she'd catch him watching her at the oddest moments, how his mood shifted at hearing Franco's name, or how angry he'd become when Maria would sometimes accompany them on their walks. It was clear to her now: Luca was obsessed with her, and if he couldn't have Gianna, no one could. As difficult as it was to accept, Gianna knew that if Luca were to ever find out she was alive he'd probably kill her. If he chose not to kill her, he'd keep her uncomfortably close, never quite trusting her to keep her mouth shut about what happened. He'd try to control her life. Her childrens' lives.

The police would never believe her story over his. The Italian police were still threatened by the influence of Luca's father. Luca sometimes even boasted that he and his father had connections with Mussolini, but then he'd laugh and say he was only joking. Gianna was sure the police or any authority figure in power would believe whatever Luca wanted them to believe. The more she thought about it, the more she realized Luca must never know she had survived his attack.

But she was determined to get out of the woods and find her daughters, and she knew she couldn't do it alone. Someone had to be her eyes and ears. Someone she could trust. After what her mother had done—taking her daughter, Grace, and giving her away—she could never be trusted let alone allowed back into her life again. Gianna's sister, Maria, meant well, but she wasn't good with keeping secrets. And her oldest sister, Sienna, was the most reliable and stable, but her husband, Rico, would never allow Gianna to stay with them. He was an abusive drunk with a big mouth. Nina, her best friend, was the only other option, but she was too far away.

Gianna knew she had to get moving. She ran back to the hole she had crawled from and began to fill it in, pushing the dirt, scooping and pulling all of it back to where it belonged. Cool soil flowed through her fingers and over her hand as she smoothed it and patted it down. Then she pulled the vines and branches back over top as though it hadn't been disturbed. As she stood over her disguised burial site, a chill ran through her, affirming that the life she once knew would never be the same.

Gianna knew the direction she needed to go was directly opposite the vineyard. She stood before the thicket that only hours before she and Luca had contemplated cutting their way through to the clearing on the other side. Gianna was determined to get to the clearing. She knew that was her only chance at safety.

She pushed her whole body into the wall of shrubs and tightly wound branches that scratched her arms and tore at her clothes. She closed her eyes to protect them while her arms and hands pushed and moved the stubborn bracken, allowing her to advance bit by tiny bit.

Push.

Move.

Step.

Low-hanging branches caught in her hair and pulled her back, slowing her progress, but not for long. She swept aside branches that sliced her skin and fought the tightly entwined vines that clung to her legs. Sweat poured down her back and dripped from her face. Her body was weak and bruised on the outside, but on the inside, she was empowered from the progress she'd made thus far and determined to get through that thicket.

Gianna began to think the task was impossible, but eventually, she noticed a slight ease in the branches as she pushed them aside. Some were not connected as tightly, seeming to break away easier with less effort. She kept going.

Push.

Move.

Step.

Unrelenting, finally she reached the clearing at the end of the thicket and stepped to the other side. She dropped to the ground, depleted of energy, and cried.

When she looked up, she saw a small meadow of amber grains ahead, waving to her as butterflies swooped and danced upon them. Her cheeks were warmed by the sun, and a cool breeze pushed back her hair and nipped at her scratches. Small houses scattered like sheep among the hills in the darkened valley below. Lights flickered in some of the windows, and Gianna imagined herself running and knocking on their doors, begging for help. Would they ask her who she was or where she was from? Or why she'd been with a man alone in the woods? Could they possibly recognize her face? She feared that asking for help might lead her back to Luca.

Even if Gianna didn't ask for help, she needed to get as far away from the woods as possible. She bolted across the meadow, praying she wouldn't be seen. Her legs flew fast through the tall grass; she was vulnerable but free. Each step emboldened her, strengthening her confidence in her decision. Just as she neared the small neighborhood in the valley, she slowed her steps, observed her surroundings, and calculated the risk. She kept still and listened to the silence of a neighborhood not yet awakened.

Gianna's throat was dry and sore. She desperately needed water.

She placed her hand against her neck and froze. The necklace that Franco had given her just before he left for the war was gone. It could be anywhere—in the grave that was dug for her, in her hiding spot among the bushes, lost in the thicket or in the tall grasses she'd just run through. She shook out her clothes to see if it had gotten stuck, but there was nothing there. Distraught over the loss of her necklace, her gaze drifted to the woods once more.

Chapter 19

Luca

Italy, 2 years ago

Luca was dizzy with emotion as he leaned against the kitchen doorframe of the old house. Food and dishes stood as they'd been left, on counters, in the sink, on the table caked with black residue. Luca recalled having to escape quickly that day following weeks of heavy surveillance by the FBI. He'd had minutes to grab as many essential items as would fit in his arms, including a blueprint for a new house that was well underway in northern Tuscany. He'd left a copy of the blueprint in his old basement office, locked in a secret compartment that no one would ever think was suspicious. He'd left other valuables he couldn't retrieve.

Since that day, he swore he'd never be back, but here he was standing right in the middle of it. He needed to know if Gianna had come here after her escape from the woods. She might think Luca was keeping Gabriella here, at least temporarily. Gianna had never been to the house, but Luca had told her where it was, assuring her it would provide safety if Mussolini's troops advanced any closer. He had shared some of what he knew about Mussolini, but he couldn't tell her everything.

Luca stared through the kitchen to the living room. He recalled seeing his father dance with another woman right in that room. He saw his father gaze into her eyes and hold her close, the way you would hold someone you loved. Luca had stared at them in disbelief, watching through the window from the front yard. How could his father humiliate his mother in front of friends and family yet treat this woman like a princess?

Luca was caught staring and his father pulled him aside to talk to him. He'd said that Luca was just like him and that he wanted to start involving him in the family business. To outsiders this meant masonry and farming, but to the innermost select few, it was something vastly different. Luca soon learned that what began as simple drug trafficking would turn into something much worse, often involving crime, prostitution, and murder. But he was excited at the idea of his father choosing him over Franco, and that was enough for him.

Eventually he came to hate the woman his father loved almost as much as he hated what his father was doing. The urge to put a stop to it, to make her disappear, was strong, though he hadn't meant for it to go as far as it had. Luca felt a piercing in his heart and his eyes welled up, just as they had when he'd seen them dancing that day. He chose not to walk through the living room, eyeing the basement door off the kitchen instead.

The pull to the basement was strong, like the day he'd been lured to it by his own fascination as a child. He'd needed to know what was behind the storm door. Once inside, it wasn't the sparkling jewelry that adorned the shelves or the sharp tools neatly lined up on the table that intrigued him. It was the gravelly voice beckoning to him just beyond the half wall at the back.

He shook his head at the memory as he descended down the stairs. He opened the door, eyeing the dusty office and adjacent spacious seating area, remembering what it had become even after his aging father had secretly gifted it to him. He thought about his wife, Lena and how he truly loved her and eventually married her, yet he'd carried on with a separate life and other wives, just like his father.

The only woman he ever truly wanted in his life was Gianna. If he could have had her he'd have stayed there forever. Maybe the things he had done as a result of her absence wouldn't have come to fruition.

Luca gave one last look around the basement and then spun around and ascended the stairs back to the kitchen. He was certain Gianna hadn't been to the house. He knew he needed to leave, but he had nowhere to go, nowhere to hide. The only option he saw available was to call Lena. He wouldn't tell her everything, only pertinent information he needed her to believe so she would support him.

His driver took Luca to his private airport, and Lena picked him up after he landed back in the States.

***

Lena did more for Luca than he expected. She had a way of soothing his nerves, making him feel important and loved. She drew him a bath and brought him his favorite brandy. She dimmed the lights in the living room and fluffed the pillows on the sofa. Luca sat comfortably drinking his brandy, which Lena continuously refilled as she listened.

Lies slipped easily from Luca's lips about what had happened and why he'd gone to the old house in Italy, lies about why he was so filthy when she'd picked him up from the airport. But Luca was tired of lying and running, and his stories began to mix with what Lena had already heard from Ella after she returned from Italy. Luca knew Lena didn't want to believe he had another side to him, although she said she had suspected for quite some time. As Luca spoke, a softness in Lena's eyes revealed her loyalty to him. He still loved her, and he needed someone on his side, so that night, under the glow of a soft light, he told his wife almost everything.

Lena vowed to protect her husband at all costs, which meant she had to lie to her family, pretending she hadn't heard from him and had no idea where he was.

Chapter 20

Ella

We waited as she held the mouse in her hand, the cursor hovering over the words, "Click to see your response," her finger just above the button on the mouse. Finally she clicked, and a short message opened, captivating us at the first line:

> *Hello, Gabriella,*
>
> *I've waited a long time for this. Thank you for reaching out. My family is very private and no one knows about my ancestry research. I had hoped someone might reach out to me as you have, because I certainly couldn't initiate contact. It seems we share a lot of DNA but not enough to be siblings. I know who my parents are, but it's not as clear on my mother's side. I believe we may be connected through her. I am interested in talking more with you and look forward to your reply.*
>
> *Sincerely,*
>
> *Emma Peragrapo*

My mother's eyes grew wide, and she read the message aloud two more times. "Emma," she said to the message displayed on the screen, "how are we connected?" She stared at the screen as if an answer might appear. So many questions evolved from Emma's response. "She thinks we're connected on her mother's side," she said. "Gianna could somehow be connected to her mother's side." She looked at us and then sat down, squaring the laptop in front of her. "I have to reply. What should I say?"

"See if she'll chat with you," Liv suggested, "you know, a video chat."

"Good idea," I said.

"You see what I mean by connections?" Angelina added. "I'm eager to see how this all unfolds." She clasped her hands in front of her and smiled.

"She might not want to do that yet," my mother said, "but it's worth asking." With very little input from us, my mother crafted her response:

Dear Emma,

I am very excited to hear from you. I'm curious to see how we are related and if we are connected on your mother's side. I've recently become aware that there is someone from my family whom I've never met or even knew existed. It is possible they are part of your ancestry and perhaps even from your mother's side. Would you be willing to do a video chat to discuss our connection further? If not, or if it's too soon, I understand and would be more than happy to continue emailing.

Best regards,

Gabriella

After my mother sent the message, she closed her laptop and looked at us. It was the first time I'd seen hope in her eyes since everything that had recently happened.

Liv suggested we go to Castello Ruffo, the ancient legendary castle where Poppy and Gianna had spent many days together. She thought we should go while it was still daylight for a quick visit to clear our minds and relax a bit before we set out to accomplish what we really came here for. Angelina decided to stay behind with Vinny. I agreed to go but said I'd meet Liv and my mother there because I wanted to try and find Nico first, since he had no idea I was already in Italy.

Before setting out, I called Nico, but it went straight to voicemail again. I called for a driver to pick me up and take me to Nico's house. I'd waited long enough to see him.

***

We parked far enough down from Nico's house so he wouldn't see me if he happened to step outside or look out the window. It appeared quiet and empty like no one was home. The car crept quietly down the road, slowly passing Nico's house. His car wasn't in the driveway.

I checked my phone; still nothing from Nico. Sometimes he volunteered at the library, so I asked the driver to take me there next. But as soon as we entered the neighborhood, I could see from the road that his car was nowhere in sight.

"Can you take me into the village?" I asked the driver. "There's a little restaurant called Rocco's. Do you know it?"

"*Sì,* I know Rocco's," he said, turning back onto the main road.

Soon we entered the mini shopping district, and a flood of memories filled me with nostalgia. Naturally, I reached for the diary in my bag but stopped, remembering sadly that it wouldn't accompany me along the Italian hillside this time. Memories popped up in every corner. I looked at the outdoor seating area at Il Pirata, where Nico had pulled me close to dance. Butterflies raced through me now as they did then. It was the moment I'd first admitted to myself that I had feelings for him.

A small crowd of people exited from the restaurant next to Rocco's, and one of them looked like Nico—his gestures and body language, the way he swung his arms and tossed his hair to the left. I asked the driver to go a little further, and the closer we got, I was sure it was him. Was he alone in that crowd or part of it? Soon the crowd dispersed to their cars, leaving Nico and a beautiful woman standing in the middle of the road. I observed how they walked and spoke to one another with such familiarity.

My breath caught in my throat as the wind swept the edge of her jacket and sent her long brown hair behind her shoulders. She slipped her arm so naturally into his and they walked to her car. At the driver's side door, they hugged and kissed one cheek and then the other as many Italians did. She got into her car and backed away slowly, offering a friendly wave. A smile spread across Nico's face.

I felt like vomiting. I stared harder to confirm it was him, and, yes, of course it was. I'd recognize him anywhere. I thought of jumping out of the car and approaching him to see what he would do, but I knew my anger and confusion would turn a surprise visit into a confrontational one. Instead I chose to wait and see if he'd text or call me, give me an explanation for all of this.

Or maybe I was a fool and he was not who he said he was.

I asked the driver to follow the woman. I needed to find out who she was or at least where she was going.

As we circled the shopping district, I kept my eyes on Nico. He walked to his car, his head low, his hands in his pockets. *Check your phone, Nico.* Had the distance finally come between us? How stupid of me to think I could have something special twice.

I sent him another text: *"U there?"* I saw him check his phone and slip it back in his pocket as he got into his car.

My stomach was in knots as we followed the woman's black

BMW for a few miles until she pulled into a hotel. She unloaded her luggage and rolled it through the doors to the lobby. I wanted desperately to follow her inside, but now she was beyond the locked double doors and out of reach. I contemplated getting out of the car, walking up to the door, and banging on it until she turned around, but chose not to. At least not today. Maybe tomorrow if I still didn't hear from Nico.

The only thing I wanted to do was go back to Angelina's and cry until I went to sleep, but my mother and sister were waiting for me at Castello Ruffo, so that's where we headed next. I wanted to tell my mom and Liv what I'd seen, but if I was wrong about Nico then that would stain their first impression of him before they even met him.

When I got to the castle, I knew exactly where to find them—the one place I had spoken so much about after I returned from Italy. I ran up the steps to the stone balcony overlooking the sea, a familiar escape in Poppy's diary.

I emerged at the top and saw the backs of my mother and Liv as they peered out to the sea. They must not have heard me coming because they both jumped when I called for them. I knew by their expressions that they were reading mine.

"Ella! What's wrong?" Liv said.

"It's nothing. . . . Nico had to work today," I said, gritting my teeth. "Something came up last-minute."

"I'm sorry," my mother said. "Will we see him tomorrow?"

"I don't think so. Maybe the next day," I said. "Isn't that beautiful?" I opened my arms toward the Tyrrhenian Sea, changing the subject.

"It's unbelievable," Liv answered. "It's surreal to be standing in the same place Poppy and Gianna stood." She looked at me. "Are you sure you're okay?"

"Yes, I'm fine," I lied. "Just disappointed that I can't see Nico yet.

I'm sure I will tomorrow." I swallowed hard on the knot in my throat, pushing down the rising sob.

We stayed at the castle until the setting sun spread shades of pink and orange across a darkening horizon. On the drive back to Angelina's, we agreed to revisit Castello Ruffo sometime before our stay in Italy came to an end. I'd lead them, like Poppy's diary led me, throughout the streets of Tropea where Poppy and Gianna grew up.

Back inside the villa, we said goodnight and I headed straight to my room. I held my stomach as I lay in bed. Then I shut down my phone and switched off the light.

Chapter 21
Gianna

Italy 1939

The ghostly trees in the distance dared her to return. Gianna cherished the necklace representing Franco's love for her and had worn it every day. She imagined one day telling Gabriella and Grace about its significance and sharing the special bond she and Franco had. Gianna shook her clothes gently, hoping it had caught within the threads of fabric, but it wasn't there. She looked at the ground near her feet and glanced again at the woods, wiping her cheeks. There was no way her body could take that punishment again. It would be dangerous and unwise to go back now. For all she knew, Luca might have returned. And if he had, he might notice something was awry.

Gianna glanced once more at the woods and then turned toward the houses in the valley. Each step filled her with uncertainty as she neared the village. The fuzzy scene she'd viewed from the hilltop was sharper, tangible now. White lights flashed intermittently from behind the houses, reflecting into the sky. Curious, Gianna scurried the rest of the way, stopping short of touching the closest house. She paused for a moment, placing her hand against the rough brick wall as the soft hum of a motor floated through the air. She listened carefully as wheels pressed into gravel and cars swooshed by on the roadway. She hadn't realized until then how close she was to a road.

As the sky brightened, Gianna knew she needed to stop lurking and appear as normal as anyone who might live in the neighborhood. She studied the road and its distance and location to the woods behind the vineyard and, once she got her bearings, she understood its connection. This road clung to the village, eventually connecting to the main roadway on the other side of the vineyard. If she could reach the main roadway without drawing attention to herself, she might be able to get to Sienna's house before Rico returned from work. She knew she couldn't stay, but perhaps Sienna could help her in some way. Sienna was her only hope.

Although she trusted her friend, Nina, the most, it would take several hours and possibly a whole day to get there on foot. Her sister Maria's house was closer than Nina's and, although she meant well, Maria was loose-lipped, and Gianna couldn't risk a slip in conversation. Sienna adored her youngest sister, Gianna, and looked after her when they were little. She could count on Sienna to protect her and keep her secret; she just needed to be careful of her husband, Rico.

Gianna stepped cautiously along the tree-lined road, hoping the towering pines would conceal her movements. When she reached the end, she sighed, realizing she had been holding her breath the entire time. Before her was Via Roma, the road she needed to cross which led to Via Carmine, the highway to Sienna's. Gianna's legs felt heavy, but she pushed herself, saying the names of her daughters aloud with each step. Via Carmine eventually led to a fork in the road, and Gianna stopped walking when she saw the plaza she and Franco had frequented as a couple. She recalled fond memories of escaping to Castello Ruffo, not far from the plaza, so they could be alone. The church where they'd professed their love for one another was only steps from the castle. All were within walking distance of the vineyard. Her throat tightened at the memories.

But the hilly road continuing to the right was where she needed to go. Once she reached the top, open farmland greeted her, and she knew she was close to Sienna's house. Her shoulders relaxed and her heart steadied for the first time since she'd awakened in the woods. In minutes she'd be at the home of her oldest sister.

The soft grass a few feet from Sienna's front porch tickled her knees. She tried to calm the shaking in her arms and legs and even in her heart. She swallowed hard as her eyes filled with warm tears that spread down her cheeks. Gianna could hardly wait to hug her sister, but she feared involving her in her troubles. Every part of her yearned for her babies and the life she used to have.

A light above the door glimmered, and the screen door slowly opened. Gianna flattened her body against the side of the house and prayed that if Rico appeared in the doorway he'd be too drunk to notice her. She wanted to sink into the soft grass and disappear. But it wasn't Rico who stepped out onto the porch; it was Sienna. Gianna pulled herself up to standing. Sienna still hadn't seen her, but Gianna noticed a crimson ember glowing near Sienna's face, the smell of tobacco hovering in the air. It reminded her of Luca.

Sienna shifted from one foot to another, squared herself toward Gianna, and squinted. She flicked her cigarette to the grass, walked to the edge of her porch, and stepped down. "Gianna? Is that you?" She leaned closer.

Gianna waved and stumbled toward Sienna, collapsing into her arms as they embraced. Sienna studied Gianna's face, taking in her ragged appearance. She gently guided her little sister inside the house, locked the door, and closed the curtains. Then she brought Gianna to the sofa, gave her a glass of water, and sat beside her.

"What happened?" Sienna asked.

"I don't know where to begin," Gianna wept.

Sienna peeked through the curtain and returned her attention to Gianna.

"Has Luca been here at all or called you? Has anyone called to see where I am?"

"No. No one," Sienna said. "Why? What's going on?"

"He tried to kill me, Sienna. Luca did." Gianna brought her hand to her neck, and Sienna's eyes widened.

"He tried to kill you?" she gasped.

"It happened so fast," Gianna continued. "He tried to kiss me and—"

"Kiss you?"

"I tried to stop him, but he wouldn't let go. I got free . . . I ran . . . He was too fast. The last thing I remember were his eyes—dark, bulging, bloodshot. The Luca I thought I knew was not behind them." Gianna felt a tightening in her chest and had to stand. Sienna stood too and wrapped her arm around Gianna's shoulders.

"It's okay," Sienna said, rubbing Gianna's back. "You got away. You're safe now."

"I'll never be safe!" Gianna shouted, and stepped away from Sienna. "He *buried* me, Sienna. He thought he'd killed me and buried me in the woods! When I woke up, I was below the earth . . . buried . . . alive!"

Sienna looked as though she might get sick.

Tears filled Gianna's eyes. "The worst part of all this is that we'd taken Gabriella with us on a walk."

"Oh no."

"Parked her carriage so we could wander just a few feet away. I looked everywhere in those woods for her, but . . . she wasn't there!" Gianna began to cry hysterically. Sienna quickly embraced her, holding her close as Gianna sobbed into her arms.

"Gianna," Sienna said, handing her a handkerchief, "you said Gabriella wasn't there at all, including her carriage, right?" Gianna nodded. "I think maybe it's a good sign. Luca must have taken her with him. She's probably with him right now. I could call or make a surprise visit." Sienna appeared strong and sure of herself. In the past, this bold exterior drastically disguised the traumatic thoughts that had wreaked havoc on her mind. Gianna wondered if her sister had grown away from her old habits and finally felt as confident as she appeared or if she was shaking on the inside as much as Gianna.

"No, that's not a good idea," Gianna said. "Luca would know as soon as he saw you or heard your voice. There has to be another way." She shook her head. "This is my fault. I put everyone in danger by trusting Luca."

"This is *not* your fault," Sienna said. "It seemed strange that he would visit you so often. I know he was doing that for Franco, but when he started showing up uninvited at family gatherings, that was odd. Almost like he tried to fill Franco's shoes . . . *be* Franco."

"I didn't see it," Gianna said. "Maria did, though. She became cautious of Luca and started to not trust him. I thought she was jealous."

"Well," Sienna rolled her eyes, "I think Maria was in love with him, don't you? I think she *was* jealous of the attention you were getting from Luca. You know she always had a crush on him."

"A long time ago, not now," Gianna said.

"Yes, even now," Sienna said. "But you're right—she started noticing something was off about him. She's good about reading people. Sees things way before anyone else does. She probably brushed it off for so long because, you know, it was Luca." Sienna held Gianna's hands. "It's not a bad thing to see the best in people. You were always able to do that, even when we were little. You tried to empathize and understand the perspectives of the mean kids at school. That's okay, Gianna. You just have to be a little more cautious. Sadly, there are people who want to harm others and take advantage of their kindness." Sienna squeezed Gianna's hands. "It will be okay. I will help you."

Gianna gave a half-hearted smile. "Do you think Franco is dead?"

"Where did that come from? Why would I think that?"

"Luca said Franco might have been in that accident that was on the news. It was Franco's unit. He had to have been there."

"I don't know if we can believe anything Luca said."

"He was visibly upset when he told me," Gianna continued. "It didn't seem like an act."

Sienna's eyes widened. "Have you asked his mother?"

"I'd never get past his father," Gianna said. "If anyone knew how to find something out it would be you. You're smart. Resourceful."

"Me?" Sienna stood and began pacing. "I could dig around a bit when I go into town this week. You have my word—if we find out Franco is alive, I'll help you get to him, and I will do anything I can to find Gabriella and Grace too." Sienna's face grew serious. "But if I can get you somewhere safer than here, you have to promise me you'll go, even if I haven't found out anything at all."

Gianna promised, feeling a small twinge of hope.

"You'll sleep in the attic tonight, and in the morning, when Rico leaves for work, you can bathe and change your clothes, and then we'll talk some more."

As Sienna led her to the attic, Gianna noticed her staring at the darkened imprints of Luca's fingers on her neck. Instinctively she placed her hand there, feeling embarrassed and ashamed.

Chapter 22

Gianna

Italy 1939

The first night in the attic, Gianna awakened with every noise, fearing Rico had discovered her. She'd slip into a deep sleep and awaken abruptly to his harsh accusations thrown at Sienna. Rico didn't deserve Sienna. His vicious words cut through the attic walls, enraging Gianna, filling her mind with disturbing thoughts of what she could do to him. Occasionally something shattered against the wall, and she feared the next sound would be the thud of a physical altercation.

Gianna imagined bursting through the attic door and savagely attacking him. He was even worse than her own husband, Carlos. Although she was thankful to be away from Carlos, she'd go back to him in a heartbeat if it meant she could have her babies again. A sharp pain shot through her stomach and wound its way to her heart, but she pushed it down as far as she could, knowing it wouldn't stay there long.

In the quiet moments between Rico's outbursts, she thought about Franco and their babies and often slipped into a pleasant dream. But her dreams quickly shifted: *Two babies crying, arms outstretched in the dark. One viciously snatched by the hands of a stranger, the other abandoned in a dark forest.* Gianna awakened twisted and contorted in the sheets. There would be no good night's sleep.

The second night in the attic wasn't much better. It was hot and uncomfortable and smelled of rotting wood. Intense quarreling between Sienna and her husband escalated, stretching long into the night, before they'd fade to Sienna's soft whimpering. Gianna decided she needed to convince Sienna to leave Rico as soon as possible.

Her weary eyelids had closed for only seconds when the attic door screeched open. Sienna stood in the doorway, her body silhouetted by daylight, her eyes sunken, her cheeks wet.

"Maria called just now," she began. "She's a mess, as you can imagine. She said you hadn't returned from your walk and that both you and the baby were missing." Sienna blotted her eyes with the hem of her dress. "I felt guilty not telling her the truth, but I know it's for the best." Sienna put her hand out to stop Gianna from hugging her. "That's not all. Maria called the police to file a report. They're searching for you. It won't be long before they're here."

Gianna sat up quickly. "I have to go."

"What if you tell them what happened? They'll arrest Luca," Sienna said.

"You know that's impossible. Luca's father owns half the police force. They'll never take my word over his. If Luca knows I'm alive . . . he won't rest until he has me, alive or dead."

Sienna nodded, staring at the floor. She left briefly and returned with a leather purse filled with money and handed it to Gianna. Sienna promised first thing in the morning, after Rico left for work, she'd get Gianna to the train station. Gianna would take the train to Rome and stay for a few weeks with Amelia, one of Sienna's closest friends. Sienna would come later to check on her.

"I can't take this money," Gianna said. "You need it. I know you do."

"Then let it be a loan, but take it. There's no other way. I promise you I will do what I can to find out if Franco is alive, and somehow I will find Gabriella and bring her to you. And Grace. If you're right about Mamá, then she needs to pay for what she did to Grace." Sienna panted as if the weight of those words exhausted her.

Gianna's heart ached and her eyes filled. She took Sienna's hand in hers. "That's too much for one person to bear. I know you mean well and you would if you could. Just promise one thing."

"Anything."

"If Luca is searching for me, convince him somehow to stop. As long as he's far away from me, I will find my babies."

Sienna nodded.

Gianna's chest squeezed against her ribs and her mind raced. She stood and paced about the room, a crazed look in her eyes.

"What is it? What are you thinking?" Sienna asked.

"It upsets me to think you might not believe me about Mamá. I can't stop thinking about what she and Aunt Mia were talking about that day."

Gianna recalled the terrible conversation she had overheard just days after she'd given birth to Gabriella. She had awakened in the guest bedroom at her mother's house where she'd been staying since her last months of pregnancy. Gabriella was sleeping soundly in the bassinet beside her bed. Voices floated from the kitchen, and Gianna's excitement grew as she recognized her Aunt Mia's voice speaking to her mother. Aunt Mia, her mother's younger sister, had been Gianna's favorite since she was a little girl, and it had been months since she'd seen her.

Gianna had tiptoed down the hallway to surprise her aunt but stopped suddenly as their voices became muted, then hushed. She heard her mother say, "Shh! It's for the baby—for Grace. Take it." Aunt Mia replied, "No, it's not the money." Her mother added, "Well, what is it then? What's wrong?" But the creaky floorboards had betrayed Gianna, and she hurried back to her room as quickly and quietly as possible. No one came to check on her, but Gianna wondered if they knew she'd been spying on them.

"I do believe you," Sienna insisted. "When I said 'if you're right' I meant—"

"I know I wasn't well after I had Gabriella. I'll admit it. I was delirious—awake one minute, passed out the next—but I know . . . a mother *knows* her babies' cries. And there were two of them!" she yelled. Gianna could almost hear their cries again; Gabriella's high-pitched wail followed by Grace's low, mumbling whine. The midwife and her mother insisted she'd been hallucinating, that the second push Gianna questioned was just the placenta and perfectly normal after giving birth. But Gianna knew otherwise and believed a sinister plot had been conspired between the two women.

"Why do you think Mamá would do something like that? For what gain?" Sienna asked.

"Money." Gianna walked about the room, waving her arms as she spoke. "We almost lost the farm last year. You know how Mamá and Papá always wanted to provide for us, and they know I can't depend on Carlos. One more mouth to feed would be too much for them . . . but *two?*"

Sienna shook her head. "What kind of person does something like that? Take away a child—from her own daughter?" She faced Gianna. "Yes, it sounds absurd and twisted and unfathomable, and I can't wrap my head around it. But if you believe this to be true, then . . . I believe you. I believe you had twins. I just don't know what to think after that. I can't imagine it."

Gianna felt her body relax. She had spoken those awful words out loud, slightly freeing the torturous thoughts that had stolen both her sleep and her sanity. A slight feeling of hope rested in her bones.

Before Sienna left the attic, she reassured Gianna that she would stand beside her no matter what. She would find Gabriella and uncover what had really happened to Grace. And, perhaps most important of all, Sienna would pretend in front of Luca that she too believed Gianna was missing and never allow him to discover the truth.

The last thing they discussed before she closed and secured the attic door was that Gianna would hide far away from Tropea. Sienna quickly arranged for Gianna to stay with her dearest friend, Amelia.

***

A crisp morning wind whipped through the tiny local train station. Gianna and Sienna had arrived early and waited for the train scheduled to arrive on time. Gianna stared for a long time at the distant steel rails until a yellow light glimmered at the end. Several people stood and gathered nearby. Businessmen in well-tailored suits holding leather briefcases rushed ahead of the assembling crowd. Gianna gasped at the distant sounds of babies wailing above the noise. Bells clanged as the train rumbled into the station, whooshing and screeching until, finally, it stopped.

Gianna squeezed Sienna's hand. "It's time," she said with a frightened smile. She took Sienna's hands in hers and pulled her close. "If Franco is alive, please make sure he knows I am too. Don't let him believe what they're saying about me," she said, "and take care of yourself—stay out of Rico's way as much as you can."

"I will," Sienna said as her eyes welled up. "You take care too."

"And you'll visit soon and call me as much as possible," Gianna reminded.

"Yes, I promise."

"Oh, Sienna," Gianna cried as she hugged her tight, "I can't imagine not seeing you every day. What will I do without you?" She buried her head in Sienna's shoulder and whispered, "I'm scared."

Gianna stepped back, and Sienna placed her hands on Gianna's arms with confidence. "You will be okay," she said. Then she kissed Gianna on each cheek, helped her with her luggage, and finally let her go. Gianna boarded the train with her head low. At the top, she stopped and faced Sienna one last time. She wiped her cheek and blew her a kiss. Then she turned away and proceeded down the aisle to find her seat.

Chapter 23
Ella

Early in the morning, before the sun was up, I was awakened by a soft tapping on the bedroom door. Angelina peeked in, her plump face framed by the sun's rays behind her. A faded yellow-and-purple bruise spread below her eyes to above her cheekbone.

"Ready?" she asked.

Liv's head popped into the doorway next to Angelina's, as did my mother's. "Coming?" Liv said.

I knew they were talking about the abandoned house.

"Bring your pendant, Ella," Angelina said. "Throw something on. It'll take a couple hours to get there. Let's go before it gets late."

I stared at them, saying nothing, still caught by the image of Nico and that woman from the night before.

"The house—remember? Let's go."

I was torn. Vinny clearly had no idea this was happening.

"We should wait for Nico. It'll be safer," I said, trying to buy some time. Everything inside me told me this was a bad idea.

"Ella." Angelina's eyes warmed. She entered my room and sat beside me on the bed. "We want to make the most of your time, right?"

I nodded. "Yes, but don't you think—"

"There's something about this house. Something more than what you see and hear." She scratched her head. "Maybe it has nothing to do with what's been happening at your house or what happened to me, but maybe it does. I think the sooner we go the better. Shouldn't we at least find out?"

"Nico said—"

"I know," Angelina interrupted. "I know he'd want to come with us and you don't want to upset him. But what if you don't hear from him until later tonight? That's a whole day wasted. You might discover something important. The sooner we go, the better."

I couldn't argue with that, and I shouldn't care what Nico thought, especially after last night. I glanced at my phone. *Nico, where are you?*

"I know it's early, but Vinny's asleep," Angelina continued. "That gives us a few hours before he wakes up and goes to the market. What do you say?"

Angelina was very determined and willing to risk a lot to help me. I threw back the covers and stepped into my jeans. I pulled my hair into a ponytail, grabbed my jacket and my purse, and popped a piece of gum into my mouth. Their eyes brightened as they waited. We tiptoed cautiously down the hall, one behind the other, until we reached the front door. Angelina snatched the car keys hanging on a hook beside the door, grabbing them carefully so they wouldn't make noise. We followed her through the fog toward the car.

At the driver's door, she handed me the keys.

"I'm driving?" I asked. "But you know where to go. Shouldn't you drive?"

"The fog makes me nervous," Angelina said. "I can think better and we'll be safer with me as your copilot and not the driver."

I didn't feel prepared at all to drive to somewhere I'd never been.

Angelina must have read my thoughts. "You have nothing to worry about. All you have to do is pay attention. I'll be your guide."

I took the keys from Angelina. "You owe me big," I joked.

"How about a big pasta dinner!" she chuckled.

I glanced in the back seat at my mother and Liv, who looked uncomfortable with the driving arrangements.

"You're sure?" my mother asked.

I squared my shoulders. "If Angelina's sure, then I am too," I said.

My hands adhered firmly to the steering wheel, and adrenaline pumped through my body as I prepared for just under a three-hour drive to the abandoned house. The morning mist became a heavy cloth which clung to the car, making it difficult to decipher the road ahead. Occasionally a street light popped through the grey, offering a brief moment of reassurance as it illuminated the lines on the road.

Angelina, having lived here all her life, knew the roads well, even through the fog. Her voice was a comforting guide as we navigated our way to the house.

As we entered the village of Positina, Angelina noted the Church of Saint Januarius, its steep peaks poking through the clouds. Just past the church, we followed a one-lane road under a dark bridge, which led to the road of the abandoned house. It was reminiscent of my visit to Via Rosa—not the fog or any of the roads but the heaviness I'd felt right before Jamie and I had found Maria. It made me as uncomfortable now as I'd felt then, maybe worse.

Angelina alerted me to the road ahead where I'd be turning right. About halfway down on the left-hand side, we could identify a shadowy outline of the abandoned house where the fog was thin. I kept my foot lightly on the gas pedal as we crawled up the steep, narrow driveway to the top and pulled into an area where it widened. Before us stood a three-story mansion partially obscured by overgrown bushes and the remains of an old iron fence. We stared at the house, peeking through the mist before exiting the car. A feeling of dread came over me as I thought about what had happened to

Angelina in this house. It felt wrong to enter, as if we might awaken something that had finally fallen asleep.

Angelina handed me a flashlight and then gave one to my mother and Liv.

"Are you sure about this?" I said to Angelina, giving her one last chance to change her mind and turn back.

"I'm sure," she said, eyeing each of us. "Let's go."

She opened her door and stepped out. Together we stood in front of the car, our combined lights scarcely slicing through the fog. It was difficult to see the entirety of the house, but I felt its looming presence. Angelina stepped toward it as my mother, Liv, and I followed, our free hands connected one behind the other, flashlights aimed at the ground.

Halfway to the door, Angelina stopped and directed her flashlight at a rope hanging from a tree, similar to the one in the picture. "Do you see it?" she whispered.

"Yes," we whispered back.

We followed her and paused when she did at the steps leading to the front door. Four grand pillars stood before it with a porch as wide as the house. I thought she might lead us inside right then, but she continued walking around the far right side of the house. She was quiet and methodical in her movements, illuminating parts of the house with her beam and occasionally peering over her shoulder. When she stopped at the right corner of the house, she swept her flashlight at something protruding slightly behind it.

"I need all of you to aim your light in the same spot as me," she said.

We did as we were told, and slowly an odd-shaped structure appeared through the mist.

"That," she said confidently, "used to be a swing set and an outdoor play area, or what's left of it. I used to play here when I was a child, and I sat on the swing that used to be there. My father, God rest his soul, used to bring me here when he made deliveries. I used to love coming along with him. I met lots of people."

We studied the dilapidated structure that didn't look like anything at all to me. I wondered how much of it could be seen in the picture.

"I just wanted to show you that. I needed to see it too. Now, let's go back to the entrance."

We returned to the grand, colorless pillars and climbed the steps to a wooden door curved at the top. At one time this entire entrance might have given an appeal of warmth and coziness, but now it exuded coldness, loneliness.

"I already know this door is locked," Angelina explained. "Everything is. I wanted you to see it, though, and get a feel for this stately mansion. We'll go around to the back. There's an old servants' entrance which is unlocked. That's how I got in before."

A damp, musty smell caught in our throats, making us cough and gasp as soon as we entered the narrow corridor leading from the servants' entrance. We walked by several old shoes of various sizes that lined one side of a crumbling wall and eventually emerged into a kitchen. Our lights flashed against the walls, counters, and floors, across signs of a life abruptly ended.

A mouse scurried across a mold-filled bowl and knocked over a cereal box on the table, making us scream. The corresponding chair was pulled away from the table. Another chair lay upended, blocking the path of a small wagon transporting dolls and stuffed animals across the dirty kitchen floor. Dishes sat in the sink caked with food which had mutated into a hardened black mass. A folded highchair leaned against the fridge. As I walked among the wreckage to the doorway at the other end, I imagined the souls that might have inhabited this life.

The doorway opened to a living room, its contents also in disarray. It was as if each family member had been plucked from amid their normal routines. I feared that Angelina's attackers might be somewhere in the house, lying in wait to ambush us.

Angelina, who was right behind me, whispered, "I want to show you what's upstairs. Follow me."

We climbed the ornate staircase and followed Angelina down one of three hallways to a bedroom at the end. I paused in the doorway as an uneasy feeling rippled through my body. She entered the room and went straight to the closet door, opened it, and stepped inside, motioning for us to follow. My mother, Liv, and I looked at each other with uncertainty as we entered behind Angelina. We brushed against old furs and mildew-laden clothes, and, where the closet should have ended, another door existed which connected to another room.

"Watch your step," Angelina said as we spilled into another bedroom, coughing from the dank air. It was a simple bedroom: one dresser, a nightstand, and a bed that looked like it had never been slept in. "The other basement entrance is off this room."

I thought it was strange to have access to the basement from an upstairs bedroom.

"Other basement entrance?" my mother said, echoing my thoughts. "There's more than one?"

"Yes," Angelina said. "The main door is off the kitchen, but it's locked. I found this one by accident. I was surprised too."

"I wonder whose bedroom this was," Liv said, "to be between a hidden closet and a private door to the basement."

"And no access to the main hallway," Angelina said as she walked to a mirror standing beside the basement door. She turned the mirror so that it faced the wall. "Don't look at that," she said, "or any old mirror you don't know. Mirrors in old houses are not to be trusted.

Sadness and fear may overcome you . . . like the one you'll see in the basement. That's where—"

"Where it happened?" I asked.

Angelina made the sign of the cross and nodded.

"Angelina, are you sure about this?" I said.

"It's okay. Give me a minute."

"What did you mean about the mirror?" Liv asked.

Angelina faced Liv and stared into her eyes. She brushed the dark, wavy locks away from her face. "You have beautiful eyes," she said. "Did you know your eyes are a window to your soul? It's true. And mirrors act in the same way, like a window, but to a life. Over time they absorb the emotions of the person or people who look into it. They also reflect the truth within ourselves—about our lives. If you live a life of happiness and good intentions and you gaze into that mirror each day as you're combing your hair or talking to yourself, the positive energy you emanate will come back to you abundantly."

"What about people who are truly kind and honest but they come upon hard times and feel sad or angry for a while?" my mother asked. I wondered if she was thinking about Poppy or herself.

"Everyone has hard times," Angelina answered. "It's not about those passing moments but more about how you internalize it, how you deal with it. Do you eventually let it go or do you hold onto it and let it define who you are? That's the difference.

"But some say—and I believe them—that a troubled mind seized by darkness and secrets . . . over time it can create a strong negative energy which can not only be absorbed by the people around him or her but also by any mirror they regularly use." Angelina gestured to the one facing the wall. "And that negative energy will be reflected back to them and into their lives. The danger that occurs with an old mirror is that, as time passes, the negativity can intensify and become trapped. That's why you should never accept a mirror from someone you don't know and never buy one from a yard sale. You'll never know the condition of the soul that gazed into that mirror each day, and eventually that negativity could come to you and affect your life."

I wondered if this could really be true or if it was merely an old superstition.

Angelina spoke quietly and softly about her experience, her eyes framed by wrinkles. She was spiritually strong with keen intuition, a strong wit, and a sharp sense about her, similar to Nonna. Not long ago I'd doubted what she'd said about the *malocchio*—that one could curse another because of jealousy or anger. But I had watched the drop of oil mix with the water and form an oval as she tried to dispel the curse she believed gripped me. I recalled how it had happened for me but not when she did it for Nico. She was right about the *malocchio*. Could she be right about the mirror?

"The person who used that mirror," Angelina said, pointing, "was deeply burdened with a powerful mixture of sadness, anger, and hatred. I turned it away because I felt the dark presence captured in it, but . . . it is nothing like the one in the basement."

"Did you look at it?" I asked.

"Oh yes, and I was quickly overcome with a feeling of intense sadness and fear. When I finally broke from the trance, that's when I realized I was no longer alone," she said, opening the door to the basement.

Chapter 24

Ella

Although I had my doubts about mirrors absorbing energy, I couldn't deny the heaviness I felt in that house. My steps as we descended into darkness were rigid and labored, and my thoughts were muddled. The air grew dense. My mother and sister remained quiet as we followed Angelina down the long staircase to the basement.

Angelina continued whispering about the fine line between good spirits and bad ones. No one questioned why she would dare take us where she knew something bad existed. Where she'd been attacked.

My phone chimed and we jumped. I quickly silenced it, fearing it might give us away, and saw a text from Nico. We had a brief exchange:

Nico: Where are you? Why haven't you called?

Me: I did…several times.

Nico: What? No missed calls. No texts. Are you here??

Me: Yes. That doesn't make sense.

Nico: Call you now?

Me: Can't…helping Angelina.

Me: I saw you yesterday…with someone.

Nico: What? When?

Nico: Can I see you tonight?

Me: Okay
Nico: You okay?

I wasn't sure how to respond to that or how to feel. I was relieved to finally hear from him but confused at why he was ignoring my calls and disturbed about the woman I'd seen him with. I also felt guilty for coming to the house without him, but Angelina was determined to go with or without me, and I couldn't let her go alone again. But now I needed to be alert. I texted him back, but it failed to send. Whatever signal I had was gone.

When we reached the base of the stairs, I saw a door hanging on one hinge, dented in the middle. The walls crumbled around its dilapidated frame. We squeezed through a small opening in the doorway and entered a peculiar room. A small beam of light peeked through a window just enough to expose the dust-covered hardwoods and an arched doorway leading to another section of the room. We followed Angelina straight to the back. Where hardwood ended, concrete flooring began. It was cold and dark, not finished like the rest of the room. My feet chilled atop the cold floor, and I felt a sinking feeling, a sense of foreboding. Blue floral wallpaper, shredded in spots, exposed chipped cinder-block walls behind it. An old desk was tucked into a corner beside a filing cabinet. A few steps away was a twin-sized bed and a tall object concealed by a sheet leaning against the wall.

"We should go," I said, trembling.

"Yes," my mother agreed, and Liv nodded. "I don't like this."

"Shhh," Angelina whispered. "We'll go in a minute. You have your necklace?"

I touched the Italian horn at my neck that Angelina claimed would ward off evil spirits and nodded.

"You feel it, too, then?" she asked, looking at each of us.

We stared back at her wide-eyed, not answering, but if she was talking about the feeling of complete dread, then, yes, I felt it, and I think they had too. Something about this area of the room felt very different from the other parts of the house—a shift . . . a burden. Chills swept through me. I swallowed the fear in my throat.

Angelina walked to the tall object leaning against the wall and pulled the sheet away, revealing an antique swivel mirror turned toward the wall.

"I found it facing out," she said. "I knew I shouldn't have, but I looked into it and—such heartache!" she said, placing her hands over her face. "And lust and greed . . . and regret. After that, I remember nothing. The doctors think that's when they hit me the first time. I thought it was a dream—that someone was yelling at me. It sounded like we were in a tunnel. The police think I was dragged across the floor over there." She pointed at drag marks from the traces of her blood that led from the mirror to the doors at the back. "I tried to fight them but they were so strong. . . ." Her voice trailed off. "When I woke up at the hospital, that's when I realized it wasn't a dream."

I put my arm around her shoulders. "Did anything else—"

"No, dear. Thank God. I think they thought I was dead. I vaguely remember another voice—a female, I think—and then . . . ," she shrugged, "nothing."

"I'm so sorry, Angelina," my mother said, coming to her side.

"I know terrible things happened in this room," Angelina continued, "and someone went to great lengths to keep it secret." She dipped her hand into her pocket and pulled out an old skeleton key. I immediately thought of Poppy's diary. She held it before us. "This was taped to the back of the mirror. I felt something on the back of the frame as I turned the mirror away from me. I had forgotten about it until the day I was released from the hospital. I put my hand in my pocket and there it was."

"May I?" I asked, reaching for the key. Could this have been the missing key to the diary?

"Maybe it opens that filing cabinet," Liv said, walking over to it. The top drawer was open a few inches, and papers and files were strewn about. The second and third drawers were the same. Some of the files were stuffed with odd items, souvenirs, and mementos from travels. Liv aimed the flashlight as we stared at the contents. It looked as if someone else might have been here before us.

I searched through the files, examining each piece, when something caught my eye, something that might have been overlooked had it not been for the light: a long, rolled-up scroll fastened by a rubber band on both ends. I carefully unfurled the yellowed parchment and saw that it was an old blueprint of a house. My heart leaped.

"Oh my gosh!" I said, pointing to a scribbled name and the word Tuscany. "I can't read the name, but that says Tuscany, doesn't it?"

My mother took the paper and examined it. "It does say Tuscany," she said, looking at me.

"I know how this sounds, but humor me for a minute." I paused, contemplating if I should say it.

"I think I know where you're going with this," Liv said.

"Could this blueprint possibly have anything to do with the house in Tuscany that Poppy talked about on the DVD?"

"What's happening here," Angelina said, moving her hands in exaggerated circles, "is not a coincidence. Everything is linked together in some way." Nonna always said the same thing.

A shuffling sound emerged from behind us. We slowly turned our heads toward the stairs. I cringed. No one else knew we were there, not even Vinny. No one would know if we needed help. I glanced at the text I had tried to send Nico an hour ago, but it was still pending. I wished I'd told him we'd gone to the house. Now it was too late.

We stood like statues, afraid to breathe. The shuffling noise stopped. Angelina pointed to a door at the back of the room, not far from where we were standing. Maybe it was another closet. We treaded lightly across the floor, and, as we resumed, so did the shuffling. When we stopped, the shuffling stopped.

"Run to the door," Angelina whispered.

We bolted as shuffled steps turned hard and followed quickly after us. Together we pushed against the heavy door until it finally gave way. We ascended the stairway as fast as possible all the way to the top, where we were met with cold, crisp air and freedom.

I glimpsed the back door one last time as we stumbled away from the old, disheveled mansion—a mansion with a private back entrance to a secret room in the basement, hidden among the wild brush of the backyard, unassuming to anyone.

Although the fog had mostly lifted, the white clouds and thick canopy of trees surrounding the mansion darkened the ground below. We ran around the side of the house until we were back at the car, breathless but safe.

"Did someone lock the doors?" I yelled, frantically searching my purse for the keys. No one remembered locking it. My fingers anxiously fumbled through the keys until I found one that fit. We slid in and locked the doors as I turned the key in the ignition. The engine turned over, but it wouldn't start. I banged my hand on the steering wheel as the tension in the air thickened. Finally it revved to life and I threw the car in reverse, but I overshot the curve and ended in the grass. I shifted into drive as the wheels spun crazily, carving the moist ground below.

Suddenly a bright light pierced the windshield. Angelina screamed, and we dove for the floor.

Chapter 25

Ella

My heart raced as the blinding beam sliced through my vision and trailed along the windshield, stopping at the driver's-side window. The shadow behind the light drew close, and I closed my eyes tightly, preparing for the worst.

But a light tapping on the glass confused me. A muffled voice was talking to me. "Ella," it said.

Who knew it was me hiding in this car?

I stayed crouched low, only turning my head to look at my mother's worried face.

"Ella," it said again.

This time the voice and the way it said my name seemed familiar. I turned toward the window and stared at the face pressed against the glass and knew immediately who it was, but how . . . how could it be Nico?

I sat up all the way and rolled down the window. "Nico?" I said incredulously, but still wary. "What are you doing here? How did you know—"

"All your texts came in at once except the last one," he blurted. "I went to Angelina's hoping you were there. Vinny was upset and had no idea where you'd gone. He hoped Angelina hadn't come back here but he said it was possible. I told him I would come and look for you so he gave me the address. He decided to stay home in case you returned before me. You know you shouldn't be here," he said. "None of us should." He flashed his light to the passenger seat and back seat, exposing my mother, sister, and Angelina.

"Nico, the car is stuck," I said, panicking, "and someone's in the house!"

Panic made his eyes bulge. "You should have waited until I could go with you!"

So many thoughts ran through my head. "Did you go inside?" I asked, hoping maybe it was Nico's footsteps we'd heard.

"No, of course not."

I wondered how he could have gotten here so quickly. How long had we been in the house?

"I'll get you out," he said. "Step on the gas as soon as I start to push." He ran to the rear of the car and pushed until we were free.

"Nico, get out of here!" I yelled as he ran to his car. From the rearview mirror, I watched as he pulled away, and I thought I saw someone standing near the garage.

***

Despite the balmy breeze, a chill stayed with me as we raced the lonely roads from the car to Angelina's house. When we arrived, a quiet argument ensued behind the door between Vinny and Angelina. I waited on the porch for Nico, but after a few minutes I stepped inside and found my mother, Liv, and Angelina in the kitchen. Angelina reassured us that Vinny was upset with her, not with us. He'd join us a bit later after he cooled down.

"That was frightening, and we are very lucky," Angelina said.

"Who do you think could have been in the house?" Liv asked. "Maybe a transient? That mansion is enormous; several families could be living there at once and never run into each other."

"What if it was your attackers?" my mother added.

"I'd like to think it could only be a transient," Angelina answered, giving Liv's hand a condescending pat, "but it didn't feel like that. It felt like someone was purposely there watching us. When we got too close to something they didn't want us to see, that's when they made themselves known." She looked at my mother. "If it were my attackers, they would certainly have come at us again. No, I think it was someone closer to us. Someone afraid of what we might discover."

"Luca," my mother suggested.

"I'm not saying that," Angelina answered, "but it's not impossible."

"You were right," I said to Angelina. "Something bad happened in that house. I felt it everywhere, especially in the basement." The more we talked, the more we were convinced it might have been Luca running behind us in the basement.

Nico finally arrived looking a little disheveled and slightly distracted. I fell into his arms immediately and snuggled my head into his neck, breathing in his woodsy pine scent I'd missed for so long. I still had many questions, but now wasn't the time to figure out the strange miscommunication we'd been having. It wasn't the way I envisioned our first encounter after being apart for months. But all was right in that moment while we hugged, and I held onto it tightly.

For the next hour, we recounted every detail from our visit to the abandoned house right up until the point when Nico arrived. Then Angelina laid the skeleton key on the table. I picked it up and studied it closely, marveling at its existence and possible connection to the diary. Tomorrow's plans would include a drive to Via Fosse Ardeatine, the neighborhood where Nico saw Luca, and then to the library or the town center to see if anyone could help us with the blueprint.

We were getting closer to Gianna. I could feel it.

Eventually, exhaustion sent us to our rooms. I was comforted by the soft, downy covers of the bed as they hugged me, but as much as my body needed sleep, my mind craved answers. I sat up, switched on the light beside me, and rolled out of bed. I grabbed the blueprint from my bag, brought it back to the bed, and spread it open beneath the light.

What had first seemed to be messy scribble marks near the bottom of the paper next to the word Tuscany appeared now like a faint scrawling of a name—a signature. Using my phone's camera, I zoomed in as close as possible and saw clearly what had been purposefully written, not scribbled: *Giovanni Luccetti.*

Fascinated by the discovery of the blueprint's author, I researched Giovanni Luccetti for several hours, until dawn peeked below the window shade.

Giovanni, originally from Pistoia, a city in the Tuscany region, had lived in Rome for several years studying the architecture of the holy city, Florence. He was well-known for designing a famous railroad station and a church in Fiesole, the small town in Florence where he was last known to have lived. I devoured everything I could about his family, his designs, and his connections to famous people, including the Pope. But what excited me most about everything I'd read was that Giovanni was still alive.

We'd have to change our plans a bit and visit Via Fosse Ardeatine, where Luca was last seen, later in the day or even the next day. A trip to Florence would now take precedence over anywhere else. I hoped we would find Giovanni and, even if the blueprint wasn't of the house in Tuscany, perhaps he could give us information that might lead us there or explain the significance of the blueprint.

The sun climbed above the horizon as I ventured to the veranda to sit in the breeze and make plans. A directory search on my phone revealed three Giovanni Luccettis in Tuscany. Of the two who lived in Florence, one was ten years old and one was in his upper seventies. A third Giovanni, in his eighties, lived in Pisa, but that was as far as the public information went, so I signed up for a premium subscription which would allow me all the access I wanted.

A soft pattering of footsteps entered the veranda from behind. The familiar short-strided, part-limping gait that I had come to know well was Angelina's. She handed me a coffee mug already mixed with cream.

"Up already?" Her voice cracked.

"I didn't sleep. Too much on my mind," I said.

Angelina sat on the sofa across from me and placed her mug on the side table, eyeing the blueprint.

I held the warm mug in my hands. "I figured out who designed the blueprint. And guess what? He's still alive."

Angelina's eyes widened. "That's amazing detective work," she said. "How did you do it?"

"The scribble marks in the corner were actually a signature," I said, handing it to her. She pushed her glasses to her nose and studied the corner. "The architect's name is Giovanni Luccetti and he lives in Fiesole up in Tuscany."

"*Meeska,*" she said, shaking her hand. "And you think he's still alive?"

"My internet search says he is," I answered, "and I'd like to visit him."

"Fee-ez-olee," Angelina said, enunciating each part. "I haven't been there in years."

"I have it all planned out," I said. "Will Vinny mind if you come with us?"

"Don't you worry about Vinny. He won't mind," she said.

"We'll go to Fiesole today, and Castello Ruffo and Via Fosse Ardeatine will have to wait until tomorrow," I said, feeling a little guilty for putting off Castello Ruffo again. My mother and sister wanted to visit the places I had while following Poppy's diary as a guide in Italy two years ago. My stomach squeezed at the thought of the diary in someone else's filthy hands, someone who might also want to follow in the footsteps of the past as well. Or worse—destroy it.

Chapter 26

Ella

Bells chimed as the train approached the station, hissing and screeching as it slowed to a stop. A small crowd of people exited and several others climbed aboard, squeezing into what little space was left. A frazzled mother pushed through the aisle, and five mini replicas marched close behind her with the same expression, carrying themselves like she did. She arranged her children in their seats one by one as four men behind her rolled their eyes, waiting impatiently for her to move. When the men could finally pass us, the third man caught my eye and did a double-take. He looked familiar, but I reasoned that he had to be just one of those familiar faces since I didn't know anyone in Italy besides Nico, Angelina, and Vinny.

"That guy's flirting with you." Liv elbowed me, and Nico looked up.

"Which guy?" he asked.

"They're already past us," I said. "I don't think he was flirting. He probably thought I was someone else." But the way he had looked at me was curious and eerily reminiscent of the times when Marco had conveniently appeared in the same places I was two years ago.

I suddenly felt flushed and hot. And paranoid. Nico stared down the aisle behind us and then returned his eyes to the book resting in his lap and placed one hand on my leg. I opened a private investigating book and pretended to read it, but the feeling that I was being watched remained the entire ride to Florence, even as we stepped off the train.

I thought it was odd that the four men who sat behind us were already off the train and waiting for their driver. Two of them were sitting on a bench while the other two stood nearby, knapsacks slung across their shoulders. As we passed them, I wondered how they had gotten off the train before us when they were seated a few rows behind. The familiar one was busy talking with his friends as he adjusted the buckle on his bag, but occasionally he'd glance over to where I was. I felt his eyes follow me as we sat two benches down from them. I watched as he separated from his friends and quickly stepped toward us. Nico was watching too. Our driver pulled in and stopped his car so that he was between us and the approaching man.

Nico stood outside the car as we got in. He glared at the man and said something I couldn't hear. The man said something to Nico and then turned away. Nico didn't move as the stranger returned to his friends, then he slid into the back seat beside us.

"What did he say?" I asked.

"He said he knew you and wanted to talk to you. I told him he *didn't* know you and, no, he couldn't talk to you." His jaw tightened. "I don't think he liked that. He just stood staring at me, as if I might change my mind. Finally I said, 'Get lost, you don't know her,' and he turned around and went back. *Idiota.*"

Nico looked at me with concern and anger in his eyes. I wondered if this man reminded him of Marco too. Thoughts of the man's familiar face lingered in my mind, but I couldn't place him.

Liv helped change the subject with talk of Tuscany and her excitement about exploring the unknown side of our ancestors, and before we knew it we had emerged onto Tuscan roads, greeted by waves of rolling green blanketing the countryside—gradual immersion into a magical world. Small homes scattered among the hills just like in photographs. Cypress trees lined the horizon silhouetted by a bright-orange sky. Every so often olive groves, vineyards, and quaint farmhouses slipped into view. I couldn't absorb it fast enough.

About an hour into our ride, the scene shifted as wide-open hills hid behind houses and narrowing streets pulled us to the small towns ahead. The city streets were lined with a smattering of impressive buildings, businesses, ancient churches, and modest homes. Soon the roads climbed just above the countryside and finally opened to fascinating panoramic views of the renaissance city below, another hidden gem of Italy: Fiesole.

Giovanni's modest home sat upon a small knoll surrounded by beautiful land. I had expected something more grandiose for a well-known and successful architect of his talent—something more intricate and modern—but perhaps Giovanni's most prized value, honor, and wealth came from within himself, as Poppy's had.

I looked at the address on my phone and compared it to the street sign and house number: Via Torre di Buiano, 4 in the town of Fiesole. "Fee-ez-olee," I said, stretching each syllable, as Angelina had, enjoying its sound. I hardly had the car in park before everyone poured out.

We walked up the driveway past a small, round, worn table set for two in the middle of the front yard. We continued along the cobbled path leading to the front porch. The house was as still and quiet as its surroundings. My mother, Liv, Angelina, and Nico waited at the bottom of the steps as I walked across the porch to the front door and rang the bell. After a few minutes with no answer, I began to doubt myself and worried that my visit might seem like an intrusion. I contemplated turning back when I heard dragging footsteps on the other side of the door. The curtains in the side window moved, and a face peeked through quickly and disappeared.

Footsteps shambled to the door again, followed by the sound of metal sliding and clicking. The door opened slowly revealing a small, portly, older woman. Her eyes were soft and kind, her thin lips displayed a gentle smile. One hand rested on a cane and the other on the doorknob. When she leaned forward, her smile disappeared and she whispered to me, "I told you they're not here anymore."

Confused by this greeting, I said, "Perhaps you were expecting someone else? I've never been here before. My name is Ella Perri," I turned to the porch, "and this is my family."

The woman squinted. "Do I know you?"

"No, you don't."

"Then you shouldn't be here," she said, closing the door.

"Please, just one moment of your time," I begged. "I think I may have something that belongs to your husband—something he designed."

"My husband hasn't designed anything in years," she scoffed, continuing to close the door.

"Yes, I know. It's from forty years ago," I said.

She opened the door about an inch more.

"Hold on," I said, pulling the blueprint from my bag and quickly unrolling it to the point of the signature. "That's his name, right? Giovanni Luccetti. Is that your husband?"

The woman slid on her glasses and looked at the name. "Where did you get this? Did someone send you here?" she asked.

"No . . . but I think your husband might have known my grandfather or my uncle. And they've both recently passed." The woman stared at me, but I continued. "They often talked about a beautiful home in Tuscany designed by a famous architect—your husband. They dreamed of meeting him but were never able to." I felt bad for lying, but it seemed easier, more believable, than what I could have said. "I was hoping to honor their wishes—"

"My husband is very sick," she retorted, furrowing her brow and pointing her finger at me. "You should know better than to bother someone when they're struggling to stay alive!"

"I'm so sorry. I didn't—"

The woman turned around and seemed to be talking to someone. Muffled voices behind her grew louder and heated. She faced me again, her eyes downcast. "Perhaps you can speak to my husband. For a moment." She lifted her gaze. "But you mustn't stay long, and please don't upset him. He needs to stay calm. If you can't agree to that, you should go now."

"Of course," I said. "I would never want to upset him. I only want to meet him and ask a couple questions. Then I'll go."

The woman gave a slight nod and stepped aside to let me in, but she pushed her hand out when Nico, my mother, and Liv approached. "I'm sorry," she said. "You will have to wait here," and closed the door behind her.

Chapter 27
Gianna

Italy 1939

Amelia lived in a modest home on Via del Lago in Bracciano, a quaint town in the Lazio region thirty kilometers northwest of Rome. When Gianna arrived, Amelia had been waiting behind a small iron gate at the steps to her house. Amelia stood as the driver pulled into a cobbled inlet near a closed gate to the driveway. She waved to Gianna, opened the gate, and met her at the car, offering her a brief hug.

"It's so nice to meet you," Amelia said, smiling. Her long black hair, swept into a ponytail, bounced as she spoke.

"And you as well," Gianna said. "I can't thank you enough for letting me stay with you."

"My pleasure. Stay as long as you need," she said. Her eyes disappeared behind slits when she smiled, like Franco's always had.

Gianna followed Amelia up the brick walkway to the entrance of her home. Once inside, Amelia showed her the kitchen, living room, and two bathrooms, taking her last to the bedroom where she would sleep. Amelia opened the door to a good-sized room that had a white writing desk, a chair, a dresser, and a bed. Gianna could tell that much care had been taken to prepare her room. The bedding looked recently fluffed, and its fresh scent floated through the room. A white cotton throw lay diagonally at the end, and beside it was a shallow basket containing a vase of white peonies, a teapot, and some cookies.

"You're so thoughtful," Gianna said. "Thank you."

Amelia smiled. "I'll let you get settled," she said. "Help yourself to anything, and if you don't see something you need, just ask." On her way out, she stood in the doorway and said, "My husband will be home in a couple hours. We would love to have you join us for dinner, if you'd like."

"Yes, I'd like that very much," Gianna said, although her stomach was in knots and she didn't feel hungry.

Gianna sat on the bed, eyeing her new surroundings while unpacking her suitcase. As she filled the dresser drawers with her few clothes, a beautiful, mature oak tree outside the bedroom window caught her eye. It was the main focal point in the middle of the backyard and had to be hundreds of years old. She marveled at its branches, twisted and bent, dipping low to the ground as if scooping its leaves so they'd never touch. Dozens of branches far thicker around than she reached toward the sky and down to the earth in all directions. Gianna placed her hand against the window and gazed longingly at the tree, captured by its breathtaking beauty, which comforted her. But as her body relaxed, she felt something loosen and shift within her, and the stabbing pain returned, wrapping again around her heart. Instead of pushing it down, denying its existence, she allowed it to rise within her. She threw her hands to her head and sunk to the ground as the ache tore through her body.

Gianna knelt on the floor, sobbing and gasping for air. She grabbed a pillow from the bed, put her face into it, and screamed with a force and sound she never knew she had. The names Gabriella, Grace, and Franco would slip from her lips into the pillow between grunts, screams, and hot, painful air consumed with unimaginable loss. She was seized in her sadness and hardly heard the knock at the door.

"Gianna?" Amelia said from the hallway. "Are you okay?" When Amelia got no reply, she poked her head in and saw Gianna bent on the floor, her head buried in the pillow. She rushed to her and wrapped her arms around her. "You poor thing," she said.

Gianna sat numb and silent in her arms, occasionally hiccuping as she tried to catch her breath.

"How about I draw you a bath and bring dinner to your room? You should eat a little bite of something."

Gianna nodded, wiping her face with the handkerchief Amelia handed her.

The warm bathwater gave small consolation to Gianna as she floated weightlessly in the tub. She pulled herself below the surface, allowing it to cover her head and massage her face. When the water cooled, she stepped out of the tub, changed into warm clothes, and sat at the desk where a covered tray of tortellini soup waited for her. Its warmth soothed her as she swallowed, but she quickly became full, covered the bowl, and put it aside. Then she climbed between the soft cotton sheets and closed her swollen eyes, not opening them even once until the following afternoon. It had been the first time she'd truly slept in weeks.

But she immediately felt ashamed. How could she sleep when her babies were lost?

Gianna existed in a fog the next few days, her mind miles away, her body heavily anchored to the ground, laboriously moving as if through a pool of water. The old oak tree outside her window was the one thing that provided any comfort. As days turned to weeks, she gradually spent a little more time outside of her room than in it. She even met Amelia's husband and occasionally had dinner with them. But regardless of what brought her downstairs, it was never long before she'd wander back to her room, to the tree.

***

Deep-green leaves turned golden-orange before browning and floating to the ground. Sienna called Gianna every day as she'd promised, but even months later she still hadn't been able to visit, and she had no news to share about Franco or the babies. Gianna felt her heart grow weaker as each day passed without them.

One morning Sienna called, Gianna could tell that something was different in her voice. About ten minutes into their conversation, Sienna paused.

"I'm so sorry, Gianna," she said.

"For what?"

"For not being there by now. It's hard with Rico. He's keeping a closer eye on me than normal. I'm trying to get to you. I will somehow."

"You need to get away from Rico," Gianna said.

"I know. I'm working on that," Sienna replied.

"Really?"

"Yes, but I can't talk about it right now. I wanted to let you know they called off the search for you. I don't know how to feel about that. It makes me sick . . . the things they've said . . ."

"What things?"

Sienna sighed. "You already knew they called your case a suspicious disappearance, but . . . they're also saying you might have . . ." Her voice trailed off.

"What? Say it."

"They think you took off with someone."

"And left my baby behind?" Gianna pounded her fist on the table.

"No . . . remember Gabriella was missing too," she said.

Hearing Gabriella's name and the weight it held made Gianna sick.

"They think you either left her with someone in our family if you didn't take her with you, or there was foul play. Nobody really believes you would leave, Gianna. It's just two theories the police have come up with since there is no solid evidence. And since there isn't anything new to go on, they're closing the case."

"What about Mamá? Has she stopped looking for me? What does she think?"

"Mamá is depressed," Sienna said. "She doesn't say much anymore. She says she doesn't know what to think but she prays you're still alive. At least that's what she tells Maria and me."

"I don't believe anything she says," Gianna sulked.

"Oh, there's something else I want you to know," Sienna continued. "You have nothing to worry about where Luca is concerned. He was ridiculous for a while, pretending to be so consumed with your disappearance and worried about you. He even led his own search through the park where you were supposedly last seen. I loathed every moment I saw him, and I had a hard time not telling him I knew he was a liar. It took everything I had not to. But over the last few weeks, strangely enough, he hasn't even mentioned you. I've made sure he has given up on his fake search for you."

"That worries me," Gianna said. "I wonder if he's scheming. You said 'over the last few weeks'—do you see him often? Is he bothering *you* now?"

"Oh, no, nothing like that," Sienna said. "I've just put some things in place that I cannot divulge now over the phone, but it's keeping his mind occupied, that's all."

"I suppose that's good," Gianna said. "Just please be careful."

"I will," Sienna said. "Now, let's stop talking about Luca. What's important is that you're all right, and I hope you know I think about you all the time. I feel so guilty not being there with you. It's not right to leave you there all this time without family."

"Don't feel guilty; it's not your fault."

Gianna knew a lot about guilt and how ingrained it could become until it consumed a person. She recalled moments when her guilty conscience had ruled her: the time she and Franco had reunited after years apart and had quickly fallen in love, she knew she had to tell him she was already promised to Carlos. The shame she had felt telling him!

And again when she learned she was expecting Franco's baby, the guilt she'd felt in Carlos's presence, pretending it was his baby she carried. Carlos had been difficult and not often in a pleasant mood, and the only thing that brought a hint of a smile to his lips were the moments they spoke about the baby.

After Franco left for the war, guilt and remorse remained as Gianna reluctantly carried out Franco's wish for her and Carlos to marry as planned. She never doubted Franco's love for her and knew he didn't want her to be with Carlos, but Franco believed marriage would protect her from gossip and provide a stable life for their child. It was a heartbreaking decision and not something either of them wanted, but they knew it would be for the best.

Of course, Gianna's most cumbersome burden of all derived from regret she'd felt in trusting Luca, the result of which led to losing everything precious to her.

At the end of their conversation, they agreed that if Sienna couldn't get all the way to Amelia's at the end of the month, she and Gianna would meet at a café halfway between their two homes. After saying goodbye, Gianna couldn't shake the eerie feeling at Sienna mentioning Luca's name. She wasn't sure if it was how Sienna said it or if hearing his name alone did that to her.

Chapter 28

Gianna

Italy 1939

Gianna's bedroom brightened earlier than normal as a soft white glowed from behind the curtains. Curious at such brightness in an otherwise cloudy November, Gianna rose from her bed, pushed aside the curtain, and smiled at what lay before her. White snow, like sifted confectioner's sugar, delicately covered the grass and leaves of the oak tree in Amelia's backyard and the neighboring yards. Snow was rare in Tropea, where Gianna had grown up, and she had hoped to see it come Christmastime at Amelia's, but experiencing it in November, much earlier than normal, was a treat. How beautiful it looked resting on the leaves and branches of the oak tree.

The phone rang, startling her, and she ran to answer it so as not to awaken Amelia and her husband, Matteo. It was Maria, and she was out of breath.

"Gianna!" she gasped. "I can't believe it! I can't believe it's really you. Sienna told me everything." When the search for Gianna was called off and the case had been closed, Gianna and Sienna had discussed telling Maria what had happened to her and where she had been all this time.

"Maria," Gianna said with a catch in her voice, "it's so good to hear your voice."

"I was upset at first," Maria began, "when I learned Sienna had known for so long and all that time I had no idea. I thought you were dead." Her voice cracked. She took a deep breath. "But I'm okay. I understand. I know you would have come to me if you could. I am just thrilled that you're alive. I can't wait to see you."

"Are you coming?" Gianna asked, hopeful.

"Not yet," Maria said, "but I have something I'm working on for you. I can't tell you, but—well, hopefully I can tell you in person."

"What is it?" Gianna begged. "I'm dying!"

"No," she said, "sorry, you're gonna have to wait. I just had to call you to hear your voice. It's like a dream. Mamá doesn't know, though. Will you tell her soon?"

"No, Maria, we can't tell her. Did Sienna talk to you at all about Mamá?"

"Yes, she did, but—"

"I know it sounds absurd and unreal, but it's true," Gianna said firmly, "and you can't—"

"I believe you," Maria blurted.

"You do?"

"I know she's hiding something," Maria said. "I can tell. She hasn't been herself ever since you had the baby. She mopes and paces, looks out the window, hardly talks. And it's not worry, it's guilt."

"How do you know?"

"She walks around like someone with a guilty conscience would," Maria said. "She hardly makes eye contact, and when she does you can see it in her eyes. They're dark, brooding. I plan to find out what she's been up to. In fact, I'm going there for a visit tomorrow. I'm just going to pop in to say hi and stick around for a while. I'm going to watch her and figure this out."

"That's risky," Gianna said. "You need to be careful. Her head is not well."

"Speaking of 'not well,'" Maria continued, "I'm watching Luca, too, and I don't like how he's been hanging around Sienna so much."

"I knew it. I knew he'd start doing that. I just wasn't sure which one of you he'd try it with."

"Oh, he knows I'll tell him like it is," she said. "Sienna's nicer, more patient. But don't worry. He won't get away with anything as long as I'm around. I started noticing how creepy he was when he came to see you after the baby. He was blushing when he saw you—sweating even. It was disgusting how obvious it was, to me at least."

"You were always good at seeing people for who they are," Gianna said. "I never could. I don't remember how Luca was toward me that day, but I do remember he acted as if he'd already seen Gabriella and yet he was supposedly there to see her for the first time. Remember that?"

"Yes. When you invited him into the room to come closer so he could see the baby, he said, 'I saw her,' but then added, 'when I came in.' It seemed strange and out of place. And Mamá had insisted on walking him in and walking him out. Just seemed secretive to me."

"Yes, I see that now," Gianna said.

"I don't want to keep you long. I just wanted to hear your voice and to tell you how much I love you and miss you, and I'm so happy you're okay. I believe you, Gianna, about the baby. I believe you had two and Mamá took away one. I know we have a lot to catch up on, and I'll see you soon in person. Sienna and I have a plan."

After Gianna and Maria hung up, Gianna closed her curtains and slid back under the covers, feeling light and happy. She closed her eyes and drifted into sleep.

Owlish green eyes stare at Gianna as cackling gasps float from behind the midwife . . . air entering lungs for the first time . . . a high-pitched wail turns softer, cooing.

A crooked smile exclaims, "A girl!" A baby swaddled in soft cotton rests in Gianna's arms but slips away. Whispers ensue in the shadows.

"Can you push again, my love?" the midwife softly urges. "You're gonna need to," her crooked smile turns grave, "as hard as you can." Water spills from cracks in the walls and floor, filling the room, surrounding Gianna who is dizzy and weak. She reaches for her mother's voice, her baby's cries, as water rushes in faster. Her eyes roll back as her mind searches the sounds around her.

Her mother's voice faintly says, "Will she live?" And nothing more.

Her own voice cries, "Mamá—my baby!"

"She's asleep," her mother answers.

"I need her," Gianna pleads.

But the midwife's voice is loudest and shakes the room as she speaks. "Can you push again, my love?"

"Thank God you're okay," her mother's voice echoes.

"Can you push again, my love?"

"You're confused, Gianna," whispers her mother.

"Push again."

"Push now."

"Again."

"Now!"

"There we go. . . ."

Gianna slips away; she hears another sound, soft and low, becoming louder, impatient. Another cry, different from the first one but familiar. Home.

Rough hands, worn and old, reach in and harshly grasp her babies, two girls she holds fixed to her chest. Gianna clutches them, but rough hands pull harder, diminishing her strength.

"No!" she screams. "No!"

"I can't believe you are mine," the woman with the rough hands says as Gianna sinks into a dark, cavernous hole. . . .

"No!" Gianna heard someone say, but quickly realized it was her own voice waking her, pleading from the shadows of her dream.

It wasn't the first time this had happened, and it wouldn't be the last. But instead of allowing those horrible thoughts to remain, Gianna recalled the day she held Gabriella in her arms for the first time, how she had kissed the top of her head and smelled her sweet skin, and then she—no one else but she—whispered, "I can't believe you are mine. All mine."

Then Gianna threw back the covers, pulled on her robe, and went downstairs to have coffee with Amelia and talk about the snow.

Chapter 29

Ella

Giovanni's wife led me to a room just off the entry where an elderly man was sitting in a leather recliner. A trail of smoke from a cigarette sitting in an ashtray floated toward the oxygen tube resting in his nose. The smoke-filled room reminded me of Poppy and Nonna, always a cigarette between their fingers or on their lips. When he saw me he waved his hand through the smog and snuffed out the cigarette. Then he smiled and exhaled a cloudy, "Hello," followed by a brief coughing fit.

"Hello," I said. "I'm Ella Perri." I pointed to a chair just outside the cloud of smoke surrounding him. "May I?"

He nodded, extending his hand toward the chair.

"Thank you for seeing me. I—"

"Perri," he said, coughing. "I know the name."

"You do?"

"What brings you here, *Signorina* Perri?" he said. "I don't have a lot of time, and I mean that literally," he winked.

"I'm very sorry to bother you," I said. "I won't stay long." I pulled the blueprint from my bag and unrolled it. "This is a house you designed many years ago. I'm wondering if you might share what you know about it." I handed the blueprint to Giovanni. "It's possible I might know who lived there once."

Giovanni pushed his bifocals onto his nose and pulled the paper close. His eyes narrowed as he studied the blueprint. They brightened for a moment and then became fierce. He removed his glasses and looked at me almost angrily. "Where did you get this?"

I tried to think of a simple explanation without admitting I'd broken into an abandoned home and found it in the creepy basement. So I continued the lie I'd told his wife, that I was pursuing the house on behalf of my beloved grandfather and dear uncle. I stressed the importance of meeting the blueprint's brilliant designer.

He eyed me sharply as if contemplating my story. "I don't believe it," he said.

I wasn't sure how to respond, but I was prepared to embellish my story if needed.

"I just don't believe it," he repeated, and began a coughing fit that brought his wife into the room.

"You are upsetting him," she scolded, shaking her finger at me.

He shook his head as he coughed, waving. "It's fine, *cara,* dear," he said between coughs.

She cupped her hands around his ear, attempting to whisper, all the while speaking as loudly as ever, just like Nonna. "What are you talking about? I hope it's not what I think. You promised," she said.

Giovanni looked at her. The wrinkles around his eyes gathered in desperate pleading. They filled as he stared at his wife.

She stared back with concern and love. Her shoulders dropped and her body softened. "Please," she said. "It's too much for you."

"My time will soon end, Lia," he muttered softly. "I don't need to hold onto this anymore."

She gave a heavy sigh, placed her hand on his shoulder, and kissed his forehead. Then, without looking at me, she left the room.

Giovanni snatched his cigarette pack from the table beside his chair and proceeded to tap it against his palm. When he was finished, he removed a cigarette, placed it between his lips, struck a match, and lit the end. It crackled and smoldered as he walked to a partially opened window, smoke trailing behind him. He exhaled through the window and then faced me. "Montepulciano," he said. "That's where the house is."

Montepulciano—still in Tuscany, but farther north than I thought. I waited for more, but Giovanni seemed mesmerized as he pursed his lips on the cigarette, drawing in an exceptionally long drag, closing his eyes and smiling as orange embers glowed at the tip. He seemed to savor each drag, and I wondered if he craved it as much as Mr. Jones did. When he finished, he returned to his chair, adjusted his oxygen, and cleared his throat.

"I promised not to ever speak of this," he began, "but I also never imagined facing the end of life so soon. It changes things . . . your perspective. When my time comes, my wife will live with her sister in Rome. We never had children, so I have nothing to lose by talking now. But back then it was a different story."

He ran his hand over his fuzzy head and paused for a moment as if lost in thought.

"That house in Montepulciano was beautiful," he said, his eyes shining. "One of the most interesting designs I've ever completed on a home. The man who ordered it—and I mean he *demanded* it—knew exactly what he wanted in that house. I don't know where he came up with his ideas, but he must have been planning it for a very long time. He was very specific about the details, and if it wasn't to his liking, he made sure I knew it," Giovanni said. "Anyone who stood in front of that house or walked by it was easily fooled. I was proud of it, for a while at least."

"What do you mean?" I asked.

"All was not what it seemed," he said, tapping the blueprint. "Many things about that house were inconspicuous. Camouflaged."

His expression shifted from serious to fascinated. His eyes brightened, and he smiled wide as if something ignited new life within him. "The man who ordered this house wanted it to be similar to another house he owned in southern Italy . . . or was it up in Florence?" He tapped his chin. "Florence, I think. Yes, that's it. He already had two houses, so I'm a little fuzzy on the details of which one it was."

"Two houses?" I said. If this man was truly Uncle Luca, then his southern home could be the one he had shared with Aunt Lena, but if he also had one in Florence, that could be the abandoned mansion.

"Yes," Giovanni said. "He wanted something very unusual. Something I had never designed before, and neither had any of my colleagues. He wanted the outside of this house to obscure the inside: a house within a house. Do you understand what I'm saying?" I shook my head. "The house I designed in Montepulciano had hidden walls, doors, and secret rooms. Complete hallways you'd never know were there."

"Secret hallways?" I said. "How is that possible? For what purpose?"

"Yes, it was possible," he said. "After it was built, I saw it with my own two eyes. He said it was for his business and that he worked for the government, but I wondered what kind of business needed something like that. What kind of person would need it?" He leaned in closer to me. "I'll tell you what kind of person: someone who has a hidden agenda, a shady business, a scandalous double life. The kind of life you can't keep secret for long. And it didn't take long for people to notice that something wasn't right with that house or the people who came and went from it. Some started asking questions, and one by one, they disappeared," he said, his eyes blazing. "It became an unspoken understanding—an acceptance among the townspeople—because they had no choice. Who would dare argue with such a monster?"

"Why didn't the police ever get involved?" I asked, cringing.

"Fear," he said. "Everyone feared him and his connections to the *'Ndrangheta*, the mafia. I pretended I didn't know a thing, but I think he wanted me to know."

"The mafia?" I was not expecting this, hoping maybe it wasn't Luca after all. But I knew deep down it was. "So . . . drugs? Crime?"

Giovanni stared at me until I blinked uncomfortably.

"That was just the beginning," he said. "It was far worse than that."

It made me sick to think what he might mean. I didn't ask. Instead, I changed tack. "I noticed that you haven't mentioned the name of this man.You keep saying 'he' but you don't say a name. Why is that?"

"I've learned not to say it out loud," he answered. "Say your last name again?" He squinted.

"Perri?"

"Perri," he repeated. "That's why it sounded familiar. His name was Pierri. Luccia Pierri, and he was very adamant about how we pronounced it."

"Looshia Pee-airy," I repeated, pronouncing it as Giovanni had. Eerily close to "Luca Perri." I held my stomach.

"Did you know him?" Giovanni asked, furrowing his brow.

I nodded, ashamed. "My uncle's name is Luca Perri," I said. "I think they may be the same person."

"Are you working with him?" he asked, his lips trembling. "Is he alive? Does he know you're here?"

"No, no, nothing like that," I said. "I'm sorry, I didn't mean to frighten you, and I didn't mean to lie. He has no idea where I am right now. What I said about my grandfather was true. He knew his brother, Luccia, had a secret house somewhere in Tuscany, and he knew he was involved in something bad. When I found this blueprint

I thought it might be the house my grandfather had talked about. I wanted to find out for him."

"Where did you say you found it?" he asked.

I explained what had happened at the abandoned mansion in Florence, what we found in the basement, the filing cabinet, the unfinished room. What I wasn't prepared for was that Giovanni seemed familiar with the house.

"That house you went to is the same one Luccia's father lived in for a while before giving it to him," he explained. "It appears both father and son, at different times, had separate lives in that home neither of their wives knew anything about." The more Giovanni spoke about it, the more sure he was that it was the house in Florence, not Tropea, where he'd first met Luca. "We met several times in the office of that house to discuss the new one. Luccia was very particular and meticulous about details and wanted to be involved in every step, almost to the point of annoyance. I remember often having to reassure him that he could trust me. I felt more or less forced to do it for him. Only a select few were aware of the new house in Montepulciano," he said. "And *mio Dio*, my God, were we surprised to hear he'd brought a beautiful woman there to live with him. They married and have been together for as long as I've known."

"Married?"

"Yes. After they got married, there were rumors he'd stopped his old ways, but no one knew for sure and they didn't want to find out. It sure was quieter, so maybe he did, or maybe he just got better at it."

"Do you know who he married?"

He stroked his chin and looked at the ceiling. "I can't remember. Silvia? No. Simona . . . ? No, that's not it. Samantha? Oh, I don't know."

My mind was addled, trying to connect everything he'd told me.

Who was this woman? It couldn't have been Gianna. Maybe it was Aunt Lena. Maybe they had a house in Tuscany no one knew about?

I looked at Giovanni. "You're sure this man's name is Luca?"

"Loosheeah," he corrected. "Remember, that's how it's pronounced."

Pronunciation didn't matter; he had recognized Perri. My heart raced as I sent a quick group text to my mother, Liv, Nico, and Angelina, who had been waiting on the porch for at least an hour.

"Please tell me everything you can about the house," I said to Giovanni.

His eyes widened and the corners of his mouth turned up with renewed vigor.

Chapter 30
Ella

Giovanni's wife peeked her head through the doorway. "It's been a while, Gio," she said.

He nodded and said, "It's okay, we won't be too much more." Then he walked to a bookshelf and took out a trunk about the size of two shoe boxes stacked on top of one another. I watched, curious, as he unlocked and opened the trunk and pulled out a folded white paper. He glanced at me and opened the paper, laying it over the blueprint on the table. Then he moved the paper next to the blueprint. "Do you see this?" he said. "No one but Luccia, me, and now you know about this part of the blueprint. I have the only copy."

I was in awe looking over both blueprints. The one Giovanni kept was an exact layout of the house but with other details—hidden features.

As we stood side by side in the small, smoky room, Giovanni revealed explicit particulars about the house in Montepulciano. He said that if I followed his instructions precisely, I would find on the second floor a concealed hallway obscured within the whimsical wallpaper. He showed me how to obtain access to the hidden hallway and pointed to the area where I'd see three doors, each with a separate and specific room behind them. "None of this," he said, "Can be detected in plain sight. You will need to have precise knowledge of what to look for and where to find it, and I will show you how."

His expression glowed as he spoke about the intricate details and special features he had added to the house at Luca's request. There wasn't a moment when he stopped, not for a glass of water, not one glance at his cigarettes. Giovanni placed an X on both the main blueprint and the private one in the exact location of the hidden hallway. On a separate sheet of paper, he scribbled notes with arrows and drew smaller diagrams as well as a numbered list of steps of what to do once I arrived at the house. He wrote the house address at the top of the notes. When he was finished, he went over each step, referring to his notes and the blueprints, asking me to repeat back to him what he'd said to make sure I understood. Finally, he stacked and clipped everything neatly together and handed it to me.

"You'll need to be very careful," he said. "Last I was aware, Luccia was still living in that house. He may still be there. I don't know what you'll find or who you'll encounter, but if you don't want to be seen, you will need to go when you know for sure no one is there."

He pulled something else from the trunk and placed it in my hand, folding my fingers over top and squeezing gently before letting go. I uncurled my fingers and saw a brass key in the palm of my hand.

"The locks have probably changed by now, but in case they haven't, you can try this."

I couldn't believe I held the key to the house in Montepulciano.

"You'll be quite taken by the exquisite beauty of the house when you see it, even as you enter. Just remember there is darkness roaming within."

I felt a compelling urge to go and see it right away. "Thank you so much for all this, *Signor* Luccetti," I said.

"Giovanni," he insisted. "I was excited to design such a house, even though it was against my better judgment. But there was a part of me that felt guilty because, in a way, by designing this house, I felt

I may have indirectly contributed to the bad things that happened there. As if I condoned it."

"You can't blame yourself for that," I said. "You made the best decisions you could based on the limited choices you had. Like you said, you were expected to do it, and who knows what might have happened if you'd said no."

He looked at me with a serious expression. "In over forty years no one has ever come to me about a house I built. But today, here you are. I always knew, somehow, even after shaking Luccia's hand and walking away from the completed job, it wouldn't be the end of my involvement in that house. I'm happy to say, though, I never thought it would be his niece standing at my door seeking answers, seeking justice . . . but here you are. I'm happy to help you find your answers, and I almost don't even care anymore if he knows your information came from me. I guess it's a way of making amends for my part in it."

"I will never divulge how I found out about the house," I said. "I'll put my own life on the line before yours; don't worry about that." I felt my fear and disappointment dissolve as anger rose within me. Anger and exhaustion of the unending story of my uncle's lies and betrayal. A story I needed to end.

Giovanni sipped his water and then he sat back in his chair. For the first time since I had arrived, he seemed relaxed. His face looked smoother and less strained, his eyes full and bright. His mouth revealed a soft smile showing his upper teeth. He looked five to ten years younger, no longer burdened by the heaviness of someone else's secret and his involvement in it.

"Thank you, Giovanni, for everything," I said, rising. He hoisted himself up as well. "I can't thank you enough for taking the time to—"

"No, no, no," he said, smiling. "Thank *you. Molte grazie.*"

I placed my hand on his arm and he gently hugged me. He

insisted on walking me out, and his wife joined us in the hallway as soon as we entered. She examined his expression and relaxed her own. Together they stood in the doorway smiling as Nico, Liv, my mother, Angelina, and I walked down the path to the driveway. At the end I turned to say goodbye and saw Giovanni's hand already raised in a friendly wave, his wife smiling at his side.

"Take care now," I said.

A wave of sadness fell upon me as we drove away.

Chapter 31

Gianna

Italy 1939

By mid-December, after nearly eight months since her escape, Gianna became slightly more comfortable with her new surroundings and routines at Amelia's house as well as her blossoming friendship with Amelia. Although nothing could fill the hole in her heart, and nothing could take away her promise and hope of finding her daughters, she was thankful Sienna had connected her with Amelia. Amelia was an honest, caring, and genuine person who had willingly opened her home to Gianna without question. Gianna felt safe with Amelia and her husband and valued her friendship, so eventually she told her everything about her life. Amelia shared some of her own private details, including her involvement in *La Resistenza*, the Italian Resistance. And in that short time together, they had formed a lasting bond.

One cold evening, as snow fell scantily over the town of Bracciano, Gianna helped Amelia set the table for four instead of their usual three.

"Are we expecting company tonight?" Gianna asked as the doorbell chimed.

Amelia smiled. "Yes. One second," she said as she ran to answer the door. She returned with a tall, handsome man with dark hair and striking blue eyes who followed her into the kitchen as Gianna was placing the last glass on the table.

"Gianna, I'd like you to meet my brother, Lorenzo," Amelia said. "He's here on business and he'll be joining us for dinner." Amelia then turned toward Lorenzo. "Gianna is Sienna's sister. She's vacationing in Rome and has been staying with me for a while."

Lorenzo looked at Gianna and smiled. He took her hand, brought it to his lips, kissed it, and said, "It's a pleasure to meet a friend of Amelia's."

Gianna's face felt warm. "Pleased to meet you as well," she said, and quickly went to help Amelia bring food to the table.

Before long, awkward conversations between bites of eggplant parmigiana and red wine flowed normal again, and Gianna felt as if she'd always been part of Amelia's family. Gianna, Amelia, Matteo, and Lorenzo sat at the table after dinner and talked long into the night. It was the happiest Gianna had felt since everything that had happened to her, but she also felt guilty for feeling that way.

Lorenzo decided to extend his stay for the week, and over the next few days Gianna spent less time staring out her window and brooding over the unanswered questions about her life and more time listening to stories Lorenzo told about his work and his family. She'd come home from working at the market and catch herself checking the clock to see if it was time for Lorenzo to arrive for dinner. She was intrigued and curious about this man who seemed so accomplished, although he couldn't have been more than a few years older than she. She was so captivated by him during that week that she missed a couple phone calls from Sienna and Maria.

***

One late afternoon, just before Christmas, Gianna had almost finished knitting a blanket for Amelia and Matteo. She was deep in thought within the fibers of the yarn as she turned and pulled one piece around the wooden needle through a loop she held with her other hand.

A knock at her bedroom door startled her. Amelia peeked in, grinning from ear to ear.

"What are you smiling about?" Gianna said.

"You have visitors downstairs who are dying to see you," she said.

Gianna's heart jumped. It had to be her sisters, but why hadn't they told her they were coming, and why hadn't they come upstairs to her room? She placed her knitting aside and sprang from her chair to follow Amelia down the stairs. As she neared the last step, she saw Sienna and Maria talking closely in the living room. Maria was facing Gianna, and Sienna's back was to her. Maria stopped talking immediately when she saw Gianna and threw herself into her arms, hugging and kissing her cheeks as tears spilled upon her own. Both sisters tightly embraced, crying in each other's arms.

"When is it my turn?" Sienna asked in a cheerful voice.

Gianna thought it was strange that Sienna continued facing the wall.

Then Maria said, "We're ready."

Sienna slowly turned around to face them.

Gianna's heart stopped when she saw the soft cotton blanket, angled and full, snuggled in Sienna's arms. She knew of only one thing that would lay so gently. So perfectly. Her heart raced and her body trembled. She pinched herself to confirm it wasn't a dream. Her legs almost gave out as she stumbled to Sienna, who was smiling widely, tears falling from her eyes. She pulled back the cotton blanket so Gianna could see the round, pink cheeks, little nose, and long lashes sleeping within the blanket.

"Oh my God, Sienna—is she—?"

"Grace," Sienna said. "This is your Grace."

Gianna fell to her knees, put her head in her hands, and began to weep silently, a deep release of grief overpowered by joy. But she promptly pulled herself up and held out her hands. She dipped her arms against Sienna's and scooped her fourteen-month-old baby, holding her close against her breast. She nuzzled her nose into the child's plump cheek and in the crook of her neck, inhaling her sweet scent. "My baby," she said. She kissed her cheek, pressed her own against it, and closed her eyes, tears spilling effortlessly. A warm embrace around her soul. Gianna looked up at Sienna and Maria. "Thank you," she whispered. "I could never thank you enough."

Grace began to stir and slowly awaken. Gianna removed the blanket and lifted Grace so they were face to face. Grace was immediately captured by Gianna and smiled as she listened to her mother's voice softly telling her how much she loved and missed her. She gurgled back as Gianna spoke, a private conversation between mother and daughter.

Soft brown curls wisped against Grace's cheeks. She thought of Gabriella and how small she was the last time she'd held her. She too would be heavier and filled out like Grace was now.

She sat on the sofa and placed Grace on her lap as Sienna and Maria sat beside her. Amelia poked her head through the doorway to the living room and asked if they'd like some tea. Gianna invited her to join them as they explained what had happened and how they had found Grace.

"You were right, Gianna," Sienna said, "to be suspicious of Mamá and Aunt Mia. They *had* been plotting something terrible."

"Sienna and I visited Mamá and Papá a couple of weeks ago unannounced," Maria added. "We knew they'd be in the backyard like they usually are, so we went around the side of the house to the patio. We heard them talking to Aunt Mia, and we remembered what you had said that time you'd overheard them, so we stopped to listen. I heard Aunt Mia say, 'The baby is fine, but I don't know if I can keep her.' Sienna didn't hear her, but I did." Sienna leaned in closer as if to say something but stopped.

Gianna put her hand to her mouth, confirming in her mind what she'd always known.

"Aunt Mia sounded stressed," Sienna agreed. "You're right about that. I didn't hear her say that, but I heard Uncle Charlie threaten to leave her."

Maria rolled her eyes at Sienna. "Yes, if she kept the baby. You were preoccupied that day because of Rico, but I know what I heard. Even Papá was pushing Aunt Mia."

"What about Mamá?" Gianna asked.

"Mamá just kept begging her," Maria continued, "reassuring her that it was best for everyone. But Aunt Mia insisted the baby should be with her grandparents if she couldn't be with her mother."

"You heard her say that?" Gianna blurted. "'She should be with her grandparents'?"

"Yes, that's when we knew for sure," Maria said, "that this was real. And Aunt Mia didn't like being part of it . . . or being deceitful. She's the only one who seemed the least bit remorseful."

"We left without ever telling them we'd been there," Sienna added.

"How did you do it?" Gianna asked. "How did you get Grace?"

"The next day we took the train to Aunt Mia's and broke into her house while she was out."

Gianna looked at Sienna. "You could have been arrested if you'd been caught. How did you get away without Rico stopping you?"

"That's a whole other issue you won't believe," Sienna said. "Rico left me."

"Left you?" Gianna said. "How? Why?" Gianna had a hard time imagining that Rico, who never let Sienna out of his sight, would one day get up and leave her. Something seemed odd about that, but she wasn't about to get into it then. Her sister was away from Rico and that was all that mattered.

Sienna and Maria took turns explaining how they had stealthily examined every room in the house, looking for clues of a baby. When they got to Aunt Mia's and Uncle Charlie's bedroom, upon first glance it looked like an ordinary bedroom. It had a bed in the middle, a nightstand on both sides, and a dresser. They almost turned away except Maria thought she saw something sticking out between the wall and the bed. When they walked to the other side of the bed they saw a wooden cradle, larger than a bassinet but smaller than a full-sized crib.

"We knew then that there really was a baby there," Maria said, "and we started looking more closely at everything." She explained how Sienna found a picture in a dresser drawer of their aunt holding a baby. "We weren't sure at the time if it was Gabriella or Grace."

"We put everything back in order and planned to come back and steal Grace, but we heard something downstairs—and then footsteps coming upstairs," Sienna chimed in. "We were so nervous and had nowhere to hide. It's not a big house."

"We heard Aunt Mia in the hallway near the door talking to the baby, and all of a sudden the bedroom door opened," Maria said. "You should have seen her face when she saw us. Her jaw dropped. We could see she was panicking. She stuttered when she said she was babysitting for a friend. I shoved the picture in her face and called her a liar. I said you had been right all along about having two babies and how could she deceive you like that. She looked so defeated."

"She said it was all Mamá's doing," Sienna continued. "Mamá said you could never handle much less afford two babies. Mamá actually considered selling her if Aunt Mia didn't take her, and she already had an interested family lined up. Aunt Mia said she offered at the last minute because she couldn't imagine Grace in someone else's family with people she didn't know. She cried a lot after she told us."

"I asked her why she hadn't confided in us," Maria said, "but she wouldn't give a straight answer. I threatened to involve the police, but she begged us not to. It was pitiful to watch—Aunt Mia crying as she kissed and hugged Grace. She handed her to Sienna and said she was wrong and apologized—begged for forgiveness. I actually felt sorry for her."

Maria went on to explain Aunt Mia's plan to tell Mamá and Papá that Grace had been kidnapped in the middle of the night. Aunt Mia offered to help Maria and Sienna and insisted they take some money. She also asked if they would allow her to be part of Grace's life somehow and would continue to send money to help with raising Grace.

"She doesn't know about me, does she?" Gianna asked.

"No, we won't tell her, at least for now," Maria said.

It was a lot for Gianna to absorb. She was hurt by the betrayal of her parents yet touched deeply by the love and loyalty of her sisters. She held Grace close to her heart and almost felt whole again. She was hopeful that if her sisters could help her find Grace, maybe there was hope for Gabriella.

Early the next morning Gianna waved goodbye to her sisters as they drove away, recalling every word they'd spoken and each loving action long after they left.

Chapter 32

Luca

The sun was a yellow dot in a sea of blue, emitting warmth as the cicadas loudly sang in the yard. It was a perfect day to spend outdoors among the colorful gardens and chirping birds, but Luca remained inside, sitting at his kitchen table across from Lena, windows and curtains closed, lights dimmed, voices hushed.

"They're on to you, Luca," Lena said. "Gabby and everyone else is different around me now. They're suspicious. They think I've been hiding you—and they're right. I can't look them in the eyes anymore."

"Did you say anything?" Luca asked. "Hint at anything?"

"No, never," Lena said, her eyes shifting left. "But . . . the other day when I was at Gabby's for lunch—Olivia was there too—Olivia insisted that she spend the night at our house. She kept saying, 'We're both alone,' 'Wouldn't it be fun to have a sleepover?' 'We shouldn't be alone,' things like that. She kept pushing me—you know how she is."

"Yes," Luca said. "She can be relentless when she wants her way. When the kids were little they called her Nagging Nonna," he chuckled. "She could be so obstinate."

"You came up with that name," Lena said, partially smiling.

Luca noticed Lena nervously tapping her foot on the floor. "What is it, *cara,* dear?" Luca asked.

Lena sighed, straightening herself. "Well . . . I might have slipped. I was so frustrated with Olivia and wanted her to stop asking me to—"

"What do you mean, 'slipped'?"

"I don't think they caught it. No one said anything, but Olivia kept repeating that I shouldn't be alone, and I think I said, 'I'm not alone.' But then I pretended I'd misspoken. I told her I meant to say, 'I'm not afraid to be alone' . . . or something like that."

Luca shook his head, "Oh, Lena."

"I'm so sorry. Do you think they knew?"

"Was Ella there?"

"No, just Olivia, Gabby, and me."

"It's probably okay, then," Luca said, "but you must be more careful. You can't let them get to you."

Lena nodded. "There's something I want to show you," she said, standing. She walked to the kitchen island and opened a drawer. She pulled something from the drawer and placed it in front of Luca.

Luca's eyes widened as he touched the worn cover, running his fingers along the jagged edges where corners of the pages protruded. Firmly he gripped what he'd coveted for so long: Franco's diary. He'd now know everything Franco had been keeping from him about Gianna. Although Lena wasn't aware of all Luca's reasons for wanting the diary, she knew it was important to him, and that was all she needed to know. Holding the diary, Luca stood and hugged Lena tightly.

"She did it," he marveled. "She wasn't sure if she could, but she actually broke into Ella's house and got it."

"Well, Cecelia didn't get out unscathed," Lena remarked.

"Shh—don't say names," Luca said. "What do you mean?"

"That dog chased after her—bit her on the leg and wrist. She showed me her bite marks. Luckily it wasn't worse and she didn't get caught."

"What about the painting?" he said. "Remember, no names."

"Her helper planned to get it, but the police arrived and she got stuck. The only place she could hide was in the attic. Ended up staying a couple nights and was able to listen to conversations between Ella and her mother. That's how I knew about Italy. Police have been everywhere, Luca, and not the ones you know."

"Lena," Luca smiled, "thank you for everything you've done for me—and always have done. I promise it will be for good reason. We'll be able to leave Skaneateles soon and go anywhere you'd like. I only have one more trip to Italy and then we can go."

Lena smiled and kissed Luca on the cheek. "I thought you already had your last trip to Italy."

"I know," he said. "It would have been if things hadn't gotten so complicated. This is it, I promise."

"Don't make me wait so long this time," she said.

***

When Lena was asleep, Luca slipped from their bed, slid into his slippers, and went to his study. He read several pages of Franco's diary and became anxious and irritable. He ruminated on what Lena had said about the family questioning her slip in front of Gabby and Olivia.

He knew that if Ella was going back to Italy, that meant she had found something. It might also mean she knew where Gianna had been hiding. It enraged him to think Ella might find her after all his efforts and resources had failed. It was imperative to return to Italy as soon as possible. He had to think like her, anticipating her next move, and get a few steps ahead of her.

He thought about her friend, Angelina, in Tropea. Ella would undoubtedly be staying with her again. He needed to send them a cryptic message and thwart their combined efforts.

After immersing himself in the diary and thinking about Ella, he devised a plan and made two phone calls, one to the airport to book his flight to Italy and the other to one of his connections in Italy who had already been following Angelina. Apparently, the message he'd previously sent when she'd broken into his old house in Florence wasn't enough. He was confident Angelina would go back there again and take Ella with her.

Before returning to bed, Luca went back to the diary and read a few entries that Franco had written when he'd first learned Gianna and Gabriella were missing. His sentences were short and choppy, his words as desperate and frantic as his penmanship. Luca read the entry, skimmed a few that followed, and stopped at the next two that caught his eye.

It was shortly after he'd told Franco that Gabriella had been found in her carriage on their parents' porch, and it was likely Gianna had left them both. Franco's fear and helplessness were prevalent in the words on every page. Although Luca was the one responsible, he had mentally distanced himself until it no longer affected him.

17 February 1939

I'm frantic. Out of my mind. I don't know what to do or who to tell. I opened Luca's letter today and cannot believe what my eyes were reading. A baby carriage was left on the front porch of our house very early in the morning. The wheels were locked so it wouldn't roll away, and the carriage faced the front door so it would be the first thing you would see when you opened it. The top of the carriage was pulled down to shield things from getting in. Luca noticed the carriage right away as he was leaving early in the morning to go to work. He lifted the cover back and inside was a baby soundly sleeping. Upon closer examination, he saw that it was Bella! My Gabriella! My baby girl. There was no note, no other information.

Why would Gianna leave our baby? If she had to go somewhere, she would have left her with her sister or her friend, Nina. Where would she go without her? Luca knew Papá wouldn't like this and might do something careless, so he told Mamá right away. Mamá pretended her friend's granddaughter needed to be cared for while she went away for a while, which isn't unusual in these times. It's very risky, but it's the only choice we have to keep Bella safe. Thank God for Mamá. But WHERE IS GIANNA? I'm distraught and don't know what to do.

14 April 1939

Luca wrote me a letter that Gianna is nowhere to be found. He went to check on her after the baby carriage was left at the house. He normally follows her home after their visit, never going farther than the cypress trees at the edge of her property. He said when he stands in that spot, the wide oak at the foot of the yard blocks him so he can't be seen, but he can still see if her husband's car is there, and sometimes he can see movement from the windows. But on this day, there was no car and, since it looked like no one was home, he took a chance and walked up to the door. When he peered through the window near the door he saw nothing. No furniture, no toys, nothing. Gone. Without a trace. He said he was fearful and didn't know what to do. I can see it in the frantic scratches of his handwriting: fear. My stomach is in knots and I cannot sleep. Other than my own survival, I think of nothing else.

A second letter from Luca arrived a few days later. In it, he says he has convinced our parents to get their papers processed in order to leave Italy for America. He and his girlfriend, Lena, and my Bella will go with them. He said he and Lena will get married, and they can care for Bella until I arrive. Luca said he can get the papers processed in one or two months. I thought this was unusually short, but he said he has connections. I will write to him and ask him to wait for me. I am due to be discharged in just a few months. I know things are not safe in Italy right now, and it's good timing as well as a good opportunity to go to America, but if only they could wait so we could be together. But I can't imagine leaving Italy without Gianna. Maybe I shouldn't go. Maybe Bella should stay here with me. Maybe I can find Gianna.

After reading the entries, Luca reflected on the day he'd buried Gianna and brought Gabriella, nearly ten months old at the time, to his parents' house. He had almost forgotten about the baby until he heard her crying. He'd taken her to a private location where he'd fed and changed her, wrapped her in blankets, and rocked her back to sleep. He'd placed her inside the carriage, tucking the blankets around her and placing two full bottles of milk at her feet. He'd cleaned the dirt from Gianna's broken necklace and tucked it deep inside the carriage so Gabriella would have a part of her mother with her. Anyone who found it would simply think it had broken and fallen into the carriage as the baby had been tended by her mother.

The sun hadn't yet peeked through the trees when he'd parked the carriage on the front porch of the only woman he knew would love and protect the baby no matter what. His mother would rise early and enter the porch with a cup of coffee first thing that morning and then she'd see the baby. She'd take her inside and, if no one claimed her, she'd raise her as her own. His father wasn't around enough to notice or even care.

After they moved to the United States, he'd tell his mother the truth.

But it hadn't gone exactly as planned. His mother awakened later than he'd expected, so Luca pretended he'd noticed the baby carriage first on his way out to work, then everything else fell into place.

Luca wanted his niece to grow up with a family, and he wanted Franco to be with his daughter once they were together in the states. Luca wasn't completely heartless. He knew the townspeople in Italy would speculate and gossip about what had happened, that two sides would form—those who believed Gianna left freely to start over with a new lover and those who knew her better, who believed she hadn't left of her own free will, that her husband or a random stalker had taken her.

Luca, being the last person to have seen Gianna alive, had also been questioned. But it never once worried him; the highest suspicion always fell on the lover, and that was Franco. He'd counted on that. Although Franco had been fulfilling a commitment to his country at the time, people speculated there were ways he could have left his post unsuspected using the tunnels. Luca had only had to sway them a little.

After he'd had enough of the diary, Luca took a swig of brandy and went back to bed, prepared and confident in his next move.

Chapter 33

Luca

On the day Luca planned to go to Italy, his flight was delayed because of the heavy fog that rested upon much of Florence. His driver had also been delayed, arriving much later than Luca expected. As soon as he got to the airport, Luca threw his bags into the trunk, flashed his money, and they sped to his old house in Florence.

This time when he entered the old neighborhood, he didn't feel anxious. Rage and adrenaline had replaced anxiety, racing through his mind and body. This time he sifted through the chaos and carefully scrutinized the details of the house. He'd know if Angelina or anyone else had returned.

He'd take those files containing old papers and empty promises, papers he should have gone back for but never did. He should have known that someday Ella would grow up and become just like her grandfather, wanting to rid the world of injustice and put things back to the way they belonged.

As Luca approached the steps, he thought again of his brother. If it weren't for him, he'd have Gianna's heart. "Damn Franco," he muttered as he placed the key into the locked door and entered the house. He remembered his plans to remodel and reconstruct the house shortly after his father had given it to him. He'd hoped to bring Gianna there and live with her forever.

Luca still couldn't fathom how Gianna had survived and escaped from the woods. All those times he'd gone back to her burial site to tell her how sorry he was and how differently he'd wished things had gone—all that time, he'd been talking to an empty grave. His blood boiled warm and angry every time he thought about it.

But sorrow replaced anger as Luca walked through the kitchen, a reminder of the time when sadness had first entered his life. He'd learned that, to get the approval of his father, he'd have to turn against his mother, pretending not to know what went on in the house. Although it seemed like a fair trade at the time, protecting his mother from heartache, living a lie in front of her smothered his heart. When it was too much to bear, he'd convince himself that the more time his father spent at his secret house, the less opportunity for cruelty toward his mother.

Luca inspected every room, doorway, drawer, and cabinet on the main floor of the house, and when he was satisfied, he headed for the basement. He treaded lightly to the shadowy landing and ascended the stairway to a dark room. He stopped abruptly and held his breath when he thought he heard voices, not voices trapped in a box like that day as a child but alive and well, sharing the same open space with him.

A small beam of light from the top of the stairs cast a dim path to his feet. The noises, far beyond the light, seemed to come from behind the unfinished wall. It aroused an unfamiliar feeling in Luca: fear. Fear captured him, squeezing his heart and anchoring his feet to the ground, and he couldn't turn away.

It was the same kind of fear he'd experienced as a child when a gravelly voice had pleaded from inside a box in the basement of this house, and he hadn't turned away then either. Instead, as before, he walked past the office to the dingy unfinished room at the end, observing the desk and chair to his right and a table that once displayed knives and sharp tools to his left. He glanced at the stairway and waited, contemplating. The same as that day as a child when he gazed at the cellar doors on the other side. The first time he'd entered the basement.

Scurrying sounds echoed, footsteps shuffled. But Luca, refusing to be caught or threatened, flattened himself against a wall and listened, hoping to glean information about his trespassers. He inched against the wall, closer to the sounds, but his watch dragged against the concrete, alerting the intruders.

Luca saw three figures running toward the storm doors at the back. He no longer cared about revealing his whereabouts; he needed to know who they were. As he ran toward them, he stumbled into the desk chair, costing him time. As he got to his feet he saw the tail end of three, possibly four people fleeing through the doors and up the stairs. By the time Luca reached the top, they were gone, lost among the fog and thickened trees, obscured within the shadows.

Luca closed and locked the doors outside the stairway and returned to the basement. He turned on all the lights, and that's when he saw the opened file drawers and knew what would be missing. He knew without a doubt who had been there and where they were going next. Luca's quest to find Gianna had been of utmost importance, but now there was someone else whose life and secret identity could be compromised as well—someone he'd loved and cared for since she was a young girl. Luca felt his life was quickly unraveling, and this time the stakes were even higher.

***

Several hours passed in an instant. The narrow roads from the south spilled into the wide terrain in the north, and Luca finally entered the old medieval hilltop of Montepulciano. His third home waited tucked behind the hills, obscured from the busy streets below, hills that under normal circumstances provided peace and calm, but not that day. He opened his window to let the fresh air wash over him, although it did nothing to relax his nerves.

Luca was so distracted that he nearly missed his street. He jerked the steering wheel, barely making the turn. He flew around the bend, past the farm and stables, and over a small knoll until he pulled into the private driveway of his home. His other home. His other life.

His wife was in the side yard hanging delicate garments on the line to dry, her dress clinging around her legs as she moved. Her dark hair was held back in a twist on one side while the rest flowed down her back. He loved her, maybe more than the others. She turned and waved as he stepped out of his car. A warm smile spread across her face as Luca approached her. The youngest of her three sisters, Sienna had kept her youth, looking far younger than her years.

Luca felt a small pang of guilt in his stomach as he walked slowly toward Sienna. Her smile and her lips reminded him so much of Gianna that sometimes he'd forget it wasn't her. The pain in his heart for Gianna had been unbearable at times, but when Sienna convinced Luca that they should marry, he jumped at the chance to have someone close to Gianna. Over the years, he grew to love Sienna more than he'd loved Lena and very similar to his love for Gianna.

He recalled simpler days when they were younger—Luca and Franco with Gianna, Maria, and Sienna Russo running through the streets in and out of each other's houses, playing until the sun went down. Sometimes they'd spy on their parents as they talked and laughed late into the night, but, sadly and abruptly, it all had ended. Suddenly everything had changed. There wasn't any eye contact except for an occasional glare from Mr. Russo at Luca's father. Heaviness surrounded them, making it hard to breathe at times. Luca vividly remembered that the night Mr. Russo had pounded on their door he thought he might break it down. Obscenities and accusations spewed behind the door from an otherwise quiet and gentle man. And in the middle of the night, the Russo family left without saying goodbye.

"Sometimes people disappear," his father had said when Luca asked why they no longer lived there. A chill raced through him then as it did now. Maybe they hadn't left, he thought at the time. Maybe they'd been hidden in the basement beneath the house like the others.

He recalled a few years later, the turning point in his life, the day Franco came home and told him with bright eyes that he'd seen Gianna. Luca convinced himself that if he'd been first to see Gianna and not Franco, she would have fallen for him instead. It had just been a matter of timing. Damn Franco.

"Luca!" Sienna yelled with her hands on her hips. "Do you hear me talking to you?"

"No, I—"

"You're staring right at me. Or through me. Are you okay?" she said. "You don't look so well."

"I'm . . . fine. I'm just . . . has anyone been to the house?"

"Today? No, why? Are you expecting someone?"

"No," he said, wiping his brow.

He kissed Sienna on the forehead and walked cautiously inside the house. He scanned the entryway and began searching behind doors and under beds. He entered his study on the second floor, opened his laptop, and analyzed the camera feed showing each of the rooms, including the secret ones.

Sienna knocked on the door and opened it.

He looked at her as she stood in the doorway. "Are you sure no one unusual has been here today or lately?"

"I'm positive," she said.

"Swear it."

"What's gotten into you?"

"Swear it!"

"I swear that no one besides me has been in this house since you left. What is this about, Luca?"

"Never mind. Pack your things. We have to go."

"Go where? What's happened?"

"I can't explain now. Just trust me. It's for our safety—mostly yours."

Sienna looked at him with uncertainty. "You're scaring me."

"It'll be okay. Pack as much as you can. We should be able to come back in a while. I'll explain later."

Sienna had learned not to ask questions when rare moments like this occurred. She learned to trust Luca even though he knew she questioned so much about him. Luca was aware that she also feared the part she didn't know so well, the one that had taken Gianna into the woods and returned without her.

Luca opened the liquor cabinet and poured a glass of whiskey, taking it down in less than a second. They moved hastily and silently over the next twenty minutes, stuffing clothes into bulging suitcases, jamming personal items into tight spaces. As Sienna packed the last suitcase with food, she heard a loud knocking on the front door. She looked at Luca, and he held a finger to his lips. She nodded, and they filled their arms with as much as they could and slipped out the back door unnoticed.

Chapter 34

Ella

On the way to Montepulciano, I relayed every detail of my visit with Giovanni. Quiet anticipation filled the car as I told them about the camouflaged hallway concealing three secret rooms in the house Giovanni had designed. I shared his stories of speculation on the secrets involving Luca and his house and the horrors that may have occurred there.

Everyone but Angelina was surprised to learn that Luca had once lived in the old abandoned house we had just broken into—a house his father had given him when he became too old to continue his adulterous affairs and sinister business. We incorporated the fragments of the story we knew of Luca to what we had learned from Giovanni, weaving an intricate and dark design.

Angelina summed it up simply. "Luca turned into his father, carrying on with similar affairs in that same house. Decades of deceit and betrayal—an ugliness beyond imagination. It's what's in those mirrors and still haunts that house."

I felt a chill run through me as I confirmed the same thoughts in my mind. We had been so engrossed in our conversation that before we knew it we were entering the neighborhood of Giovanni's masterpiece, roads akin to the streets of Tropea. I was sure Luca had chosen it for that reason.

Several buildings were close together, connected by warm, golden stone. Others perched high in the cliffs, weaving among the roads, similar to Fiesole. When the road ended, we made our final turn onto Via del Macellino, a gated community with a private drive. We stepped from the car and peered through metal bars at the greenest grass I'd ever seen. Cypress trees marched along the driveway beyond the gate, dipping and popping with the hills and ending a few feet before the grand entrance to Luca's most secret home.

The modern architecture of the residence was flawlessly paired with the warmth and quaintness of a modest Tuscan home. Accent lights from the ground illuminated peaks and other points of interest on the exterior. Windows glowed beneath a flattened rooftop under a darkening sky. What secrets could possibly exist behind something so beautiful?

We stood side by side with our faces pressed between the bars, staring in awe at the house. Some of the lights in the entrance near the stairway seemed to flicker in a peculiar way, not like something you would expect from an electrical short but the kind of flicker someone stepping in front and then moving away might make. I pointed as it happened again, trying to see it more clearly, but the distance blurred the details. Was someone there?

I pulled out my phone and zoomed the camera lens at a less blurred but still jagged outline of what might have been a person, maybe two. I followed the outline as it moved to the stairs, where it suddenly stopped. I feared they had seen me watching.

"What's going on?" Liv whispered.

"I think I see someone," I said. "I think they're walking."

"Let's go," Liv said, pulling my arm. But I was glued to the image on my phone and pressed record. As I watched, I became convinced that it really had been a person moving near the lights. That person had now moved to the front porch, descended the stairs to the driveway. They continued walking, still far away but becoming more focused, and I could see it was . . . a man. Trailing slightly behind appeared to be the silhouette of a woman.

"Let's go," Nico said.

I thought I heard voices, faint and high coupled with low grumbles.

"Get to the car," Nico urged.

We crept back to the car, glancing over our shoulders. The gates slowly widened, and the man broke into a run. I backed away fast, catching a glimpse of his uneven strides. He raised his arm to the headlights as they beamed into his eyes, but I couldn't tell if he was blocking the lights or hiding from them. His body language and mannerisms reminded me of the man I saw that night outside the precinct in Italy two years ago. He was standing on the other side of my car. The night we confirmed that Luca had kidnapped and possibly killed Gianna.

"It's him!" I screamed as my tires screeched around a corner. I feared that the house lights had illuminated the shiny black hood of our car.

"Oh my God," my mother gasped.

"I saw him too," Liv blurted.

"Do you think he knew it was us?" my mother said.

"I think the headlights blinded him," I said, "but I'm sure he suspected and has been watching ever since that day Nico saw him at the market."

"And now he knows we're on to him," Nico said.

"I thought Giovanni said the house was vacant," Liv said.

"He wasn't sure," I said.

"You said you heard voices," my mother said. "Could it have been Aunt Lena?"

"Could she really be going back and forth from Skaneateles to

Italy with Luca without any of us knowing?"

"It's possible," I said. "We don't see her as much as we used to. It's probably why she was so adamant about Nonna not coming over—because she doesn't want her to see something or because she's not even there."

"She probably hides him when he's home," Liv murmured. It seemed strange to hear her say the word *home* knowing Luca had more than one.

"I bet she's aware of his past and helped him hide it all along," Angelina said, holding onto the armrest door as I rounded the corner.

"Nothing surprises me anymore," said my mother.

"I don't know," I said. "I'm not even sure if the woman's voice was younger or older. We were too far away to tell."

"She sounded young to me," Angelina said, "youthful."

"That doesn't make any sense," my mother said.

"We need to go back," I said, "and get into that house. I know there's something in there."

"That's dangerous, Ella," my mother said, "not to mention illegal."

"I agree," Nico said. "There's got to be another way."

"There's no other way to know if Luca's been living there and what else he's hiding," I argued, "or if he's found Gianna."

***

Over the next couple days, Liv and I devised a plan to observe the strange comings and goings of Luca and the woman in that house. On the first day, we noticed the woman outside attending to something near the side of the house. Shortly after, a car entered as the gates opened and zipped up the driveway, stopping abruptly in front of the house. Then Luca and another woman from inside the house got into the car and left. About an hour later, Luca returned alone.

Another hour passed, and three men arrived wearing dark suits. We watched as they rang the bell and knocked on the door with no answer. They inspected the grounds thoroughly before leaving. No one returned to the house after that.

The next day, before the sun appeared and while our mother and Angelina slept, Liv and I departed from the villa, leaving behind a note explaining where we'd gone and to stay put until they heard from us.

Nico drove us to the gate of the old house and parked on a side street off the main drive with a perfect view to watch and alert us to anyone entering. Exhilaration, fear, and anticipation pulsed through my body. I glanced at Liv, whose expression told me she felt the same. Before long we would be breaking into Giovanni's creation and Luca's house of secrets.

Chapter 35

Luca

Luca exhausted every available resource and, in a matter of days, he'd learned that it wasn't only one man banging on his door but three. They were associates of the 'Ndrangheta, the most powerful and feared mafia in Italy.

Rumors that Gianna's husband, Carlos, had colluded with the 'Ndrangheta were true. His commitment to finding Gianna along with theirs seeking Luca bound them together, eventually leading them straight to Luca. Carlos must have learned that Luca wasn't with Gianna but with her sister, Sienna. How long had Carlos been following Luca, and what else did he know? Maybe it was Carlos who had shot Marco in the woods.

The 'Ndrangheta would be back, so Luca needed to be more careful. He didn't like being pursued and, except for Gianna, he'd always gotten what he wanted. He was maddened by the constant reminder that he still didn't have her but knew he needed to focus on not getting caught right now. He convinced Sienna for her safety she should move back in with her sister, Maria, for a while. He'd call Lena and explain that extenuating circumstances with work made it impossible to come home anytime soon. He'd empty the house in Montepulciano and lock it up.

His essential goal now became finding Gianna before Ella or Carlos could and preventing Sienna from leaving him. Based on his last encounter at the old house in Florence, Luca was sure Ella was en route to somewhere—and she might have been the trespasser hiding outside his house the other day. Either way, he knew he hadn't seen the last of her.

Which is why he'd enlisted the perfect spy to watch Ella shortly after she'd returned to Skaneateles about a year and a half ago, when Lena first reported on Ella's plans to go back to Italy. He'd recruited someone who knew exactly how to break in and confiscate the coveted diary. Someone trustworthy to Luca as well as someone who wouldn't seem out of place if they were to be seen near the property. This person had once proved dependable, even to the point of hiding in the attic and listening to Ella's conversations to report to Luca or Lena. The same person who had stolen the painting of Gianna which rightfully belonged to him. It was someone already comfortable being Luca's spy.

But she'd gotten sloppy as time went on, and Luca wondered if his spy was wavering again, like the last time. By now she should have already known and reported on what Ella had been up to in Italy. If he hadn't caught Nico watching him at the market that day, he wouldn't have known how close they were to finding him. His spy was slipping, and Luca couldn't afford to let that happen.

Luca and Sienna were safe in one of his private hotels, but they were anxious to return to their home in Montepulciano. The days and nights in waiting had been torturous to Luca. His mind envisioned Ella discovering other transgressions and ruining what little secrecy remained regarding Lena and Sienna. The more his life unraveled out of control the more convinced he was that, as long as Ella was around, his secret life he wanted to hold onto would no longer be sacred. At one point, he'd considered faking his death and starting over again far from the United States and Italy and everyone.

***

The next morning before work, Luca went through his usual daily routine beginning with a five-mile run on the treadmill followed by a hot shower. He then consumed two hard-boiled eggs and a full glass of orange juice while monitoring the stock market. Finally, he went to his office at the other end of their suite, closed the door, and called Lena. He explained that his job in Tuscany had become very demanding and that he hoped to return to Skaneateles within the month. Lena was angry at first as he knew she would be, but she came around and assured him that when he returned to Skaneateles she'd hide him in their renovated basement again until they could finally leave together.

Lena reassured Luca that, except for a short visit with Gabby, she hadn't seen Ella or anyone else in the family since they'd last spoken. She said no one had asked about him and, no, she hadn't slipped again.

When they finished talking, Luca locked the office door, kissed Sienna on her forehead, and left the hotel, scanning the edges of the property from the moment he exited the hotel until he got to his car. He sat for a few minutes recalling the recent turn of events, convinced it had been Ella at the old house. But the stolen blueprint alone couldn't have led them to his house in Montepulciano, so how did they do it? But the silhouettes beneath the streetlight were undoubtedly Ella and whoever else she'd brought with her. It wasn't the 'Ngdrangeta—they wouldn't hide.

An uneasy feeling perplexed Luca as he pulled away from the hotel, almost as if he'd forgotten something. It continued to nag at him when he arrived at his appointment. His heart palpitated and his skin itched. A dull headache sat at the base of his skull. He parked the car and removed his seatbelt while the engine still hummed. He rubbed his temples and shook his head. Something wasn't right. He dialed Sienna but she didn't answer. At least he knew she was safe at the hotel and not at their home. But a suspicious, troubled feeling remained, so he strapped on his seatbelt and, instead of going to the hotel, he drove all the way back to his house in Montepulciano.

Chapter 36

Gianna

Italy 1939

Gianna felt renewed now that Grace was with her. But at night, when she'd put her to bed, her thoughts consumed her. She couldn't grasp her mother's motivation for taking her away. She also ached for Gabriella to be with her and was desperate to know where she was.

Sometimes when she closed her eyes she'd recall her conversation with Franco when they'd first spoken of baby names, long before her belly became visible. If it was a girl, they'd call her Gabriella, after her mother, or Grace, her grandmother's middle name. If it was a boy they'd choose either Salvatore or Franco, both names after Franco. She remembered how her mother's eyes lit the day she told her about her choices for girls' names. She was sure that's why her mother had named the baby she'd stolen "Grace." Gianna held those memories close to her heart and cried every time she thought of them.

Amelia's voice broke her thoughts. She was calling her from behind the closed door, and Gianna knew it meant Lorenzo had arrived. Gianna had been so absorbed in spending every moment of the last couple of days with Grace that she'd unintentionally avoided several of Lorenzo's attempts to talk with her.

Amelia once told Gianna she hoped that someday Gianna might go out with her brother. Gianna assured her Lorenzo was merely a friend, although she knew something else was blossoming. But her thoughts of Franco conflicted with her feelings for Lorenzo. She'd questioned the validity of Luca's claim that Franco had perished in an accident at war. If he was alive, was she not betraying him with her new life and the people in it?

And now Lorenzo was downstairs waiting for her. Amelia had convinced her to tell him the truth about Grace the next time he was in town, and that day had arrived. Would he change his mind about her after she told him she had a child?

Gianna gently laid a sleepy Grace into her bassinet, brushed her fingers through her hair, and straightened her dress before heading to the living room to greet Lorenzo. As soon as she entered the room, a smile spread across his lips, sending butterflies straight through her.

Amelia left the room to give them some time alone. They embraced and then both began speaking at once, so Lorenzo insisted she go first. When they sat on the sofa, Gianna turned toward him.

"I know I've been distant lately," she began, "but it wasn't because I didn't want to see you. I hope you know that." Lorenzo smiled but waited for her to continue. "I haven't shared everything with you about my life—my past—but there's something I need to share with you today."

"You can tell me anything," he said. "I'll never judge you."

Gianna breathed a heavy sigh of old pain and regret. "Long before I came to stay with Amelia and met you, I was in love with someone. We'd planned to marry, but he had to leave for the war. Before he left I found I was expecting a child. I had twins—two girls, Gabriella and Grace." Gianna studied Lorenzo's face, which held the same serious expression throughout the conversation. "Then it gets complicated," she continued. "I won't go into all the details now, but shortly after I gave birth, my mother stole Grace from me and planned to give her to another family. She didn't think I could handle two babies. She told me I'd delivered only one. I was delirious that day and almost didn't survive, so I believed her at first."

Lorenzo's eyes widened. He swallowed. "She stole your baby? Your own mother? I'm so sorry, Gianna. How did you find out?"

"That's the part I'll save for another time," Gianna said as her voice caught. "But the good news is that my sisters promised to find my babies, and they found Grace."

"And Gabriella?" he asked.

"No, not yet," Gianna said. Her gaze fell to the floor. She waited to see if the weight of her words would finally register and if he'd change his mind once they did.

"I'll help you find Gabriella," Lorenzo said. "We'll find her together."

"Lorenzo," she said, reaching for his hand, "you don't really mean that."

"Of course I do, he said, tilting his head. "What's the real reason you've been staying with my sister?" Gianna froze. She wasn't ready to share that yet. Lorenzo must have noticed, because he placed his hand on her cheek. "Another time?" he said.

"Yes." Then she stood and reached out her hand. "I'd like to show you something." He took her hand and she led him upstairs to her room where Grace was sleeping. "There's someone I'd like you to meet," she whispered, opening the door. Lorenzo looked at Gianna. "That's my daughter, Grace," she said. She noticed the warmth in his eyes as he smiled. They treaded lightly into the room, and Lorenzo peeked in at a sleeping Grace.

"She's beautiful," he said, "like her mother."

Gianna's face grew warm. After a couple minutes, they stepped back into the hallway and Lorenzo hugged her.

She stared into his eyes."I wasn't intentionally hiding her from you. The story of Gabriella and Grace and how I came to be here with Amelia is long and complicated, but if you'd like, I will share it with you, in time."

"I'd like that," he said. "Whenever you're ready." Gianna felt light and relieved from his smile and his kindness.

Once they returned to the living room, and much sooner than she'd expected, Gianna explained everything that had happened to her while they waited for dinner to be ready. The conversation continued through dinner in front of Amelia and Matteo and several hours into the night. After Amelia and Matteo went to bed and Lorenzo left, Gianna realized she had shared far more than she had intended. Lorenzo knew everything that happened to her from the day Franco left for the war until that night at dinner. He seemed captivated by her story and genuinely interested in what she had to say. But Gianna still worried that later, once everything had time to sink in, he might have second thoughts.

***

A few nights later, Lorenzo took Gianna out for dinner in the village, and from that point on they were together regularly and came to know each other very well. Gianna learned that Lorenzo was a dedicated, hard worker and that he valued God, family, and friendship above all else. The oldest and most driven of his five siblings, he was employed at one of the largest textile machinery industries in Italy, a family-owned business that would one day be his.

Gianna put her hand to her heart when he mentioned fighting in the war as Franco had. She wondered if that's where he had gotten the scar near his chin. Lorenzo said that, other than the four dreadful years he'd fought in the war, he'd worked in the family business for most of his life. Lorenzo told Gianna that his family owned several homes throughout the world, and they were among the richest in Italy. Gianna marveled at how such a wealthy and privileged man could be so humble.

After dinner one night, the waiter placed two champagne glasses on the table. He removed the cork as the bubbly white wine spilled over the rim. Gianna watched as it sparkled and filled her glass. A second waiter arrived holding a beautiful display of white roses brimming atop a crystal vase. He cleared Gianna's part of the table and placed the roses in front of her. Gianna smiled and leaned in to smell the flowers. "They're breathtaking," she said. "Thank you, Lorenzo."

"There's something special about them," Lorenzo said. "Look them over carefully and see if you can tell what it is."

Gianna studied the delicate roses, gently moving and adjusting them in the vase.

"Look closely in the middle," he hinted.

Gianna saw it immediately as it caught the light. The middle rose, slightly taller than the others, had a satin ivory ribbon tied at the highest leaf. Attached to the ribbon was the most exquisite diamond ring she'd ever seen. Her heart fluttered and her eyes filled at the display before her. She looked at Lorenzo and untied the ribbon. She held it in her hands and then slipped it over her finger.

When she looked at Lorenzo again he was kneeling before her. "I know we haven't known each other long, but I have never met anyone like you before," he said. "I can't imagine my life without you and your daughters in it. Please say you'll marry me."

Chapter 37

Ella

The neighborhood slept peacefully under a starlit sky, an idyllic moment captured in time. Its cryptic beauty entranced us. We peered at the house at 2394 Via Del Macellino from the car, hidden among the trees, and waited. Although it appeared to have been empty for the last couple days, we weren't completely sure someone wouldn't be there now. But now was all we had, and there was no turning back.

"Ready?" I said, glancing at Liv.

She nodded, but we remained anchored to our seats for a few more minutes. We'd rehearsed the plan several times the night before with Nico.

At the gated entrance stood two large pillars on either side of the doors, connecting the iron fence around the confines of the property. Having previously observed the property, I had noticed a small space at the outer edges of the pillars obscured by overhanging brush. The climbing hills within the gates had also provided a natural barrier around the property, but the trees and protruding roots expanding upon them had forced a cleft at the edge of one of the doors just big enough for a small person to slip inside. A flaw in Luca's design was undetected unless one was purposely looking for it. That would be our point of entry.

We bolted to the gate, our eyes darting to the road, the trees, the house until, finally, we reached it, praying no one had seen us. I pushed aside the brush and forced my body through the crevice, pulling Liv in after me.

Fear silenced our voices as we climbed the hills through thickening trees, aware that one slip would disturb the quiet. The hills hiding behind the cypress trees at the edge of the narrow drive to the house lengthened and stretched before us, slowly bringing us close. Several times we stopped to catch our breath and rest our heavy legs.

The hills abruptly ended where the gardens began. I lost my footing and thudded to the soft grass below. Liv stepped down carefully and pulled me up, and the house just steps away towered over us. The only thing between us and the entrance was brightly lit, landscaped gardens with cobbled paths stretching to the porch and around the mansion.

We ran fast, crouching low along the path leading straight to the porch steps. As predicted, the front mahogany door was locked and impossible to break through. We circled the house, searching for an alternative entry. I thought about Luca's alternate home, the abandoned house, recalling the layout and how we'd barely escaped through the cellar door. Luca could be predictable; he thrived on routine and details, and he planned everything out precisely, as Mr. Jones had confirmed in many of our conversations at the hospital.

At the back of the house we looked for an unassuming entrance, and it wasn't long before we found one obscured by low branches and wild brush, a perfect yet now predictable disguise, unsurprisingly similar to the old, abandoned house. A solid door hidden within the brush had been bolted tightly with a series of locks. The small window beside it was also locked.

I remembered what Mr. Jones had said about the mindset of someone like Luca and how desperate they'd be to keep their secret.

I worried Luca might be on to us, waiting for us inside the house.

"What do you think?" Liv asked as we scoured the small, private patio.

"We need to break in," I said, choosing a fist-sized stone that at one time might have been part of the landscape.

"What if you set off an alarm?" Liv said.

"We've come this far, Liv," I said, hoisting the rock above my head. "We need to do this." I anchored my feet to the floor, bent back slightly, and thrust the rock out of my hands and through the window.

Nothing happened. No loud scream from an alarm. I used my jacket to clear the remaining broken shards from the window frame, still fearing Luca had other ways to be notified of an intruder. I poked my head through the darkness, then climbed on Liv's shoulders, hoisted myself through the window, and fell to the floor.

"I'll wait and watch," Liv said, but I feared our separation would be a mistake.

"No, we need to stay together," I said, unlocking the door from the inside to let her in.

Lights flashed on, and we found ourselves in a small back entrance leading to a modern kitchen with breathtaking views. Dark slate-grey hardwoods contrasted sharply against creamy cabinets. Bronze modern pendant lighting illuminated granite countertops and stainless steel appliances, more exquisite than Luca's beautiful home in Skaneateles. "Luca must be doing well for himself if this is truly his home."

"If this belongs to Uncle Luca and Aunt Lena, why keep it a secret from our family?" Liv asked.

"Because they're hiding something," I said. "At least *he* is."

I pulled Giovanni's blueprint from my bag. Once we got our bearings and understood where we were in reference to the blueprint, we investigated every room on that floor fit for a magazine spread. Nothing seemed unusual, so we moved to the second floor, where I was most anxious to go.

I ran my finger over the spot on the blueprint where the hidden door to the hallway was. Everything we encountered was an exact match to Giovanni's blueprint. Following his notes and sketched-in arrows, we found the area within the patterned wallpaper which concealed the hidden door. I pushed along the edge as Giovanni had instructed and felt it move. I pushed again and the door slid to the side, disappearing within the wall.

We stepped into the hallway and the door slid back to its closed position behind us. My skin prickled. Before us stood three doors spaced about twenty feet apart—the secret rooms. From Giovanni's description, I knew the first door on the right would be the study, which held the darkest secrets.

I placed my hand on the doorknob and glanced at Liv. "This is the one," I said.

Chapter 38

Ella

The doorknob turned with ease, and we stepped into an impeccably designed office with a library I could only dream of having. Book-filled shelves lined the walls from floor to ceiling. A grey sofa and two leather chairs were positioned on a plush shag rug beneath a painting of the ocean. In a nook beside the sitting area was a small kitchenette which included a coffee bar, a wine bar, and a stocked liquor cabinet. On the opposite side, modern industrial orb lights hung above an oversized desk. Two leafy plants spilling over marble pots stood on both sides of the desk.

Liv and I exchanged glances.

We swept through the room quickly and methodically, seeking signs confirming Luca's existence in the house, but there was nothing glaring among the knickknacks, odd statues, and other décor. I walked to a wide shelving area that faced the sofa, not easily noticeable upon first entering the room. Framed photographs of people I didn't recognize filled the shelves. I studied them closely and froze when I came to a particular picture with five people standing close together, toes beneath the sand, blue waves folding behind them. An older man stood in the center holding hands with a woman. Her eyes seemed familiar, but I couldn't place her. Next to the woman were two younger women and a child. I ran my finger over the glass. My whole body tensed when I saw him. I couldn't believe I was looking at Luca. Who were the people standing around him?

"It's him," I said to Liv. "Come see."

"What?" Liv quickly came beside me.

"Look." I handed her the picture.

Her jaw dropped. "My God, what is he doing?" Liv said. "Who are those people?"

Suddenly I felt vulnerable, as if what we'd discovered might unleash something dark and of terrible consequence.

Liv continued to scour the other pictures for more clues while I stared into Luca's eyes, wanting to read his mind.

"What . . . is this?" Liv said, squatting near a lower shelf. She stood and placed another picture in my hand, keeping her eyes on mine. She pointed and said, "Look closely."

I saw immediately what she meant. A sick feeling hung in the pit of my stomach. Shock turned to disgust and then rage as I forced reasoning for what I saw—a young woman with long blonde hair and green eyes smiling next to a man with his arm around her waist. They stood together, relaxed and comfortable, as others fanned behind them, Luca being one of them. She wore a beautiful white dress that fell to the ground and pooled around her feet. The man with his arm around her wore a grey suit with a pink tie. A posed smile for the photographer on their wedding day . . .

Jamie's and Thomas's wedding.

"Jamie," I said, her name stinging my lips. I removed the photo from the frame and looked on the back for a date or anything that would say when or where this had occurred, but there was nothing. "What is this? What is she doing?" A feeling of betrayal far worse than that of two years ago sat heavy in my bones. "Why would she do this to me?"

"She's always helped Luca," Liv said, as if realizing it at that moment. "She wasn't misinformed by Luca in Italy as she'd said. She wasn't protecting you from the alleged truth about Poppy. She was protecting Luca . . . and herself." Liv glared at the photo. "What's his hold on her?"

I couldn't take my eyes away from the photo. How was this possible? I reached back to my memories of our lives together, of our friendship, and when the fault between us had begun. Something I had missed before our trip to Italy.

I snapped a picture with my phone before returning the photograph to its position on the shelf. Liv was right, and had she been all along—Jamie wasn't the loyal friend Luca had pulled aside that day asking her to keep an eye on me in Italy. Something far deeper was going on, some kind of connection—a bond that couldn't have evolved from merely being my friend. No, there was definitely more to this relationship than I'd realized.

Fearing too much time had slipped away while I was focusing on the photographs, I knew we had to move on. Giovanni had specifically mentioned the desk and said we should focus our efforts there. The short side of the desk appeared connected to a wall of books while the longer side extended into the room. I ran my fingers over the polished wood, looking for a link to a secret passageway. Giovanni said there would be a button or a lever and that it wouldn't be obvious but I'd know it when I found it.

I pulled the leather chair from the desk, looked beneath it, spun it around, and sat down. While Liv continued to search the bookcases, I spread the blueprint across the desk. I touched the marked area on the blueprint representing the wall of books behind the desk.

"If I'm reading this correctly," I said to myself, "that wall of books is a facade." If Giovanni remembered accurately, then a secret passageway to a private room existed behind that wall of books.

Liv and I immediately began searching the wall of books that ran behind the desk across the whole side of the room. We ran our hands up and down the shelves, feeling for a handle or a button, anything that might transform the wall.

"Many of these books are fake," Liv said, removing a wooden replica of five books connected together from one of the shelves. "But you wouldn't know it just by looking at it from a distance."

"Even up close," I said. "There must be something here that opens this wall. What have we missed?"

Something I remembered from one of my private investigating books came to mind. I returned to the desk and slid my hands on the underside of the desk's edge once more. When I bent down to look I saw a slight protrusion at the center. I reached a little further and pressed it with my thumb. A loud sound of metal clicked near the door, but nothing visible happened.

"I think that's the door to the study locking," I said, confirming a related note on the blueprint. I knew we were close to finding our way behind the books.

We examined all the books on the shelves, real spines blending with imposters. "I think we need to clear the shelves," I said. We began removing large sections of books to see if something was hidden behind them, as there had been in Poppy's study.

And then we found it: a large, red, faux reference book. When we removed it from the shelf, a grinding of gears and the low hum of a motor ensued as the shelves slightly vibrated. We watched wide-eyed as a small crevice within the wall slowly parted, widening enough for entry. We entered through a small corridor that spilled into a darkened room. Liv and I stared in disbelief as we walked in together. Sensor lights flashed on, revealing an exact replica of the room we'd just left.

"What is this?" Liv said.

We moved about the room, noting the same items in the same

locations as in the other room. The desk, the sitting area, bookshelves, and shelves of framed photographs were all the same. I noticed a door at the back of the room that reminded me of the storm doors we'd escaped from in the basement of the abandoned house.

Unlike the other desk, the file drawer belonging to this particular desk slid open with ease. Tightly packed files with labeled tabs filled the drawer—Accounts, Business New York, Business Tropea, Business Tuscany, Life Insurance, Home Tuscany, Home Skaneateles, Home Tropea.

I paused before reading aloud the last three tabs: "'Gianna,' 'Grace,' and then 'Franco.'" I couldn't believe what I was seeing.

Liv removed the last three folders. I opened Franco's, and right on top was his death certificate followed by a copy of his birth certificate and his passport, his army discharge papers, and news articles surrounding the disappearance of Gianna. The last few items in his folder were the letters written to Luca from Franco during the war. I snapped pictures of each item before returning them to the folder.

"Why would he have these?" Liv asked.

"He's a sociopath," I said, recalling conversations from Mr. Jones, "and a narcissist. He does everything for his own gain. He thrives on details and being in control. He craves it. . . ." I had to stop myself although I could have gone on.

Gianna's folder included several pictures of her. One of them reminded me of a photograph Poppy had described in his diary, one that Gianna had given him. Poppy knew Luca had stolen it when it fell from one of the pockets in Luca's jacket right in front of Poppy. Luca had lied and said Gianna had given him a photo of herself, too, but Poppy always knew he was lying.

Gianna's folder also contained envelopes addressed from Gianna to Franco, sealed edges sliced open, no postage marks or stamps, their contents exposed to eyes they weren't intended for. I held them in my hand and looked at Liv. "That's why Poppy never received any letters from Gianna. He'd always wondered why she hadn't written him back after the baby was born. He was so worried about it—his diary was filled with worry."

"Oh my gosh. Poor Poppy," she said. "All along they'd been confiscated by Luca. It makes me sick."

But there was one more item in the folder I'd never expected to see. A small, clear plastic bag was tucked at the back, a fragment from a gold chain with a scripted *Forever* dangling at one end. It was the missing part of the necklace a young Poppy had given to Gianna.

I held it for Liv to see. "This is the part we never found," I said, referring to part of Gianna's necklace I'd found two years ago in the woods behind the vineyard in Italy. I'd discovered a broken golden chain with a worn-out scripted *F* with smaller indiscernible letters clinging to it. It had been hidden among the brush close to Gianna's burial place.

I gave it to my mother when I'd returned from Italy, and she connected it to her own *G* which had been tucked in her carriage bedding the day she'd been found on the steps of Luca's parents' home. My mother had saved the *G* and attached it to a new chain, thinking it stood for her own name, Gabriella. She'd worn it for as long as I could remember. And here was the part that completed it: *F & G Forever.*

Each item we found was more perplexing than the last, especially the envelope with a handful of wedding pictures of Luca with someone who was not Aunt Lena. I handed them to Liv. "Had Luca been married before Aunt Lena?" I asked. "Oh God, do you think he's a polygamist?"

"I think Aunt Lena was his first wife," she said, "but who knows for sure?"

Suddenly a loud noise like something falling came from the outside study. We stopped talking and listened as a softer sound followed—sliding, like footsteps dragging on the floor.

I looked at my phone to see if we'd missed a warning text from Nico, but there was none. Our eyes locked, horrified at the realization that we were not alone. Had Luca discovered us at the abandoned house in Tropea and followed us here?

We ran to the door at the back, hoping for a similar escape, but it was locked. Maybe the key Angelina had found at the abandoned house belonged to this door. I pulled it from my pocket as something like an explosion engulfed us. I felt myself falling and fading.

Chapter 39

Luca

Thickening clouds obstructed the starry night, casting a somber haze as Luca entered the secluded hills of his private community. His heart raced and sweat dripped into his eyes, obscuring his vision of the road. He dragged his face against his shoulder while his fingers stayed locked on the wheel, convinced the car behind him had been there from the start.

Luca's breath was ragged, and he felt he might suffocate. Sienna's voice would soothe him, so he spoke her name and his phone dialed her number. He glimpsed the rearview mirror at the car trailing him. It slowed, then revved its engine and sped around Luca and down the road. The call to Sienna went straight to voicemail, and a feeling of dread consumed him. Why hadn't she answered?

The gate widened as he neared, a shrill scraping of metal on metal. He jumped at the sound of his phone ringing; it was Sienna calling.

"Sienna," he gasped.

"Luca, what's wrong?"

"Where are you?"

"At the hotel, why—"

"Stay there," he said.

"What's happening?"

"Just stay at the hotel and everything will be fine."

"Where are *you*?" she asked.

"Tell me you'll stay there until I get back."

"Yes, but—"

"Sienna!"

"What?"

"I love you," he whispered. "Don't call me back."

He ended the call and eyed his surroundings as the car crawled to the end of his private drive. The limbs of the trees taunted him as if they were luring him further into the darkness. Luca felt like the world had turned against him, preparing to snuff out his existence at any moment.

His body trembled as he exited the car and walked around the front of his home. He examined it closely, deducing no apparent signs of foul play. He touched the front door and pressed his ear against the wood, holding his breath, listening to the silence behind it. As he unlocked the door and stepped inside, his stomach tightened and the hairs on his neck prickled his skin.

Luca laid his hand against the gun in his pocket and walked through the foyer, stopping at every corner. When he felt satisfied with his investigation of the main floor, he moved stealthily up the stairs, scrutinizing the walls and rooms for signs of anything amiss, particularly concerned with one particular area of the hallway. He placed his hand within the patterned wallpaper and pressed his fingertips at the spot known only to him. As the wall separated and the door disappeared, Luca stepped inside, treading lightly, hardly breathing with each step.

Although it was locked, he didn't have to touch the doorknob to his secret study to know it had been breached. He stepped inside and immediately saw the slight differences in the room he knew well. The crystal vase on the edge of his desk was an inch from its original position. The chair facing the desk was slightly angled to the right.

The white pillow on the couch no longer touched the blue one. More obvious disparities glared at him as he approached his desk. Several books from some of the shelves were placed in piles on the floor near his desk. The red wooden reference book replica was no longer in its rightful position, confirming that someone had entered beyond the feigned wall where old crimes and a secret life once existed.

He saw a small opening where the wall hadn't completely closed. Luca unlocked his gun and held it at his side, never thinking this day would come.

Luca slipped through the opening, his back pressed against the wall, his gun in his hand. Viewing most of the room from where he stood, he saw the papers and files strewn about his desk and onto the floor, the file cabinet drawers fully extended. But beyond that, near the room of similar design and purpose to the one in his old house, he saw *them*: Ella and Liv.

He cursed himself for not putting an end to things long ago. His great-nieces had crossed a line, and there was no turning back now. Luca inched closer, preparing to ambush them from the side, but the floorboards betrayed him, and Ella glanced over her shoulder in his direction. He knew they'd try to escape through the fake door at the back. They'd already stepped through the only exit from that room. He saw the panic in their faces as they tried and failed at opening the door, their eyes reaching back to the spot where Luca hid.

He gripped his gun, taking aim at the girls he had helped raise, sweat beading on his brow. For a moment he saw them as children, laughing and playing, their sweet voices ringing in his ears. He shook the memory, now seeing Ella's innocent expression seeking his comfort, the sadness in her eyes at Jack's passing. How close they had all been. The angry and devious part of Luca fought hard against his memories, demanding he press the trigger, but before he could, someone else decided for him.

She too must have sensed Ella's arrival. Luca watched as the crowbar in her hand met the back of Ella's head. He swallowed hard, watching Liv's horrified face as her sister fell. A small morsel of love surfaced in Luca, and he wanted to run to Ella and help her. But the stronger, darker force that had long ago taken residence within pulled him away as it always had.

Chapter 40
Ella

Pain at the back of my head forced consciousness as it rippled to my arms, bound behind me. I opened my eyes, seeing shadows through a blurry haze. My hair felt wet against my chin. Aside from the smell of the duct tape that silenced my voice, a musty, metallic odor lingered. Agitated, quarreling voices seeped from behind the walls. I wondered frantically where Liv had ended up.

Heavy, deliberate footsteps entered from behind and stopped. I turned to see who it was and winced at the shooting pain. An overhead light flashed on illuminating grey cinder walls, some of them padded. It was eerily similar to the unfinished room in the abandoned house, and I was certain I knew its purpose.

A few minutes later, heels clicked across the floor, their wearer trailing sweet chamomile and lavender and stopping just behind me. Whispers ensued, private words floating just beyond reach. Then my assumed captors walked around my chair, finally facing me. The older woman wearing jeans, a white T-shirt, and worn combat boots I'd never seen before, but the younger woman, the one with the heels, broke my heart.

I stared in disbelief at the blonde-haired, green-eyed younger woman. A low-cut shirt peeked behind her leather jacket, ripped jeans tucked into high-heeled boots. She held something behind her back and something unrecognizable in her familiar eyes, eyes belonging to a girl I had once considered a sister. *Jamie.*

"Shoot her," the older woman said.

Dread slammed into my gut as Jamie stared at me, frozen. A look of uncertainty flashed through her eyes. I desperately wanted them to remove the duct tape so I could speak to her.

"Do it," the woman said. She stormed at Jamie and snatched the gun she held at her back, taking aim at me.

"Don't!" Jamie said. "You don't have to shoot her."

"Oh, don't I?" she sneered at Jamie. Then she looked at me. "We finally meet," she said. She had to be in her late forties or early fifties and in pretty good shape. "You don't know me," the woman continued, "but I know who you are." She stepped closer, put the barrel of the gun to my chin, and lifted it. "We've been watching you. We knew eventually you'd come here." Then she slid the weapon into the waist of her jeans as if she'd changed her mind. "You're messing with the wrong family. Did you honestly think we'd let you? Your life has been a lie," she snickered. "The only reason—*the only reason*—you're not in jail or dead is because of my mother."

Her mother? I pleaded with my eyes, but the woman didn't care.

She thrust a leather-bound book in my face. "This belongs to *my* family," she said. My heart raced at the sight of the diary. "If it weren't for my daughter," she went on, glancing at Jamie, "we wouldn't have known about the diary, or the painting . . . or Gianna. We'd have nothing."

The woman bent low so we were face-to-face. Her bloodshot eyes peered into mine, and I noticed a scar above the left one. Another scar peeked beneath the sleeve of her jacket, a curved arc, like that of incisors from an upper jaw.

"*You* know my daughter," she glared. "You're both much closer than you think—not quite sisters, but close." She folded her arms and brought her index finger to her lips. "It was alarming how obsessed my father had become when you helped him realize Gianna was alive. He doesn't know my mother had kept that a secret from him. Just like you. Maybe you worked together."

I devoured the warped details of her story, still failing to understand my connection with her mother and how or why we would have worked together to find Gianna.

The woman then told me her name was Cecelia, but it meant nothing to me. And she referred to Jamie as her daughter. I remembered when Jamie and I had first met in second grade, how quickly we'd become close. Later, in our teens, at a sleepover, Jamie had shared her sad childhood story with me that she'd been taken away from her neglectful mother and placed with a new family, the one I came to know well. She'd cried that day, wishing she knew who her real mother was. So Cecelia was Jamie's biological mother, and at some point they had obviously reconnected. It was beginning to make sense—Jamie's watchful eye in Italy two years ago, the photographs in Luca's private study. As I sifted through the details, a new truth and Luca's part in it slowly emerged.

Cecelia got in my face again. "You have one chance to speak. You scream, I shoot your knees and you'll never walk out of here. Nod if you understand."

I nodded as my heart stampeded in my chest. I had to carefully choose my words. Cecelia ripped the duct tape from my mouth. The sharp sting on my lips paled in comparison to the delicious air entering my lungs.

"Where's Liv?" I asked, gasping and coughing.

"She's fine," Cecelia replied nonchalantly.

"I need to see her. I need to know she's all right."

"How did you know about this house?" Cecelia said, ignoring my plea. "Who told you?"

"I need to know that my sister is okay," I said, trying to maintain an even tone so I wouldn't lose my chance at finding Liv. I would never betray Giovanni's trust, but I feared they might have found the blueprint and his notes in my pocket.

Cecelia looked at Jamie. "Go get her damn sister."

Jamie did as she was told.

"You said something about your father," I began. "Who is he?"

"I ask the questions, not you. And don't act dumb," she said. "You know damn well who he is."

I felt dizzy. She couldn't be referring to Luca. How could he be this woman's father? If he were, that would make Jamie . . . my cousin? No, not possible.

"My father is not the dangerous one," she continued. "I will protect him no matter what. You'll have to go through me first. This is your moment of truth," Cecelia growled.

"That's why I'm here," I said, "for the truth."

"Watch your tone." Cecelia picked up the diary. "You think your truth is in here—a stolen diary from a stolen life?" she mocked.

"It's not your diary," I said.

Cecelia raised her gun.

I heard Liv's voice behind me.

"Liv—run!" I screamed, throwing my body so the chair fell to the floor as the gun cracked. "Please don't!" I pleaded. "I don't care about Luca! I just want to find Gianna . . . for *my* mother."

Where was Liv? Why couldn't I hear her anymore?

Cecelia knelt down, mumbling something indecipherable, then she got to the floor and lay beside me, her dark eyes piercing mine. "Gianna is the cause of all evil," she said. "She could have chosen which man she wanted instead of faking her death, choosing neither. She stole something from my father and he wants it back. He wants revenge." She got to her feet again and held the gun on me once more.

"Please," I said. "We can talk. Maybe we can help each other." I had no idea how, but I'd do anything to get out of this house unharmed. I feared my mother had seen our note by now. What if she and Angelina had decided to come here even though I'd told them not to?

"It's too late for that," she said, still aiming the gun. "My father has someone headed to Gianna's as we speak."

My heart sank. I worked to loosen the ties around my wrists, feeling hope as the fibers in the rope began to give.

Cecelia's eyes darted at something and back. Liv entered the room and backed up slowly when she saw us, a gun she must have found grasped firmly in her hands and aimed at Cecelia. As they faced off, a shot exploded and Cecelia fell to the ground and dropped her gun, writhing in pain.

Liv snatched Cecelia's gun and rushed to untie me.

"Hurry, Liv," I said.

She handed me Cecelia's gun as Jamie entered and ran to her mother. Liv pointed her gun at Jamie, who was bent over her mother as a pool of blood spilled around them.

"No, Liv. Let's go," I said, staring into Jamie's sad, defeated eyes.

Jamie stood as the lights flickered and went out. More footsteps drew near, and a loud clap whipped through the room. I dropped to the floor, reaching for Liv beside me.

"Liv?" I whispered, touching her arm.

"El," Liv softly replied, "I've been shot."

How could that be? Only seconds ago she stood beside me.

"What? Where?" I said as I patted her body, stopping at her warm, wet chest. I remembered assisting Dr. McCarthy during an operation to remove a bullet from a police officer's chest that had grazed his heart. It was a successful operation but, sadly, unable to regain his strength, he had succumbed to his wounds shortly after. I wouldn't let that happen to Liv. I would save her. "It's okay," I said, trying to disguise the fear in my voice. "I'll get you out of here."

"No, Ella, I can't—"

"Liv . . ." I placed my hand on her cold, clammy cheek and felt the weak pulse at her neck. Inside I screamed and raged, but on the outside I remained calm. It was my fault for bringing Liv to the house in the first place, my fault if anything happened to her. "I love you, Liv. It'll be okay." I removed a shirt tied around my waist and placed it over her to keep her warm.

There was no service on my phone. It would be impossible to get her out of the house the way we came.

Hands grasped my shoulders, pulling me up as voices from all directions entered the room. I knew the soft palms and strong grip of those hands belonged to Nico, who must have seen Luca or Cecelia and Jamie and had tried to warn us. Upon realizing he couldn't get through by phone, he came to us instead.

"I'm so sorry, El," he said, his voice choppy. "I saw she had a gun. I thought I could get to her before she could shoot Liv. We have to go."

"Nico, I can't leave her," I said as others rushed into the room, pushing us aside, pulling me away from Liv.

"We need to stay out of their way," he said. "She's in good hands. She'll be okay."

I reached my hand toward Liv. She was all I cared about.

Chapter 41

Ella

Nico pulled me close to his chest as we stood outside and waited for the emergency technicians to take Liv to the hospital. "Thank God you're okay!" he said, his eyes filling. "I saw Luca's car heading toward the house and another one behind him. I texted you but the message wouldn't send. I was scared for you, Ella. I got here as quickly as I could. I should have come sooner."

"How did you get in—to that hallway? How did you find us?"

"I remembered what you said when you went over the details with Liv. I put a chair in the doorway to prevent the door from closing so the ambulance crew could get through. I called them as soon as I realized I couldn't reach you. I'm sorry, Ella; I know you didn't want the police involved because of Luca, but I had to do it. For you."

"It's okay," I said. "If you hadn't then Liv might . . ."

Nico held me tighter.

Two police officers converged within earshot of us. "One, maybe two dead. What the hell happened here? Never seen a house like that before."

My legs weakened as, seconds later, Liv was carried out by the paramedics strapped to a cot.

Nico and I rushed to see her, thankful they let us through. "Liv," I said, fighting back tears, "you're gonna be okay." I looked at one of the technicians as he opened the ambulance doors. "She'll be okay, right?" But they were too busy to acknowledge or they didn't want to. "Stay with me," I said. "Don't give up."

In the seconds before they took her away, I held her hand and noticed a trace of blood spattered on her lips. "You'll be okay," I said. "I love you." I sensed a slight pressure on my hand from hers. The technicians stepped in, and Nico and I faded to the background. We watched as they steadied her within the ambulance, closed the doors, and sped away. My heart was heavy as we raced to our car to follow them.

"How did this happen?" I said, sliding into the passenger side. Before Nico could get into the car, an officer approached him.

"Sir," I heard him say, "I know this is a bad time, but may we have a quick word with you?"

Nico nodded and closed the door, leaving me alone inside the car.

It was hard to hear everything through the glass. Something about a witness seeing him enter with a gun. I hadn't known Nico owned a gun. He'd been against guns for years after a close friend was shot and killed when an intruder wrestled it out of his hands and used it on him.

A couple minutes later, the officer came to my side of the car and asked me to step out.

"*Signorina*, I understand you're going to the hospital to see your sister," he said.

"Yes, and I need to get there fast," I said, my voice quivering.

"I want you to get there," he said. "Perhaps we can talk at the hospital. Would that be all right? I have a few more questions for both of you."

"Yes, that's fine," I said.

The officer thanked us and got into his car as we returned to ours.

"What did he ask you?" I asked Nico on the way to the hospital.

"He wanted to know why I was there and what I'd seen."

"Did you bring a gun?"

He glanced at me. "Yes, in case I needed it, and I *did* need it. Why are you looking at me like that?"

"I thought after what happened—"

"This is different," he said, staring at the road.

I stared out the window as the houses streamed by on the never-ending drive to the hospital. My thoughts were miles away from the car, and I felt lost and helpless.

***

The nurse at the information desk told us Liv had been taken into surgery; we had just missed her. Although I wanted to see her, I was relieved that they had attended to her right away.

A trauma doctor approached from a corridor off the waiting area and asked to speak with me as the police officer who had spoken to us earlier entered and headed toward Nico. My stomach twisted, eager but fearful to hear what the doctor had to say. I glanced at Nico talking with the officer, his body language defensive.

The doctor explained that the bullet, upon entry, broke a rib on Liv's left side and pierced her lung. Liv was in the middle of surgery to remove the bullet and repair her damaged lung, which was taking longer than expected. He said that on the way to the hospital Liv slipped into shock, but the paramedics acted quickly and inserted an endotracheal tube into her lung to help her breathe. That as well as a significant amount of blood loss made it critical to operate immediately.

"She's very lucky to be alive," he said, "but she's not out of the woods yet."

Those words were repeated over and over again in my mind. I knew Liv was in good hands, but I was well aware in my own experience as a surgeon that anything could happen.

When the doctor left, I glanced again at Nico and the officer. Something about the way the officer was standing reminded me of Officer Spalina and how he'd stood as he told me someone had been in my attic. That someone I now knew had been Jamie.

With everything that had happened to Liv, I'd hardly given Luca a thought until now. He could be at Gianna's house at this very moment. But as much as I'd chased him, determined to find Gianna and expose the remaining secrets, none of that mattered now. Nothing compared to what I was feeling right now as Liv fought for her life.

After speaking with Nico, the officer approached me. We discussed my reasons for being in Luca's house. I admitted to trespassing and explained how I knew about the house and the secret rooms, why I'd done it, and what I had been looking for. It wasn't an excuse; I knew I'd broken the law by breaking into Luca's home. I wasn't sure if I'd get charged, and I didn't care. I only wanted Liv to be okay.

The shooting was of particular concern to the officer. He was trying to understand who had shot Cecelia and who shot Liv. I didn't know much myself, only that Cecelia was threatening to kill me, and someone had shot her almost at the same time as Liv was shot. It was all a blur, too hard to remember the details. I just wanted it all to go away.

Nico was vague about what he'd discussed with the police. He seemed distant and quiet, hardly making eye contact, so unlike his normal self. When he did speak, his words and tone had a hint of an edge. It was baffling that he'd gone from being so attentive at the house, never leaving my side, to aloof and standoffish. Now of all times was when I really needed him to help me quiet the radical thoughts in my mind. I wondered if something had happened when he spoke with the police or if he was perhaps feeling guilty about the other woman I'd seen him with, something we hadn't talked about yet.

I thumbed through my phone at the selfies Liv and I had taken just days before, smiling, silly, happy. Now so many pieces of my life seemed to be floating away.

I glanced at Nico as he tapped his foot on the floor and stared at the wall. Our eyes met and then he looked away.

"How are you holding up?" he finally asked, reaching his hand to mine.

"Terrible," I said, looking at him, studying his face. "What's wrong?"

"Nothing."

"Something is definitely wrong," I insisted. "You're not yourself."

"What do you mean?" Tears formed at the corners of his eyes. He looked away and back. "I—I don't know how to say this," he said. The muscles in his neck twitched and he clenched his teeth. "I need to tell you something . . . I just don't know how to say it."

My stomach squeezed. "Just say it."

"I lied to you." His eyes dropped.

What could he have possibly lied to me about? Was it the woman I saw him with?

"I think I know," I said.

"I tried, Ella—to protect you—but I'm not the hero you think I am."

"I saw you, Nico," I said, remembering the day I tried to surprise him by arriving in Italy earlier than planned. The day he ignored my texts and came out of a restaurant with that woman.

"You saw me?" Tears streamed his cheeks. "Ella . . . I'm *so* sorry."

"Why would you do that to me? To us?" I said, swallowing hard on the rising knot.

"I didn't intend for it to happen," he said. "I thought about not saying anything, but I just can't live with myself. But you have to know, I—I thought I was aiming at Cecelia and I . . ." His voice trailed away.

Cecelia? Why had he mentioned *her?*

The veins at his temples bulged and his face flushed red. "I—I thought Liv was with you. I didn't know she'd run to you when I . . . pulled the trigger."

"Nico, what are you saying?"

"I was the one who did it!" he blurted, sobbing. "I shot Liv!" He threw his head into his hands; his shoulders shook as he cried.

I stood and embraced Nico, a mix of emotions stirring within me. "No, don't say that," I said. "It's not your fault."

"I didn't think I had, but after talking with the police—the details, where I was standing, the trajectory of the bullet—it was me. I put your sister in that operating room. They might arrest me. I understand if you can't forgive me."

"Nico . . ." I blinked at the tears on my lashes and hugged him tighter. "I know you didn't mean for this to happen," I said. And although the implications of the situation and what might still happen were serious and hard to imagine, I believed him. He'd always had my best interests at heart.

The double doors opened and a surgeon stepped out. I tried to decipher his solemn expression. As he drew nearer, his eyes relaxed and he pulled down his mask to reveal a smile. My body loosened, and I released my breath. The surgeon explained the seriousness of Liv's situation, that she had lost a lot of blood and it took a while to stabilize her. The surgery was more complicated than expected, but they had successfully removed the bullet and repaired her lung. She was asleep in the intensive care unit and we would be able to see her as soon as she got to a room.

I wept as he spoke, overwhelmed by a rush of emotions that had plagued me over the last few days, especially the last few hours. But Liv has survived and she would be okay. I wouldn't lose my sweet sister, my real best friend. I couldn't wait to tell her how much I loved her.

Nico and I embraced again as the surgeon left, and the fear and pain we'd been carrying slowly melted away.

About an hour later, we were allowed to visit Liv in her room. We sat in the chairs closest to her bed, listening to the swish of the ventilator, the repetitive beep of the monitor, and the low hum from the fan. I placed my hand on hers and smiled at the warmth of her touch. I kissed her forehead and whispered in her ear that she was going to be okay. I told her I was here and I wasn't going anywhere without her and that I loved her.

My mother and Angelina arrived shortly after, and I explained to them everything that had happened. It was hard to see the heartache and fear in my mother's eyes, and I still felt responsible. While Liv slept, my mother and Angelina went to the cafeteria to get some coffee. They had been gone for less than ten minutes when a surprise visitor arrived.

Her hair, dyed platinum-blonde, curved toward her face just under her jawline. I could tell she was older by the fine lines near her eyes and lips, but she seemed far younger than she probably was. She wore light makeup and dressed well, making her appearance rather youthful. I'd seen this woman only in pictures, never face-to-face, and I knew who she was before she even said her name.

"Hello, Ella. I'm Sienna . . . your great-aunt."

Chapter 42

Gianna

Italy 1939

In the days following their engagement, Gianna and Lorenzo discussed how they would share the good news with each others' families. Other than Amelia and her husband, Gianna had never met Lorenzo's family, and likewise, he had never met hers. Although they hadn't set a date, they knew they probably wouldn't wait very long.

Under the oak tree in Amelia's backyard, Lorenzo promised Gianna he would exhaust every resource he had to help her find Gabriella and that one day they would all be a family. Having Lorenzo in her life allowed Gianna a small piece of her heart to mend, though she still ached for Gabriella and the life she once knew.

Gianna and Lorenzo made plans to visit Lorenzo's parents and siblings the following weekend, and soon after that they'd invite Sienna and Maria to dinner at Amelia's. But before seeing either family, they felt Amelia should be the first to know. She had accepted Gianna into her home without question or judgment and had been among the kindest souls Gianna had ever met.

Amelia was thrilled when they told her. "I was hoping for exactly that someday," she said as she hugged Lorenzo and then Gianna.

"You're like a sister to me already," she told Gianna. "I couldn't imagine anyone else but you with Lorenzo." Amelia brought out a bottle of wine and made a toast to their engagement and to their happiness. As they sipped, the phone rang, and Amelia got up to answer it. When she returned, Gianna saw the look on her face and knew something was wrong.

"You have a phone call," Amelia said. "Why don't you take it upstairs?" She smiled a thin smile that made Gianna's stomach turn.

Gianna raced up the stairs two at a time, fearing the voice and its message on the other end. She snatched the phone and put it to her ear. Short, rapid breathing greeted her on the other end.

"Are you sitting down?" Sienna asked, her voice strained.

"Yes," Gianna said as she sat on the end of her bed.

"I have news for you—good and bad," Sienna said.

"What is it?"

"Franco—Gabriella—they're alive!" Sienna cried.

"What did you just say?" Gianna sprang to her feet as her heart raced and something in her stomach churned. She paced around the bed and to the window, staring out at the tree and waiting for Sienna to tell her more.

"It's true—they're alive!" Sienna said. "I can't explain how, but I found a way to follow Luca and, my God . . . Gabriella has been with Luca's parents this whole time."

A rush of emotion swept through Gianna: relief, disgust, fear, in that order.

"Are you sure? How do you know it's her? Franco? My God—Franco! How do you know all this?"

"I saw Gabriella myself," Sienna said, "through the window at Luca's parents' house. She was in his mother's lap. She seemed okay, like she'd been well taken care of. Luca's mother was playing with her."

"*Uomo cattivo*. Nasty man!" Gianna spat. "I've been dying inside, and he's had her with him all this time." She let out a small cry.

"Yes, but he wasn't entirely heartless," Sienna said. "He didn't leave her in the woods to die or give her away as we feared. It could have been so much worse, Gianna."

"Don't defend him," Gianna said. "None of this would be happening if it weren't for him. It will be impossible to get her back without risking her safety—or mine—but I need to." Gianna loosened the neck of her shirt and fanned herself with her hand. "Franco . . . where is he?"

"Luca lied about his death," Sienna said. "He didn't die in the accident; in fact, he earned a medal for his bravery during the war. He was honorably discharged and came home at the end of his tour. He's living at his parents' house for now."

Gianna gasped, and her body trembled. Goosebumps raced along her arms to her head. She cried through her smile at the thought of Franco being united with their daughter. She felt solace in knowing they'd had each other. Was it possible to be reunited with her family after all?

"There's more you should know," Sienna said. "Franco brought someone home with him—a woman—and . . . I don't know how to say this . . . Franco will be going to America with his parents, this woman . . . and Gabriella."

"No!" Gianna cried. "No, that can't happen. I'll never see Gabriella again! Who is this woman? Why would he leave Italy? He's completely given up on me, that's why. We have to stop them!"

Gianna realized the selfishness of her words and cringed as soon as she had uttered them. She was the one who had left, not him. Maybe he believed the speculation of the town gossip, that she left of her own free will.

"He didn't want to give up on you, Gianna," Sienna said. "I know that for a fact. I found a book—a journal. Again, I can't say how right now, but it was in Luca's possession and I was able to get my hands on it briefly."

"A book?"

"Yes, like a diary," Sienna said. "The pages are filled with entries—almost all of them about you."

"Me?"

"I didn't have a lot of time, but the first one was when he saw you at the deli. There's one about you being pregnant and how happy and conflicted he felt. And then close to the end of the book—well, I'll just say it was obvious he was torn about this woman, Olivia, because he still didn't know what happened to you. He also wrote that he felt it was urgent to get his parents and Gabriella out of Italy because of the tension with the Nazis and his fear for their safety. Many of the pages I skimmed, but there was nothing more clear to me than his love for you."

Gianna wept as she listened to her sister talk about Franco's diary, a nostalgic, regret-filled cry that made her question everything she thought she knew.

"What should I do?" she asked, thinking of Lorenzo and the life she was building with him. If she sent word through Sienna to Franco that she was alive, Luca would find out, possibly incensing him to harm Franco and Gabriella, and then he'd come for her. But seeking Franco meant she'd be destroying his relationship with Olivia and hers with Lorenzo. They'd be together, but at what cost? Too many obstacles had been stacked against Franco and her from the start, fate perhaps confirming they were meant to be together, but their moment had been fleeting.

"I don't think there's anything you can do," Sienna said. "I'm so sorry to have to tell you this."

"No," Gianna said. "I needed to know. I'm glad you told me and you didn't keep it from me thinking you were protecting me."

"I'd never keep something like that from you," Sienna said. "All I ever wanted was for you to be safe and find happiness."

Gianna sat on her bed for a long time after the call ended and, before she could succumb to the heaviness in her heart, she forced herself to go back downstairs. She returned to Amelia and Lorenzo, who had been anxiously waiting for her in the living room, sat beside Lorenzo, and relayed the whole conversation she'd had with Sienna.

Chapter 43
Gianna

Present Day, Italy

A beam of light from the window carried dust motes to a table beside Gianna as it had each week for the last twenty years. She gazed into it, releasing her own flow of thoughts and unprocessed feelings. After she and Lorenzo married, Gianna had regularly confided her feelings to Amelia, but it wasn't until Grace had grown into a young woman that Gianna realized she required more than that.

She repositioned herself in the leather chair, crossing one leg over the other, as she retold the recurring dream that had tortured her for so long.

It was always the same: *Carefree in the vineyard with Franco, the scent of pine she'd smelled upon awakening. Blissful sounds of nature. Franco's warm eyes become Luca's, flat and empty. Shadows lengthen, and fear steals joy. Dark clouds form in the distance as a black-gloved hand cups her mouth. Another one moves to her neck. There's a moment in the dream where she becomes aware that she's dreaming, and she tries to undo what's happening but she can't. Hands squeeze as the treetops above her swirl and blur, then she awakens breathless and sweaty.*

For a while, Gianna believed what had happened to her in the woods was her fault. She had put herself at risk by being alone with Luca and, as a result, she'd lost everything—her child, the love of her life, her freedom—everything. If only she could have seen what might have happened, how differently she'd have chosen her path. It was the one regret she had.

She'd kept in touch with her sisters; usually they would come to her, still insisting, even after Franco and his family moved to America, that it was safer that way. She was indebted to them for connecting her with Amelia, bringing her Grace, and for finding out where Gabriella and Franco were.

But it was Lorenzo she credited for saving her life. If not for him, she might not have ever trusted or loved again. Lorenzo was compassionate and true to his word, hiring investigators to search for Gabriella in the United States, although their efforts turned up fruitless.

Sometimes seeing Grace gave Gianna immense comfort, and sometimes it pained her, a constant reminder that Gabriella was out in the world without her. At times their relationship suffered because of it.

These were the burdens she shared with Dr. Garfieldo each week. Sometimes they stopped just before their session ended, and other times, like today, she wished their time never had to end.

She reached for the glass of water at the edge of the table, steadied it in her hand, and raised it to her lips as her shallow breaths returned to a normal rhythm. Dr. Garfieldo jotted a few notes but mostly engaged in conversation with Gianna, helping her to understand her feelings and offer advice.

One day after returning home from her session, her granddaughter, Emma, came by to tell her something she'd never forget. Emma beamed as she rushed in, gave Gianna a kiss, and stood breathless before her.

"*Nonnina*," she said, her eyes widening.

Gianna looked at her with concern. Emma had called her *Nonnina,* which meant "little grandma," or sometimes *Nani,* since she could speak, but today her voice sounded so formal when she said it.

"My professor in my genetics class encouraged us to research our ancestral history for a paper we'll be writing, and you won't believe what I learned."

"That's interesting, Emma." Gianna grew anxious wondering what Emma might have found. "How does it work?"

"I had to spit saliva into a collection tube and send it away to a lab," she said. "Then I created an account for my results to be sent to."

"Isn't it amazing what we can do now to learn about ourselves?" Gianna said, her lip twitching as she spoke.

"It's fascinating," Emma continued. "My report came back with interesting results, Nani, and connected me to someone."

While Emma logged into her laptop to retrieve the report, Gianna excused herself to go to the bathroom. She closed the bathroom door and stood against it, catching her breath. What had Emma found, and who did she connect with? Gianna had to think of what she might say in response to any number of things Emma might have discovered. But she calmed herself, looking into the mirror. *You have nothing to hide. You did nothing wrong.*

After a few minutes, she took a deep breath and returned to Emma.

"You see this?" Emma said, pointing to the report on her computer screen. "This shows we have a strong presence of relatives in Calabria, near Tropea, and also here in Tuscany. But that's not really the surprising part." Emma scrolled to another page and pointed at the screen again. "What's intriguing to me is that we have relatives all the way over here in the United States—in New York."

Gianna's stomach twisted. "What?" she said, squinting at the screen, pretending she didn't know.

"Yes," Emma said. "And a few weeks ago, someone reached out to me and—"

"What do you mean, 'reached out'?" Gianna asked.

"When you get your DNA tested," Emma explained, "you become part of a database, and anyone else who's in that database and who shares similar traits could be related to you in some way. They would have to share a significant amount of DNA with you."

"Go on. . . ."

"So, a woman reached out to me saying that, based on the traits we share, we're somehow related. She asked if I would speak with her over the phone or through video."

"What did she say? Did you speak to her?"

"Not yet," Emma said, "but I did reply to her message and told her I would be interested."

"Oh, *tesoro*, sweetheart," Gianna said, "how do you know this isn't some kind of scam?"

"*Nonnina,*" Emma said, smiling, "it's not a scam. It's real. Here, let me show you the message she sent me." Emma clicked on the small envelope icon and opened the message. She read it aloud.

"*Hello,*

I recently received my ancestry report, and it appears we may be related in some way. I am interested in connecting with you if you are comfortable with that. However, I respect your privacy and understand if you do not wish to connect. Thank you for considering.

Best regards,
Gabriella Perri"

Gianna threw her hand to her mouth and burst into tears.

"Nani," Emma gasped as she ran to Gianna, "what's wrong? What did I say?"

Gianna couldn't control herself. It had been years since she'd heard the name of her other daughter, Gabriella.

"Nani, let me get you some tissues and some water," Emma said, running to the kitchen and back.

Gianna dabbed her eyes with the tissues and sipped the water. "Oh, my dear God," she said. "I can't believe it. I just can't believe it. But it has to be . . . her."

"What? What is it? Do you know this woman?"

Gianna nodded, crying once more into the tissues. "Yes, *cara*, dear, I do. Gabriella Perri is the name I gave to my other daughter, your mother's twin."

"Twin? My mother had a twin?" Emma said. "Why didn't I know this before?"

Gianna looked at Emma with regret.

"Why would you both keep this from me?" she pressed.

Gianna shook her head and closed her eyes. "Your mother doesn't know. I could never bear to tell her."

"Nani . . ."

"We were separated. It's a painful story, Emma," Gianna said. "Too painful to share. The years went by so fast, and it got harder to bring it up. I'm so sorry. It wasn't to hurt either of you in any way. I wanted to protect you."

"Protect us from what?"

"Not what. *Whom*," Gianna corrected her. "For all I know, this person who reached out saying they're Gabriella could be someone else pretending to be her so they can lure us into a trap. It is not a story for now," Gianna said, "but I promise you, we'll ask your mother to come over and, when she's here, I'll tell you both everything."

"You're sounding paranoid, Nani," Emma said. "You never talk like this."

"I'll tell you everything," Gianna said.

Emma paced the room. "I can't believe I'm hearing this. . . . All this time . . ." She stopped suddenly and approached Gianna. "I'd never blame you for keeping this from us, *Nonnina*. I'm sure you had your reasons, but—you know my mom and I—we'll want to connect with her if there's a way."

Gianna nodded, placing her hand on Emma's.

***

A week later, at her session with Dr. Garfieldo, Gianna told him about Emma's connection with Gabriella. It stirred up so many emotions and years of regret that Gianna had worked hard to overcome and accept. It usurped much of their session, but she was adamant to share a conversation she'd had with Sienna which occurred only a few days after Emma's visit.

Gianna hadn't heard from Sienna in months, hadn't seen her in years, and she'd called out of the blue to tell her something urgent. The first thing Sienna had told her was that Gabriella and her daughter, Ella, were in Italy and were only a train ride away. It reminded Gianna of the phone call from Sienna years ago when she'd called to say that both Franco and Gabriella were alive.

"I almost had a heart attack," Gianna said to Dr. Garfieldo, putting her hand to her chest. "I can't believe this is happening." She sipped her water. "And you know what my next thought was? 'Where's Luca?' He still invades my thoughts, even now."

"How did your sister know they were here?" Dr. Garfieldo asked.

Gianna glared into the dust-filled stream of light. "She married him. My sister married Luca." Her voice was flat, deflated.

Dr. Garfieldo's forehead creased into several tiny ripples. "I'm so sorry," he said. "This must be devastating for you."

"She said she did it *for* me—to keep an eye on him, make sure he never knew where I was," Gianna said.

"That's quite a sacrifice," he said. "Do you believe her?"

"No, not at first," she said, "but then it made sense. She was married before to an abusive man who ended up leaving her. But then she met someone new. She seemed happy, and I was just glad she had someone to take care of her. She never said they'd married." Gianna sipped her water again and wiped her brow with her sleeve. "We hardly saw each other in person after that. If we did it was only she and I, and not for very long.

"But then, a few years into their marriage, she noticed a change in his behavior. He'd be gone 'til late at night, sometimes not come home at all. She said she worried about where he was going and feared he might find me. She hired a private investigator who discovered he was also married to a woman named Lena in New York." Gianna spit the words in a continuous stream, feeling breathless at the end. "Sienna never told him what she discovered. As long as he hadn't found me, she played along."

"You keep saying 'he' and 'him' and not his name."

"I don't like to say his name," Gianna said.

"Aren't you giving him power if you don't say his name?"

Gianna sighed and continued. "The investigator also said *Luca* went to a storage unit between his supposed work-related trips around the world." Dr. Garfieldo tilted his head. "Sienna found a key she'd never seen before in Luca's jacket. She said she knew it had to belong to the storage unit, so she went to see what was in there—" Gianna's voice caught. She placed her hand to her mouth as if to capture the words that would follow and looked at Dr. Garfieldo.

"Take your time," he said, glimpsing the clock above the door.

"She said the unit wasn't very big but it was filled with boxes. She went through most of them. There were personal items belonging to women—jewelry, purses, wallets, a scarf, hair accessories—and then she found a box with things that belonged to me, from that day: my hat, my purse . . ." She shook her head and looked at Dr. Garfieldo. "That's not all. Sienna also said she found a book with a list of names in it. Benito Mussolini was near the top. Luca is . . . much darker than I thought."

"And she never went to the police with this?"

"Not until now," Gianna said, eyeing the clock. "There's one more thing I need to tell you." He nodded. "Luca and Sienna had a daughter, Cecelia. She said he created a wedge between Sienna and Cecelia, and she never knew why or how until recently. Sienna found out that Luca had poisoned Cecelia's mind with hatred, lies, and contempt for Gabriella and Ella. He instilled fear in Cecelia that Sienna wasn't safe with Gabriella and Ella around and warned her to be vigilant. He even went as far as to involve his granddaughter in his affairs.

"He planted his granddaughter in New York well before she went to elementary school, purposely close to my granddaughter, Ella, nurturing their relationship for his benefit. He got her into a prestigious law school and pulled strings to get her a job waiting tables at a restaurant in the city where Ella also worked while she went to school. His granddaughter—I think her name is Jamie—wasn't aware for a long time that she was put there purposely, and she genuinely had gotten close to Ella. Luca became threatened by their closeness, so he and Cecelia planted doubt and mistrust of Ella in her mind." Gianna's face was hot. She looked away in disgust.

Dr. Garfieldo glanced at the clock, which had run fifteen minutes over their usual ending time. "Why do you think she has chosen to tell you this now, after all this time?"

"Ella and her sister broke into Sienna's home, and Cecelia

followed them and trapped them. Jamie was there too. But something went wrong and Cecelia was shot—and killed. Sienna is devastated and regrets not doing something sooner. She said she'd make sure Luca would never hurt anyone again. She finally went to the police and took them to the storage unit. It's . . . it's all over with now."

Chapter 44

Ella

I gasped at hearing her name and seeing her—Gianna's older sister—before me. I looked at Nico, whose face was frozen. We stood at the same time and I walked around the bed to meet her. A nurse poked her head in to remind us of the two family members rule, so Nico stepped out into the hallway.

"You're surprised to see me," Sienna said, "yet you seem to recognize me."

"I've seen pictures," I said. "You haven't changed that much."

Sienna's smile was fleeting. "How is she?" She looked at Liv and the machines connected to her.

"She'll be okay, thank God," I said. "She's strong."

"I'm glad she's okay." Sienna blinked and blotted her eyes with a handkerchief. "It's not the same for my daughter."

"Your daughter?" I said.

"She was brought here at the same time as your sister, but . . . she didn't make it." Sienna made the sign of the cross and looked away.

"I'm so sorry for your loss," I said, still unsure why she'd come to see me.

Sienna straightened herself and wiped her nose with a tissue. "Actually, I'm the one who's sorry—for my daughter Cecelia's actions, which led us to this moment."

Cecelia is Sienna's daughter? The pieces began to fall into place.

"She was obsessed with you, or a version of you she was made to believe," Sienna explained. I listened as the fibers of the story knitted together. "She'd been in and out of hospitals and institutions for years, diagnosed with just about everything you can imagine: schizophrenia, bipolar disorder . . . No one knew how to help her. She refused medication and therapy and continued to spew hateful ideas to her own daughter, Jamie. By the time I realized the damage my husband had done, how he'd corrupted her mind, it was too late. So, I'm the one who's sorry."

"Your husband . . . Luca?" I said.

"Yes," she said. "It was not at all how I thought things would turn out."

It was too much to comprehend. Sienna was Jamie's grandmother. . . . Jamie—my closest friend and confidant for as long as I could remember. I'd told her things I'd never tell anyone else. I thought of the memories we shared growing up at the cottage. She was by my side every day following Jack's death. Had it all been a lie from the start? I'd begun to question her loyalty only two years ago in Italy when I'd exposed Uncle Luca, but never a moment before.

"It was all a lie," I said to myself as my heart broke again.

"You're referring to Jamie," Sienna confirmed. "She'd only recently—a couple years ago—learned of her purpose in your life. So, if you're referring to her friendship with you before then, *that* was not a lie. Even shortly after Luca pulled her into his world, I learned that she had struggled with the decision to help him. She thought she was protecting you . . . at least in the beginning. Maybe she regrets it now. I don't know. But I don't think I can trust her anymore."

It felt like I'd been punched in the gut. I couldn't believe what I was hearing. I recalled the time she'd helped me find the box Poppy had hidden in his study. Her actions and even the expression on her face seemed so sincere. Had she known then? That same face, the kindness in her smile and eyes, also existed in the frame in the private study at Luca's mansion.

"In case you're wondering," Sienna added, "Luca and I are no longer together, and I've notified the authorities."

I felt as though part of the burden that had encompassed much of my life had been slightly dislodged. Before Sienna left, she confirmed that both Cecelia and Jamie had been the ones stalking me at the cottage. It was Jamie who had snuck into the attic, becoming trapped there for a few days once the police arrived. And Cecelia had been the one Hercules chased after and attacked. I recalled the bite mark on her wrist at the mansion.

The last thing Sienna said before leaving the hospital room that day was that she knew where Gianna and Grace were and that she would call her niece, Emma, to arrange a visit.

Chapter 45
Ella

The Tyrrhenian Sea carried a crisp, salty breeze that jostled the petals of the terrace pots. Our stay in Italy had drawn quickly to an end, but I was not ready to go. I smiled at the sea that had greeted me each day since I'd been here, staring into the white wisps that licked the horizon. *This is where I belong.*

We'd extended our stay, just like the last time, only this time our purpose was different. Liv had regained her strength during her weeklong stay at the hospital, and my mother and I had hardly left her side. Sienna and I had exchanged phone numbers the day she stopped by the hospital,and three days later she contacted me to arrange a visit with Gianna and Grace.

We decided to make it a surprise. My mother had received Emma's reply to her request to connect. Emma obliged and invited her to meet in person at her apartment in Tuscany, never divulging her true identity. Emma also invited Gianna and Grace to lunch at her apartment as she frequently had. Liv, my mother, and I would take the train first thing the next morning. It would feel like an eternity until then.

A text from my phone chimed. It was Nico asking if I'd meet him at Castello Ruffo as soon as possible. I felt anxious as I replied that I would be there in an hour. What did he have to tell me that was so urgent, and why, of all places, the castle? Why couldn't he just come to the villa?

I arrived at Castello Ruffo in just under an hour and climbed its numerous steps to the top. I saw Nico standing at the edge gazing out at the blue sea. He turned as I arrived and I walked over to him, analyzing his expression and body language.

He clenched his jaw as he smiled, taking my hand. He seemed to struggle with what he had to say.

"Nico, are you okay?" I said.

"Now that you're here with me in Italy," he said, "I can't let you go."

I released the breath I'd been holding and gazed into his eyes which disappeared with his smile, as Poppy's always had. He pulled me in and we kissed, but I stepped back.

"I have to ask you something, and I'm afraid of your answer."

"You can ask me anything," he said.

"I'm committed to you," I said. "You know that, right?"

"Of course, as I am to you," he said, smiling. "Why are you asking?"

"I'm confused," I said. "I arrived in Italy a day earlier than I'd planned, hoping to surprise you. . . ."

"You did?" he said, scrunching his nose. "Why didn't you tell me?"

"It was supposed to be a surprise," I repeated. "You weren't home when I got to your house, so I asked the driver to take me to Rocco's. When I got there, I saw you with a bunch of other people . . . and a woman."

Nico's eyes flashed to the side as if trying to recall that day. Then they widened as he ran his fingers through his hair. He pulled his phone from his pocket, tapped the screen, scrolled down, tapped again, and turned it toward me to reveal a photo of the beautiful woman I'd seen with him. "Is this who you saw?"

"Yes," I said, bewildered.

He tossed back his head and laughed. "Ella . . . This woman—the one you saw me with—is Anna. She's my sister," he said. My face flushed as he chuckled. "She lives in Rome and was here on business, so she took me out to lunch."

"How did I not know you had a sister?" I laughed, feeling relieved and embarrassed at the same time.

"That's another story, but you will meet her one day soon, I promise," he said. "I can see how that might have looked—seeing me with another woman—but you shouldn't have doubted me. Why did you wait until now to ask?"

"It never was the right time," I said, "and then with Liv—"

"It's okay," he said. "I wanted you to come to the castle to ask you something too." He took my hands. "We've been together for two years already. People questioned whether we could make a long-distance relationship work, but I think we have."

I nodded, waiting to see where he was going with this.

He looked at the sea and back. "I don't want to see you through video call or once every four months anymore. I want more than that. I want to see you every day."

"Every day?" I echoed.

"Every. Day."

A warm glow spread through me. "Nico," I said, "are you asking me . . . *something?*"

"I'm asking you to live with me, here in Italy," he said. "You said so yourself that you belong here. I think you do too."

"And let's say I take you up on that," I said. "Do we live together forever?"

He chuckled. "Are you wondering if we'll get married?"

"Yes, because I can't imagine my life without you," I said, "and that's what *I* want."

"I want to marry you, too, Ella," he smiled.

During our last few moments together under the arched ledge of the castle, I told Nico about the Doctors in Italy fellowship program I'd been accepted into, and we made plans for our future. Although it would be torture being so far away from my mother and Liv, I knew it was something I needed to do, and they would understand. We'd never let distance come between us. We were just too important to each other.

***

Emma greeted us warmly at the door. She wore a floral sundress, cinched at the waist. Her light-brown hair fell just below her shoulders. She hugged us one by one as we introduced ourselves and then she led us through her apartment and out to the terrace.

A small sofa sat to the left, just off the back door, and a serving table stood to the right with a variety of cheeses, salami, capicola, bruschetta, bread, and fried eggplant on various serving plates. As she filled our wine glasses, Emma talked about the recipe she used for the eggplant parmigiana—her mother's recipe. Several feet away was a beautiful table set for six, overlooking the sea.

As we took in the view, we could see two women nearby, speaking closely to each other. I wondered who they were.

We followed Emma to the table, and I watched as my mother's gaze shifted to the women near the water. She participated in our conversation, but her attention stayed on them. The older woman had wavy salt-and-pepper hair that came to her shoulders. She was animated, waving her arms as she spoke to the woman across from her and tipping her head back to laugh. She wore a navy sundress and beside her was a wide-brimmed sun hat. The other woman, whose back was to us, pointed at something on the water, and together they stared.

I looked at Emma when my mother wasn't watching and pointed to the women. Emma nodded and mouthed, "Yes." My heart fluttered and my body trembled for a moment. I couldn't believe we were here and right before us were Gianna and Grace.

"Emma," my mother said, "thank you for having us today and for all of this." She waved her hand at the food. "You didn't have to do anything. I just wanted to meet you. I'm so curious to know our connection. But I want you to know that even if you're not connected to the person I'm wondering about, I really appreciate you taking the time to have us here."

Emma smiled. "It's my pleasure. I'm curious also. If it hadn't been for my class, I might not have sent away my DNA for testing, and we wouldn't have connected. Now, who was the woman you were thinking we both might know?"

"Well, two women, actually. . . ."

"Hold on one minute." Emma looked at the women near the water and called, "Nani!" Both women turned to look at her. "*Vieni qui.* Come here."

As they neared, I gasped as another version of my mother approached. Liv grabbed my hand, and my mother sat up anxiously, drawing her hand to her mouth. I watched it all unfold before me. My mother's eyes drifted from one woman to the other, then to Liv and me. And then to Emma.

"Is that—?" she turned to me and then looked at Grace.

"This is my grandmother, Gianna, and my mother, Grace," Emma said. "I think you're right—we are connected by the same person."

My mother stood shakily, her knees slightly buckling, her hand covering her mouth and looking as if she might cry or throw up. Liv and I stood beside her as Emma guided her grandmother and aunt forward.

"Nani, Aunt Grace, I'd like you to meet some friends of mine," Emma said, her eyes sparkling. But neither of them had to be told anything else. One look at my mother and they knew.

Gianna caught herself, resting her hand on Grace to keep from falling. Then her hands reached for my mother's, and my mother's stretched toward both Grace and Gianna, pulling them toward her. The three womens' hands intertwined and drew tightly into a hug that never stopped. At different moments one would step back, look at the other two, begin to cry, and hug again, gestures revealing more than words ever could.

When they had cried and hugged enough until their arms were tired, finally, my eyes locked with Gianna's. *All this time and here you are,* I thought in amazement. My heart was lighter than it had been in years, filled with a sense of pride for no one more than Poppy. If only he were here to experience this moment. Maybe he knew his life with Nonna in the present was more important at the time than his life with Gianna in the past. Maybe he was okay with this part of his story coming alive now, in this way and at this time.

And how courageous and selfless Nonna had been when we'd told her we were returning to Italy. Especially after feeling so displaced when I'd come home from Italy the first time and brought the truth about Gianna and all she encompassed into our lives. I had reassured her that, no matter what happened, whether we found Gianna or not, that Nonna would forever be my Nonna whom I loved so deeply. Nothing would change that.

As we watched them, Liv put her arm around my shoulders. "You did it," she said. "You made this happen, and I'm so proud of you."

Gianna stepped from her daughters and walked toward me. They followed her and stood behind her arm in arm. "Ella," Gianna said with wet eyes. I was wrapped in the warmth of her voice. She placed her hand on my cheek. "My granddaughter. I hear you are responsible for bringing us all together. I never thought I'd see it."

"I did it for Poppy," I said. "Franco."

"Franco," Gianna repeated wistfully.

"He knew I'd find you," I said.

"One day soon, I would love to hear everything you know about him and how he sent you to me," Gianna said, smiling.

"I would love nothing more," I said, reflecting on that day when my Poppy had slipped away, whispering about a box, the box that held a diary, Gianna's picture, Poppy's partially written manuscript, and a gun.

I would bring her the diary and watch as she opened it, saw his familiar handwriting, and read his words—words about her. I would show her the letters I'd found hidden in his paintings and in the pages of scrapbooks. I would tell her how I exposed Luca for who he really was, how I became connected with Sienna—everything.

And on a separate day, I would bring Angelina and Vinny to meet them, since they too had a part in this journey.

There we were, six women in the Perri family, talking, laughing, and crying as we ate dinner and sipped wine by the sea, sharing stories from each others' pasts. The sun lowered itself in the sky and we stood close together, peering at the unending view of turquoise blue.

We kicked off our sandals and walked along the beach, our toes disappearing in the sand as we stepped in unison. Emma, Liv, and I walked ahead of Gianna, Gabriella, and Grace, arms linked and smiles wide. Soon they caught up to us forming one line of six as waves crashed at our feet. A balmy wind tossed the edges of our dresses and danced through our hair, embracing us as we walked arm in arm, finally together. Finally complete.

Acknowledgements:

Many people have supported me throughout the journey of this book and I am grateful for their love and encouragement. I am especially thankful to my editor and friend, Megan Basinger, whose integrity, honesty, and editing expertise helped steer me straight when I was losing my way. Her guidance, encouragement, and her insight into my story's structure and characters made the final version so much stronger.

Thank you to my friends and colleagues for taking the time to read and offer your support, which helped me launch this book with confidence. I couldn't have done this without you.

I am thankful to my first readers of the earliest versions of my book, Yolanda and Dennis Parnell and Corrine and Gary Baccaro, all lovers of books and especially mysteries. Their feedback let me know early on that I was on the right track with the plot of this story and eagerly cheered me to the finish.

Most of all I would like to thank my family: my children, Sarah and Michael, who were ready at a moment's notice to lend their opinions and insights into the direction of my story, and my husband, Jimmy, who continued to lift me up and push me forward when I felt discouraged, reminding me at times to slow down and be proud of what I'd accomplished along the way. It was exactly what I needed.

Dear Readers,

Thank you for choosing to read *One Last Secret.* Perhaps you started with the first book in the Ella Perri Mysteries series, *Buried Secrets,* or maybe you happened to begin with this one. I hoped to portray Ella's, Gianna's, and Luca's stories in a way that was both appropriate and satisfying to my readers. And now that the mystery is complete and most of the questions have been answered, I'll be delving deeper into the Perri world in a prequel of what happened before *Buried Secrets* even began.

I hope you enjoyed *One Last Secret* and, if you did, I would be very grateful if you would leave a review on Amazon or my Facebook page. I always love hearing from my readers.

If you would like to know more about my next book or if you like free mysteries and thrillers, please visit my website and join my mailing list. I promise you will not be spammed, and you may unsubscribe at any time.

Gratefully yours,
Krissy Baccaro

About The Author

Krissy Baccaro writes mystery and suspense. She recently published her debut novel Buried Secrets (Ella Perri Mysteries Book 1) as well as her short psychological thriller, LUCA. She also collaborated with authors from around the world to publish two anthologies, *Once Upon a Story: A Short Fiction Anthology* and *The Rearview Mirror: An Anthology* which feature her short thrillers "Luca", "Monster", and "In the Shadows".

As a child, she picked up the book, From the *Mixed Up Files of Mrs. Basil E. Frankweiler* by E.L. Konigsburg and became enthralled in mysteries forever. She writes every chance she gets and is currently working on a prequel to her Ella Perri Mystery series.

When she's not writing mysteries, Krissy teaches writing and reading to 5th-grade students and loves to share with them all she knows about writing. The author resides in upstate New York not far from Skaneateles, where the Ella Perri mysterious puzzle begins.

Be the first to know about Krissy's next release plus get free thrillers & mysteries when you visit her website and join her mailing list.

https://krissybaccaro.com/

Amazon Author Page:
https://www.amazon.com/Krissy-Baccaro/e/B0862CXFFP

https://Twitter.com/BaccaroKrissy

https://www.goodreads.com/author/show/18891057.Krissy_Baccaro

https://www.instagram.com/krissybaccaro/

https://www.facebook.com/Krissy-Baccaro-Books-100566741650751

Other Books By Krissy:

Buried Secrets (Ella Perri Mysteries Book 1)

Luca

Once Upon a Story: A Short Fiction Anthology

The Rearview Mirror: An Anthology

Made in the USA
Middletown, DE
21 December 2022